UNFORGETTABLE

Recent Titles by Gloria Cook from Severn House

The Meryen Series

KEEPING ECHOES
OUT OF SHADOWS
ALL IN A DAY
HOLDING THE LIGHT
DREAM CHASERS

The Harvey Family Series

TOUCH THE SILENCE
MOMENTS OF TIME
FROM A DISTANCE
NEVER JUST A MEMORY
A STRANGER LIGHT
A WHISPER OF LIFE

The Pengarron Series

PENGARRON DYNASTY
PENGARRON RIVALRY

The Tresaile Saga

LEAVING SHADES
REFLECTIONS

UNFORGETTABLE

Gloria Cook

This first world edition published 2011
in Great Britain and in the USA by
SEVERN HOUSE PUBLISHERS LTD of
9–15 High Street, Sutton, Surrey, England, SM1 1DF.
Trade paperback edition first published
in Great Britain and the USA 2012 by
SEVERN HOUSE PUBLISHERS LTD

British Library Cataloguing in Publication Data

Cook, Gloria.
Unforgettable.
1. Widows–Fiction. 2. Village
3. Dysfunctional families–Ficti
Conservation and restoration–
Social conditions–1945- –Ficti
I. Title
823.9'2-dc22

ISBN-13: 978-0-7278-8068-0 (cased)
ISBN-13: 978-1-84751-369-4 (trade paper)

Except where actual historical events and characters are being described for the storyline of this novel, all situations in this publication are fictitious and any resemblance to living persons is purely coincidental.

All Severn House titles are printed on acid-free paper.

Severn House Publishers support The Forest Stewardship Council [FSC], the leading international forest certification organisation. All our titles that are printed on Greenpeace-approved FSC-certified paper carry the FSC logo.

Typeset by Palimpsest Book Production Ltd.,
Falkirk, Stirlingshire, Scotland.
Printed and bound in Great Britain by
MPG Books Ltd., Bodmin, Cornwall.

Dog lovers will understand this.

To my gorgeous, adorable, black and tan King Charles puppy, Grady Max. My newest love and my utter delight, and I could go on and on . . .

One

'Dorrie Resterick, now there's an enigma for you.'

Dorrie raised her neat ginger eyebrows at her brother, Gregory Barnicoat. 'Must you be so boring, Greg, forever repeating old sayings? That saying didn't even start with you. I'm merely putting on my walking shoes to take Corky along to Shady Lane for his walk. Then we'll sit together by the stream and I'll write some poetry.' She patted the pocket of her hip-length, pre-war cardigan where her notebook and pencil were tucked down inside. 'There's nothing remotely unusual or strange in that.'

Dorrie did not mind hearing widower Greg's oft-repeated kindly or mocking maxims, but the enigma one about herself had been started by her beloved late husband. It had been a special thing between Piers and herself, and it had remained special to Dorrie throughout her seven years of widowhood. Special, for Dorrie was not the slightest bit enigmatic, but handsome, successful Piers, used to being surrounded by beautiful, wealthy city women, had seen Dorrie, everyday and unassuming, as fascinating and desirable. Her parents had always described her, the youngest child of their brood of five as, 'Little Dorrie, she's as ordinary as people come, and a good thing too.' Her eldest sibling, at fifty-eight, Greg's usual declaration about her was, 'Good old Dor, you always know where you are with her.' While Greg and her other two brothers and sister continued with old grudges, notwithstanding a feud or two, Dorrie, the peacemaker, got on with them all.

After a lifetime of learning about and watching all manner of scandal unfold, and of being confided in – all too desperately at times due to her open, trusting face – with the secrets and fears of young and old, Dorrie was pleased she was not remotely puzzling or mysterious.

I'm not an enigma at all, Dorrie thought, but they do rather seem to find me. During the war she had, or rather Corky had, sniffed out a scrap of evidence in a dreadful local crime. It turned out to be part of a poorly written blackmail note, which had led to a double murder. It had not been a straightforward case. The murderer, a young member of a small-time gangland operation, had been clumsy and was soon traced to his lair in Bristol, where he had died an ignoble death with his own gun rather than face the hangman's noose. The torn-off part of the scribbled note Dorrie had handed to the police had stated '*found out about Ch . . . bring money to Merryvale . . .*' Merryvale was the wrong spelling for Merrivale, a nearby property then empty, where the young murder victims, Neville Stevens and his girlfriend Mary Rawling, had been found. The authorities had decided the couple paid the price for foolishly trying to blackmail a black-market gang with a widespread operation. It seemed the most feasible explanation but Dorrie felt that wasn't really the case. Neville Stevens had been a slow-witted petty thief who had never travelled far. The whole village had been questioned and no one had admitted to knowing anything, but a few people, Dorrie included, felt someone among them was keeping evil secrets. The murders were often mulled over but Dorrie felt too troubled to join in with the morbid speculation.

Leaving the cosy, comfortable sitting room for the hall she now pulled her beloved floppy crocheted sun-hat over her naturally curly hair, which glowed as bright as polished copper but was now prettily stranded through with silver. The copper freckles on her face and arms were beginning to fade but rather than being worried about the signs of ageing, Dorrie was rather fascinated by them. The light wrinkles at the corners of her eyes and her mouth showed that she smiled a lot, was optimistic and caring. She was proud that her once fine hands were slightly roughened by all the years of digging for victory. Dorrie was wearing a pleated blouse and tweed skirt of twenty years service, but she had been happy to 'make do and mend' long before the war had started, and the two years of even tighter post-war rationing was not a particular bother to her. From the long row of coat hooks, she fetched the lead of lovable, mixed-breed Corky, who had a mainly short black coat, long thick body and squat legs.

Corky was more than a pet to Dorrie. She had come across him as a puppy, lying on top of Piers' grave just after his burial. Piers had been killed while answering the call, in his own little boat, to help with the evacuation of the retreating British troops at Dunkirk. He had been laid to rest next to his and Dorrie's only child, Veronica, lost to them suddenly in infancy, from croup. Strangely, the villagers, who usually knew each other's business, had no idea where the puppy had come from. The friendly little scuff had crawled up to Dorrie and dropped its tiny dirty head on Dorrie's foot, and heartbroken Dorrie, believing Piers had sent the puppy to ease her loneliness, had immediately fallen in love with him. Corky had needed her too. He was deaf and virtually blind, with a slightly lame hind leg, and there had been little hope of him getting a home elsewhere. 'You're coming home with me, little fellow. I've got an evacuee brother and sister who will be delighted to have a little playmate.'

'Hold fast there, Dor. Fetch me my panama, old girl. I'll start off with you. It's the meeting at the Olde Plough, remember? Johnny and Margaret Westlake are putting their snug at the disposal of interested parties in forming a committee to get the building of a village hall up and running. It's time Nanviscoe had one.' Greg's mellow, slightly drawling voice was fired up with the new passion in his heart. 'As you know, I've spoken to Jack Newton and he's willing to donate a parcel of land where it verges on to the main road of the village. We need a playing field for the kiddies and a building for the Gardening Club and the like to meet. You women of the WVS did sterling work in that little hut next to the general stores and in each other's houses for the war effort, but with a proper hall you could start up a Women's Institute. It would have been just the ticket for the VE celebrations. It would get lonely people out of their houses. Mrs Sanders will probably be happy to donate a good sum of money towards a fund; she's always very generous, in every way.' Greg smoothed the ends of his neat David Niven moustache. 'The villagers can build the hall themselves. I'm sure the Vercoes can be counted on for manual labour, along with Charlie Lawry when he's not too busy at The Orchards. Hector Evans is eager to pitch in and is willing to be treasurer; he's got a good head for figures. Mrs Mitchelmore, the battleaxe self-styled lady of the manor, will be bound to show up today. Nothing happens in the village without her staunch involvement – well more or less her say-so. I don't care what the opposition says. They're not important.'

Still spry and lean, with a habitual twinkling expression, he was making mock sword thrusting movements, fighting off the unseen opposition, when Dorrie returned to the sitting room. Music sheets on top of the piano were sent scattering to the floor.

'Greg, do mind the vase of lilac blossom.' Dorrie was often required to take the part of the sensible one in their joint home, but she loved her brother's lasting touch of boyishness, and he was always the best fun. 'The vicar and the Newtons from the Stores are the main opponents to the idea. The Reverend Lytton wants a new church hall. You'd never think Soames Newton is a second cousin to Jack. Then there's the question of Mr Evans. He's an eminently pleasant Welshman, but his seven-year residence in Nanviscoe may not be long enough for most villagers to feel he has the right to a say,' she reminded him. Dorrie could not be doing with the arguments that were always a part of planning meetings and committees. 'I'm a willing soldier not an officer,' she would say. 'Just tell me where I'm needed and I'll be happy to comply.'

Then she asked pointedly, 'Is Jack Newton likely to be at the pub today?'

'Yes,' Greg replied in an innocent tone but his light blue eyes were glinting.

'Go easy on the ale. The Westlakes sell their own evil brew from under the counter. Don't forget it's potent.' Dorrie passed Greg the hat and his walking stick. She was holding her own simple little cane, although neither in fact needed a walking aid. Since retiring as a major in the Grenadiers, Greg used his carved handled stick to march along on his regular long walks. Dorrie found her cane useful for prodding and poking about in the hedges and ditches if Corky suddenly pushed his head, sometimes frantically, in, under or through the herbage having sniffed out something of vital interest to him. A stiff-limbed plodder he might be, but Corky had a fearfully sharp sense of smell – a very useful thing. Corky's avid investigations had led to the rescue of a number of injured birds, a squirrel and a trapped fox cub. He had ended the mystery of the sultry Honoria Sanders' lost gold watch, flung off her wrist when she had been forced to fling herself out of the way of Jack Newton's tractor – or at least that was their story. In was in the woods below Merrivale that Corky had sniffed out the piece of evidence in the double murder.

'Fiddlesticks and fie to the opponents.' Greg flicked aside her caution with his big competent hand. 'That old creaking fossil in the vicarage hasn't a clue or a care about the needs of the parish. It's his fault the church hall fell into ruin, and besides it's only the size of a postage stamp. Soames and Delia Newton oppose anything they fear will take their self-held importance away. And the origins of Hector Evans, and the length of his residence in Nanviscoe, are irrelevant. I was born and bred in this house, as you were and our brothers and sister. I'm the instigator and the leader of this notion. A village hall will be built before this year is out; you have my word on it! Worry not, old girl, leave it to me.'

'Oh, I certainly will, dear,' Dorrie said, as they and the eager, air sniffing Corky ambled down Sunny Corner's front path which seemed to have a mind of its own, broad here, narrowing there, straight and then nonchalantly turning. They passed between the flower borders billowing with lilac, rhododendron, azalea, 'bleeding heart', pansies, violas and the like. Against the drystone walls were various blossom trees and a glorious spreading light purple magnolia. Sunny Corner's splendid gardens were something of a legend, and it was not unknown to attract photographers from far-flung places. The rear of the property, once composed of finely cut lawns, and every manner of flowerbed and free-standing shrub and then a fenced acre of paddock before the war, had all been dug over for vital vegetable crops. Dorrie and Greg also kept hens and a couple of pigs. The war years had seen world-traveller great-grandfather Barnicoat's miniature folly, a Chinese-inspired pagoda, moved near the back terrace. The evacuees Dorrie had taken in had thought it a marvellous lark to sleep out in it. The pagoda also did nicely as a summer house.

At the very bottom of the vegetable plots came the stream, flanked in turn by a high long hedgerow swathed with bluebells, lacy cow parsley, clumps of white, pink and red campion and wild violets. On the other side of the hedgerow was one of Farmer Newton's largest fields, growing wheat this year. The whole area had high quality, undulating farmland.

The fame of Sunny Corner's gardens was how Dorrie had first met Piers, he then reading English literature and history at Cambridge University. She had been cutting lilac blossom when a tall, striking man had appeared at the gateless entrance, at this very same time of the year, preparing to take a photo of the then-promising young magnolia tree. She had stared at him in wonder and awe, and as instinct had drawn his stunning dark eyes to her, he had smiled. Such a beautiful, heart-stopping smile, like the rise of the very first sun. Dorrie had drawn on that precious image every day since then.

For a century and a half Sunny Corner had nestled at the edge of a crossroads, roughly a mile outside the village. It had been built in the manner of a small manor house by the Barnicoat family, one time mine speculators, who had moved from Bodmin town to a more peaceful rural setting.

Once in the lane, Corky sniffed and aimed his solid head down the lane, known as Barnicoat Way. Dorrie was doubtful if his failing eyes and ears could see or hear much of the person he had scented hurrying their way. 'Oh look, it's the young man who recently moved into Merrivale with his mother. Templeton, I think their name is. I did call on them with a cake to welcome them to the neighbourhood but no one seemed to be at home. I've caught a glimpse of the boy a couple of times. It seems they like to keep themselves to themselves. I feel sorry for anyone living in that sorely neglected old cottage with its terrible history. They must be down on their luck. He's smartly dressed. Perhaps he's been to The Orchards looking for work. He must be the same age as Sam Lawry.'

'Well, let's say hello to the young chap then,' Greg said.

It became obvious the Templeton boy had slowed his steps and was keeping his head down.

'He seems very down in the dumps and plainly doesn't want to speak to us,' Dorrie said, feeling sorry for the boy. Charlie Lawry had a full workforce on his premises that produced many kinds of fruit and vegetables. He took on jobless ex-servicemen who pleaded for even a few hours' employment a week. It was unlikely the Templeton boy had been successful if he had been seeking work. 'We'd better get on, don't want to embarrass him.'

The pair set off to their right at the crossroads on to Newton Road, the route to the village. Dorrie soon diverted off for tree-covered Shady Lane, a sheltered footpath. The stream meandered off underground from Sunny Corner to flow in dark seclusion under the crossroads and emerged to greet daylight several hundred yards along Shady Lane, just inside Newton farmland. She would have preferred to go straight across up the slightly rising sun-dappled Meadow Hill for a change, the route the Templeton boy would take, but Corky did not fare well in the heat. Greg carried on briskly for the village.

Twenty minutes after the sister and brother had separated a young woman arrived on their doorstep. Heaving a hefty sigh, she flung down her heavy suitcases and tried the door. The greeting she was about to propel inside was stalled rudely on her pink painted lips.

'Oh, damn it!' She kicked the nearest suitcase. To avoid the village nosy parkers she had alighted from the stuffy rattling coach that had brought her from Wadebridge, outside Nanviscoe's boundary. She sensibly wore flat shoes but under the weight of her overstuffed luggage the walk had turned into a shoulder-aching trudge. The front door was locked and that never happened unless her aunt and uncle were going to be out for more than half an hour. Following a brutal double murder some years ago, they hid a spare key outside but changed the secret place once a month. It could be wedged in under an ornamental stone or one of the dozens of flowerpots, anywhere.

Verity Barnicoat clenched her fists. 'Oh, where are the pair of you when I really need you?'

Two

'Mum, I'm back,' Finn Templeton shouted up the bare stairs in Merrivale cottage. 'Where are you? Don't tell me you've gone back to bed? You promised me you'd make the effort!'

Finn met continuous silence, which hung ominously in the musty air. His mother's lack of response was nothing new. She had been down and depressed for months, since his council official father's conviction for fraud and prison sentence of four years. She was pining for the man who had left her pregnant. The unexpected event to Finn, after spending sixteen years as an only child, was a horrifying prospect that grew worse as the birth approached.

'You'd do better to forget him, Mum. He's turned his back on us. He's forbidden you to visit him in prison and hasn't even replied to your letters. He doesn't care about anyone except himself.' Finn's frustrated viewpoints always fell on deaf ears.

'But he's the love of my life, Finn, and I know he loves me!' she would wail. 'He loves all of us. He said he was really looking forward to us having another child.'

Finn believed she had conceived this baby in an attempt to cling on to his thoroughly rotten father. If his mother were not so fragile Finn would tell her exactly what he thought of his father – that Aidan Templeton-Barr, who had thought himself such a big shot, had carried out at least three adulterous affairs. Finn had learned this through the spiteful tongue of a town hall clerk. On Aidan's arrest Fiona had hidden away in their elegant four-bedroom house in Wadebridge, and she didn't know about the taunts thrown in Finn's face at school and in the neighbourhood.

Most days it was a hard task to get Fiona to drag herself out of her present ghastly bedroom or even to get her to eat and drink. She did nothing about the dilapidated place. Stale smells permeated everything like a desolate living force despite Finn keeping as many windows as possible open. Some windows, upstairs and downstairs, were boarded up, smashed at some point during the property's long years of abandonment. The straggling cottage was as dark as winter, made worse by the wooded ground that surrounded it. Finn leaned against the cold, flaking whitewashed wall and threw his dark head back in despair. In a few short weeks he had lost everything, even the second half of his surname, dropped in the hope that his father's disgrace would not become known in this backwater location. He loathed this place but it had been this or nothing and he was thankful it had been offered rent-free to Fiona by one of her old friends.

It was only when the bailiffs had turned up that Fiona had made the frantic telephone call for help to Guy Carthewy. Aidan Templeton-Barr's enormous debts had been a terrible shock to Finn but not to Fiona. Her disbelieving state over her husband's conviction had led her to ignoring the warning letters from the courts for repossession of their home and belongings. Finn was furious that Aidan had left them in such dire circumstances. The bailiffs had claimed the two cars, the valuables, the paintings and porcelain, Fiona's jewellery and furs, even Finn's bicycle, which would be handy now for speeding along the lanes to the village shops and to get quickly to and from a job – if or when he got one. It was a worry to be away from his mother for long; he was afraid that in her despair she would hurt herself. But he had to bring some money in soon or they would starve. He had been left a small legacy by his grandparents but was unable to access it until he was twenty-one, five long years away. He and Fiona had been allowed to keep some of their clothes and a few personal possessions. How the hell was he supposed to cope with all this? Living in a dump with barely a decent stick of furniture and a few basic things found lying about in it. Guy Carthewy had apparently inherited Merrivale years ago from some eccentric old relative but had yet to decide what he would do with the property. He had supplied his own spare bed linen and curtains but those, like everything else here in the dank joyless cottage, had taken on the pervading mouldy smells. Guy Carthewy had promised to see about making improvements but after he had dropped them off here he had been called away on some serious family matter. Finn had been denied his studies and his dream of becoming a graphic artist; he was shunned by relatives for his mother's devotion to her misdemeanant husband, dropped by so-called friends, and was crushed to be brought down from his comfortable, privileged, upper-middle-class lifestyle. Resentment bubbled up in him that there would soon be a bawling baby stealing the last of his mother's failing energy.

Earlier this morning, while fetching Fiona's uneaten breakfast of porridge (all they could afford now), he had sighed impatiently at her curled-up lethargic form in the lumpy bed. 'Mum, have I got a clean shirt somewhere?'

When in this room Finn's head felt heavy and his nose blocked up. Fiona insisted on keeping the curtains shut and the electric light overhead gave off a murky orangey glow. Discarded clothes lay heaped on the floor. Dust fuzzed the dressing table and the neglected make-up, brush and comb. The door of the built-in wardrobe, next to the boarded-up fireplace, had burst open, spilling out his mother's few tossed-in clothes and shoes like flotsam on a seashore. Fiona had refused to sweep the scuffed floorboards or to allow Finn to do it and they were so strewn with fluff and grit he might actually be standing on a shingle beach.

Another blow was his mother's loss of interest in bathing. 'Mum, will you listen to me for once!'

'Don't raise your voice at me, Finn,' Fiona had muttered vaguely, hardly stirring in the sagging Victorian brass double bed.

'I have to raise my voice at you,' he'd cried, tugging hopelessly at his thick dark brown hair. 'You've practically stayed hunched up in this bed the entire two weeks we've been here. The only time you made an effort was when you arranged for the midwife to call. It's the only sensible thing you've done since we arrived here. Mum, you've got to try to pull yourself together. You're not doing yourself any good. This place is in a dreadful mess. I've done my best but you know better than me how a place should look. Like it or not this is our home for only God knows how long, thanks to my miserable, rotten father.'

'Don't talk about your father like that, Finn,' Fiona wailed, struggling on her elbows to sit up a bit. Finn looked away, hating the sight of his mother, once beautifully groomed and classy even in utility clothes, now with straggling hair, gone a dull blonde, her eyes red-rimmed, her highly toned features now puffy and ghastly white. He especially hated her bulging middle. 'What was it you wanted?'

'A clean shirt. Well, where can I find one?'

Fiona shifted her cumbersome weight and leaned against the bed head, groggily pushing back tats of hair. 'I–I did some washing in that horrid sink the other day. Have you looked in that old basket in the scullery? Wait, Finn . . .' She was instantly panicky. 'Why do you need a clean shirt? You got some food in yesterday. You're not going out, are you?'

'I have to, Mum.' He suppressed a despairing sigh, knowing his mother was fast getting beyond thinking clearly. 'I've got to look for work. The money you had in your purse is nearly all gone. We can't live on fresh air, and there's even a short supply of that in this damned place. I'll try to get something part-time. I thought before I try the farms I'd ask at The Orchards. All sorts are grown there, apparently. It's not far past the crossroads that's just down the hill. I've gleaned from the couple of times I was in the general stores the Lawrys sometimes take on extra help at this time of year. Seems the best bet. So I need a clean shirt to make a good impression.'

'But it won't be their busy picking season yet and would be a waste of time. Finn, I don't want you going out today. Please stay here.'

'I can't,' he stressed impatiently. 'I've got to earn some money. In fact, as soon as you get your head sorted out and accept that this is our life from now on, I'll be looking for something full-time and permanent. We've got to make the best of it. All you need do is get out of that wretched bed and do something to make this place something like a home, and then look after the baby when it comes. Guy said we can stay here indefinitely and he's promised to do something about the basic conditions when he gets back. We've got some hope, Mum. Try to see it that way. If not for Guy we'd be on the ruddy streets.'

'I'm sorry I'm like this, Finn.' Fiona wiped away tears of desperation. 'It's not my fault . . .'

'I know that, it's my damned father's for getting himself sent down! Because he was so bloody bent he took a bribe off a building contractor, and why? Because he got himself up to the eyeballs in debt from dealing on the black market. Didn't you ever wonder why we always had plenty while our neighbours were struggling with the rationing? His war effort was a bloody joke! He's ruined our lives and sent my future down the bloody drain. Mum, you've got to get a grip on yourself. Keeping me tied to you in this dump all day isn't going to help our situation.'

Finn had felt if he stayed cooped up here he would go off his head, like the local people would say his mother was and deserved to be if they discovered the truth about the strangers in their midst, and that was inevitable sooner or later. They couldn't keep hiding away from interested callers. The small lady, casually draped, who had dropped by soon after their arrival, holding a tea towel round a promising-looking gift of welcome for them, had gazed at all the windows, showing a kind face fixed with a natural pleasant smile. Finn had wanted to speak to her on the doorstep – he was too ashamed to invite anyone inside. His mother in her condition needed at least one trustworthy female acquaintance. But Fiona had been adamant from the start that she did not want anyone to even come near the cottage. 'They would only be busybodies and soon as they find out all about us – don't forget it was in all the newspapers – we'd be the subject of spiteful gossip. People will look down on us like they did in our old neighbourhood and I couldn't cope with that.'

Finn was beginning to feel like he was a faint drawing, gradually being rubbed out. He realized then just how scared he was to face the future with his mother so feeble and in a month's time a new baby brother or sister would be depending on him.

'I don't know what to do, Finn,' Fiona groaned, tears welling up in her throat.

'Don't, Mum,' Finn sighed, but he sat down close to her and reached for her hand. 'Look at it another way, what is it that *you* want?' Guy Carthewy had counselled Finn that this might be a good question to ask her when Finn considered it the right time, to get Fiona to face up to the future. It was a critical time. Finn had no choice about leaving her alone for considerable lengths of time, and he didn't have the slightest idea what to do about the baby when it was born. He was more scared now than when the police had swooped at an ungodly hour to arrest his father.

'I–I just want your father back,' Fiona whimpered, her voice watery and frightened. 'I know things will never be the same as before but I don't care about that, I just want Aidan. I love him so much.'

Her plaintive longing made Finn's guts turn over. He had always had a good relationship with his father – not matey, for they had shared little of the same interests, but they had engaged a mutual pride in each other. Now he loathed his father, saw him for the cunning crook that he was. Aidan Templeton-Barr was an unprincipled, smooth-talking bastard. Finn thanked God he had managed to shield his mother from the most malicious taunts and gossip, and that she was unlikely to find out about it now they were several miles away from their old home. He didn't want to talk positively about his father but he had to use him to coax Fiona out of her crushing misery. 'Well, Father wouldn't want to see you like this, would he? He'd said he was looking forward to the baby's birth. Think about it, Mum, if we work together to get this place more presentable you can write to him about it and give him somewhere to look forward to living in when he's released. You can send him photos of the baby; show him you're making the best of it. A good thing for all of us, don't you think?'

For the first time in weeks Fiona had managed to look thoughtful. 'I suppose you're right, Finn.'

'Of course I am. Now how about getting up and helping to sort me out a shirt? And eat something, Mum. You'll feel much better. I won't be away long, I promise. It's a nice warm sunny day. When I get back we'll sit out in the garden and make some simple plans, one step at a time, eh?'

'All right, Finn,' Fiona had said wearily. Finn wasn't a bit heartened; she still looked as if all she wanted to do was to curl up, sleep and forget she existed.

To hide his impatience with her he had left the room. Like all the good things before his father's arrest the natural affection that had flowed between him and his mother was gone.

Now he was back from The Orchards having failed to get work there, shouting up the stairs and crushed that Fiona wasn't up and about. 'Mum, for goodness sake will you answer me!'

'Finn . . .' He heard her strained breathless groan from her room and knew at once something was seriously wrong. He took the stairs three at a time.

Three

Dorrie and Corky were back at the crossroads. Both were satisfied and at ease after their gentle amble under the canopy of trees that merged together from the long hedgerows either side of Shady Lane. Corky had taken his regular drink of sparkling water from the stream. Dorrie had composed some poetry – for the first time a nursery rhyme, about a comical young rabbit playing tricks on his meadow friends. She wrote all sorts of stuff, often loving messages to Piers. Some of her poetry she read at parties and when requested at village events. Most she kept in an ever-growing stack of journals. For years she had belonged to a poetry group, meeting in an upstairs room of the pub, but the other two members, an elderly couple, had long ago died. The three of them had been disappointed not to attract new members.

Although virtually deaf, Corky was wholly sensible to vibrations on or under the ground and he swung his head towards Meadow Hill and sniffed and stared short-sightedly and sniffed and sniffed.

'No sound of a vehicle or a pony, so it's someone heading this way on foot, eh boy?' Dorrie soon heard running steps thumping down the hill and she waited curiously to greet, as she supposed, a neighbour in some sort of hurry. Jack Newton's farmstead and some of his tied cottages, and Honoria Sanders' impressive property were further along from Merrivale. A moment passed and then Dorrie was watching the youth from Merrivale tearing her way, red in the face and puffing, his eyes wide and glittering, clearly in a panic.

Leaving Corky, Dorrie hastened to meet the youth, holding her hand out to him in a gesture of offering help. From a certain angle of the boy's head Dorrie knew where she had seen someone like him before – in a photograph in the local newspapers – and she suddenly knew exactly who Finn was: the son of disgraced criminal Aidan Templeton-Barr, who was now in Dartmoor Prison. Dorrie understood why his mother had dropped the second half of her name and had not once showed her face in Nanviscoe.

'Pl . . . ease,' Finn flung the plea forward to her, his breath coming in painful rasps, just saving himself from stumbling and plunging flat on his face. 'I'm in a terrible fix. It's my mother . . .'

He came to a shuddering halt in front of Dorrie and grabbed for her shoulder, his well-built frame heaving from lack of oxygen, all the while staring into Dorrie's eyes.

'Now catch your breath. Finn, isn't it?' Dorrie said, her voice slipping into confident-kindly-in-charge mode. 'Then tell me what's wrong with your mother. I'm sure I can help.'

Panting wildly, his eyes huge in fright, Finn got out, 'She – she's having a baby and she says it's coming right now! She says there's not a minute to lose. She needs the midwife. Please, have you got a telephone? I couldn't find where my mother put the directions to the midwife's house. Do you live far from here? Can we go there now? I'm so worried, my mother's so fragile.'

'I live just there at Sunny Corner,' Dorrie pointed the short distance to where the thatched roof and chimneys were peeping through trees. 'I'm Dorrie Resterick. You run back to your mother, Finn. I'll summon Nurse Rumford, and then I'll be straight along after you. Can I bring anything you might need?'

'I–I don't know. Please hurry the midwife.' Fear and anxiety rife in every inch of him, Finn turned tail and tore back up the hill.

Dorrie hastened home, as concerned for Finn as she was for his mother. She had learned from District Nurse and midwife Rebecca Rumford, who had called at Merrivale, that a woman and her son had moved into the tumbledown property. A pregnancy had not been mentioned. Rebecca Rumford, a born and bred Nanviscoe girl, was strictly observant about patient confidentiality. Merrivale had lain empty for seven years after its owner Elvira White had been discovered passed away peacefully in her bed by the postman. Shortly afterwards, the gruesomely murdered bodies of young courting couple Neville Stevens and Mary Rawling had been discovered in the gardens. They had been shot between the eyes in execution style. There followed the inevitable tales of ghostly haunting. Three years on, just before the end of the war, a one-armed tramp had broken in and slept there overnight. He was well known and liked in the village, a harmless veteran from the First World War, down on his luck. Known only as Freddie, and thought to have been in service before fighting on the Somme, he passed through Nanviscoe each autumn. Dorrie and Greg, like many others, gave him food and good used clothes or a blanket – he refused to accept anything new. Freddie had told Dorrie and Greg about his night in the abandoned property. 'I'll never do that again, sir, madam. The place is cursed. Heard all manner of weird and ungodly noises, I did, and I'll swear on a stack of Holy Bibles I saw the spirits of that couple. Was them and no mistake, saw them face-to-face and they had great black holes in their foreheads. Then I heard Elvira White's voice shrieking at us all to get out. She might have died peaceful but she was mean and cantankerous, well, everyone knew that. She wouldn't give me nothing, not even a sip of water. Snooty she was, but I believe her past would show she was no better than she ought to be. You won't catch me going there again. Tell the kiddies to stay away and never play there.'

Haunted or not, Merrivale, although basically sound and with a bathroom of sorts, required its water to be pumped up from the well outside and it offered no other amenities. Dorrie thought the electrical wiring might be tricky. It was no place for a vulnerable baby to be born in, especially one without a father on the scene.

At the front door, Corky used his black snout for a thorough sniffing then had other ideas to settling down on the sitting-room hearthrug. He went off round to the back. The mock pagoda was one of his favourite places to snooze in. Dorrie made the telephone call. Rebecca Rumford's landlady, Great War widow Mrs Agnes Pentecost, said she would track her down on her rounds and send her along to Merrivale directly. Dorrie had no qualms about mentioning the possibility of the baby's imminent birth. Mrs Pentecost was the soul of discretion and very protective of her paying guest. Dorrie collected some things together, dashed off a note to Greg and was soon off and out again.

Everything to Finn felt skin-tinglingly odd. Intimidating. Scary. Frightening him more than ever. With alarming clarity he knew that he wasn't in the throes of a nightmare yet it seemed he had been running back up the hill – just a length of several hundred yards and not at all steep – for hours in a kind of limbo world. The hedgerows, although draped in May blossom, bluebells, white wild garlic and cow parsley with shiny yellow celandines down near the ditches, broken in one place by a field gate, seemed to rear up either side of him, close in on him, and he half expected something suddenly to drop down in front of him and block his way back to his mother.

'No! You can't leave me, Finn,' Fiona had screamed when he'd yelled in panic that he must run and get help.

He had found her on her knees on the bedroom floor clutching her huge belly, gritting her teeth, her pale hollow face flushed and grimacing in pain. A stab of fear had sent Finn's heart thrashing so fiercely in his chest he thought his ribs would break. The woman down before him didn't seem like his mother but some gargoyle-like version of her. 'Mum, are you hurt?' Had she hurt herself deliberately? She had so often cried out that she wished she were dead.

Fiona had motioned with a taut hand to give her a moment. After an endless time she let out a long desperate gasp, an ugly breath, and slumped forward, her rat-tailed hair swinging like a piece of ripped cloth hiding her face. It was a strange thought at the time but Finn felt heartbroken over the loss of her gleaming blonde hair that had once been immaculately sculptured into luxuriant waves or chignons. Fiona lifted her face to him and Finn got the impression he was looking down at a bewildered child and he reached out to her.

'I'm in labour, Finn,' she whimpered. 'Help me up on the bed. After you left I was going to tidy up and try to cook us something, then I had a burning need to go to the bathroom. You may not understand this,' she had heaved and puffed while he hauled her up to sit on the edge of the bed, 'but my waters broke.'

'There's no immediate worry, is there?' Finn had asked, reaching round to the dressing table and picking up her hairbrush. 'Babies take hours to come, don't they?'

'I thought this one would – you certainly did, Finn – but I went straight into strong contractions and the birth is not far off.'

'What?' Finn's gut constricted. He dropped the hairbrush and it hit the bare wooden floor with a thump that startled them both.

'Finn, don't,' Fiona moaned. 'Fetch some towels and bring over that box on the chair. I did manage to put a few things together that the midwife suggested. I've put back some money to pay her for this. I kept some of your baby clothes, they're in there too, and some new nappies I bought before they sent your father away.' She spat out the last words. It was her belief that Aidan, of previously exemplary character, had been too harshly dealt with for one single act of taking a bribe, and she hated all those on the urban council she suspected had anonymously and cowardly informed the police on him.

'Midwife! That's it, I must fetch her at once,' Finn cried, springing to fetch the box for his mother. He was too keyed-up to consider that his sudden movements were alarming to her. 'Blast, there's no phone here! Where does she live? I know it's in the village but where exactly?'

'She left her address on a piece of paper. I think I left it downstairs.' Fiona screwed up her face as another pain hit her back and insides, drawing her mouth back and revealing all her teeth and gums, perspiration shining on her lined brow. 'But you can't leave me, Finn.'

'I have to, Mum,' he had squealed. 'I don't know anything about the birth of a baby.'

Fiona's hands flew to Finn's shirt so forcefully the collar cut into his neck. 'Don't you dare think of leaving me alone!'

But he did, and guilt teamed up with his worries at deserting his mother and he prayed the baby would take a good while longer before making its entrance into the world. He was rushing home at his fastest but his legs seemed to be dragging him in slow motion. He rounded a bend and a large green shape sped straight at him forcing him to leap up into the hedge, his hands finding purchase on a blackthorn bush. All he saw of the young male driver in the sporty roadster was a wide white grin under a tweed cap. Jumping down to the ground, ignoring the thorns piercing his palms, Finn shook his fist at the retreating car. 'Damn you, you bloody swine!' he swore and shouted worse. 'You nearly spread me all over the road.'

He charged on up the last of the hill, picking thorns out of his flesh and tossing them down in anger. Finally he was pounding over the rutted ground, muddy still in places from recent rain, on the path that led to Merrivale. Guilt once more nagged at him. He should have supported his mother more and complained a lot less and perhaps she wouldn't have moped so much, got so down. In her condition many women would end up the same, depressed and lonely, and ashamed to be reduced to living in a fetid dump on limited means, abandoned by family and friends. One or two friends had offered help but Fiona had only taken up Guy Carthewy's offer, the only person she said she could truly trust. What a bloody great come down. He should have thought more about the baby; he had not even wondered if it would be a boy or a girl or what a baby would need.

The cottage appeared through the elm and beech trees that hid it from the road. A sudden wash of baleful wind pierced through his angst and cooled the sweat dripping off him. The house seemed to darken before his eyes and he lost focus. It must be exhaustion brought on by his ragged nerves, he reasoned, but things didn't appear as usual. The glass windows in the quirky, mossy, flaking white walls were like spidery eyes, glaring at him darkly in the gloom. Finn had heard the rumours about Merrivale being haunted by two tortured souls despatched here by violent murder and also by a distant relative of Guy Carthewy's who had died here. The old biddy in the general stores had gleefully told him all about it while trying to pump him for personal information when he had trailed to the village shop with the ration books, he feeling conspicuous to be carrying a straw shopping bag. Was someone watching him from among the trees? Finn shook his head and his sight cleared but he could have sworn he'd seen a shadowy form. The house now seemed as it normally did, run-down, uninviting and cheerless, even in early summer. Winter here didn't bear thinking about, and as for the long-term future . . .

The front door hung out of true on its rusty hinges and was so difficult to open that he and Fiona kept it locked. Fiona ordered all the doors to be kept locked most of the time in fear of surprise nosy visitors. Finn sprinted round the rear of the property, crunching over the ash path that was partly encroached by a botanist's dream of wild herbage. Thrusting aside an overgrowth of woody shrubs choked by ivy he knocked over a mouldy concrete urn, bruising his knee. The urn crashed, spilling out its long dead blackened plant, and he hoped the noise wouldn't alarm Fiona. Finn's best shoes slammed down over the patio of cracked quarry tiles and then with his heart threatening to rip apart he burst into the kitchen.

Without stopping to get his breath back, Finn shot up the stairs. 'Mum, Mum, are you all right? I've got some help. She's ringing the midwife now.'

'Finn, oh Finn . . .'

His mother's voice echoed weakly back to him. 'Oh God.' Finn stalled a second outside the bedroom door. 'Please, Mrs Resterick, don't be long.'

Dorrie was as fit and fast as she had been forty years ago and she surprised Finn by reaching Merrivale shortly after him. The instant Finn heard her call downstairs he went to the top of the stairs, relief paramount in him. 'Thank God, come up, come up. Mum says she wants to push!' he ended with a panicked squeal.

'All we have to do is keep calm,' Dorrie said, smiling confidently as she climbed up to him, but she was feeling far from relaxed. She had been in childbirth rooms but had never seen a woman actually giving birth. She would have to call on what she had heard over the years and her own experience of pushing her daughter into the world, her darling little Veronica, whom she had lost at just fifteen months.

'Thank you for coming, Mrs Resterick, I'm so glad you're here.' Fiona murmured breathlessly through her groans as a pain subsided. 'I've done as much as I could manage to get things ready. This is no place for Finn.' She was lying on the bed on her side, half covered by a sheet and her nightdress scrunched up above her bump. She was gripping the sheet with white-knuckled hands. Dorrie saw the baby clothes, baby bottles and teats and a tin of National Dried milk. Clearly Mrs Templeton did not intend to breastfeed. There were no other infant requirements. A pile of clean towels and a face cloth were on the washstand. 'Finn has stoked up the kitchen range and put the kettle and some pans on for hot water.'

'That's good, Mrs Templeton,' Dorrie said, putting down the bag of things she had brought and taking off her cardigan and rolling up her blouse sleeves, smiling a lot, as she was wont to do anyway, but this time hoping she was showing she was completely capable of taking charge. 'Finn, bring up some hot water as fast as you can so I can wash my hands. Keep a look out for Nurse Rumford.'

Finn wanted nothing more than to leave the labour room but he was afraid for his mother and couldn't tear his eyes off her. The pain had ended and she seemed to have dropped into a stupor, panting with her mouth sagging open. A school friend's mother had been paralysed giving birth and he knew women occasionally died during the agonizing process.

'There's no need for you to worry,' Dorrie said soothingly, easing him out of the room. 'I'll call you if you're needed. Could you look in the rooms for something for the baby to sleep in? Use your imagination, an empty drawer would do, and could you wash it well with some disinfected hot soapy water.'

Finn nodded eagerly, glad to have something to do. He hoped when he got downstairs he would hardly hear his mother's cries and groans of pain. He'd had no idea a woman could grunt and howl like a wounded animal, in savage, primeval wails.

As Finn headed downstairs, Fiona screamed, 'I'm going to push!'

Dorrie whipped to the bedside. Still on her side, Fiona was trying to shove down the bed sheet. Dorrie did it for her. 'Wouldn't you be better partially sitting up, Mrs Templeton?'

'Noooo, I had Finn on my side and that's how I'll deliver this baby. Hold my leg up please.' Fiona grunted, then she cried out and screwed up a grotesque face, making guttural noises deep in her throat as she bore down and down.

Quickly supporting the woman's skinny white leg, Dorrie looked at the birth area and was shocked to see a tiny greasy scalp of fair hair. 'I can see the head.' The words were barely out of her mouth when Fiona screamed as if she was being torn apart and the whole head was out followed by the first little shoulder and then the other and then the rest of the baby slid out in a gush of stained waters. Releasing the mother's leg, Dorrie caught the baby before it twisted at an angle and hit the bed. The baby cried lustily. It was very small but at a glance Dorrie thought it healthy and whole. Fiona flopped over flat on her back, panting as noisy as a steam engine. The baby let forth more startled cries.

Her core in knots of excitement, Dorrie carefully wiped round the baby's nose and eyes, the most delicate thing she had ever done. Then with a feeling of spiritual awe that she had taken part in the beginning of a new life, she gently supported the slippery child on the length of her arm and hand and lifted it up. 'You have a little girl, Mrs Templeton, congratulations. She's absolutely beautiful.'

Dorrie's smile had never been wider and she had tears of wonder in her eyes as she turned to the new mother.

But Fiona had closed her eyes and faced away.

'Mrs Templeton . . .'

No reaction.

'Mum!' Finn had charged back up the stairs and now he peered round the door. His expression was utter disbelief. 'It's here!'

Dorrie flipped the sheet over Fiona to preserve her decency but not before she had glanced down, relieved to see Fiona wasn't gaping open or bleeding profusely from the rapid birth. While swaddling the baby in a towel she said, emotion making her sound throaty, 'You have a little sister, Finn. From what I can see she's perfect.'

Finn crept in for a closer look. Dorrie placed the tiny girl, now making low whimpers, on her mother's chest and then she lifted Fiona's arm round her child. Fiona's only reaction was to turn her head further away.

'She doesn't want to know her own baby.' Finn's voice was steeped in bewilderment and unease. 'What's wrong with her?'

'Your mother is overwhelmed by the quick birth, and she's exhausted. She'll be fine in a little while,' Dorrie explained gently, but she didn't believe her last remark. Fiona Templeton seemed to have cut herself off from reality, and Dorrie knew all about depression and wanting only to be left alone. She had been the same way for several weeks herself when she had lost Veronica, and again years later when Piers had been killed. 'It's safe to leave the cord intact for a couple of minutes or so. If Nurse Rumford isn't here by then, I'll see to it. Now, Finn, dear, we could really do with that hot water.'

'The baby's gone quiet! Has she stopped breathing?' Finn panicked, staring at the bundled-up deep pink face of his sister. There had been a time he'd hoped his mother would miscarry, but now the baby was here and had taken her first breath, and even though he hadn't yet touched her he felt a bond with her. If his mother didn't come round quickly from her stupor the baby would be depending on him, for life and safety and sustenance and possibly to keep her out of an orphanage – and against all his previous resentment and anger, he wanted that responsibility. He wanted to know his sister, to see her grow up. Now it seemed she had died.

Dorrie reached forward and caressed the baby's soft face. 'She's dozing, Finn, and that's a good thing at the moment. Now hot water, please, without delay.'

Finn let out an almighty breath of relief coupled with the release of all the stress he had gone through so far today. Then he gulped and braced himself for he had a new set of woes ahead of him, realizing how the new responsibility, although he was glad to undertake it, would also weigh him down. Today he must become a man; all thoughts of his own life and future had to be set aside. 'Right, hot water.' He sped out of the room.

Dorrie remained still and listened for the sounds of bicycle wheels and Nurse Rumford ringing her bell, as she always did, to announce her arrival. She detected nothing except the various creakings of the old house. Feeling a little out of her depth now that the immediacy of the birth was over, she folded back Fiona's stained sheet and cautiously felt about her bulbous stomach for indication that the placenta was about to be expelled. It could take several minutes for that to happen and there was no sign from the all-too-quiet Fiona that she was having another contraction. There seemed no danger of bleeding and so Dorrie covered the mother again, deciding to wait another minute. Among the things laid out in preparation for the birth was a small pair of scissors and surgical spirit. Dorrie swabbed the scissors with a wad of cotton wool in readiness should she need to cut the umbilical cord.

Moving round the bed she went to the spot Fiona was facing. Fiona's eyes were open. 'Can you hear me, Mrs Templeton?'

'Yes,' she answered miserably.

'You've done very well, a beautiful baby girl, you must be so pleased.' Dorrie had a passionate belief in encouragement being the best help in all ills. 'You have some water here. Try to take a sip. I'm sure your mouth must be very dry. Finn is doing sterling work downstairs, I'm sure. He's seems a very capable young man, you must be proud of him. Nurse Rumford will be here at any moment and you'll soon be made comfortable.'

'I didn't ask him,' Fiona murmured.

'I beg your pardon?'

'Finn went out to look for a job. I didn't ask him if he got it.'

'Well, he can tell you about it in a little while,' Dorrie said cheerily.

'He mustn't get a job,' Fiona whispered in desperation as if she was giving up all her strength. 'I can't cope with this baby. I don't want it. Take it away . . . Just want to sleep . . .'

'I'll take her for now,' Dorrie said, with sympathy. Poor woman, she thought, as she gathered the newborn into her arms. It must have been so hard facing this in her circumstances, without her husband at her side, wondering how she was going to manage in the future. She heard a persistent ringing and gazed down at the baby, now yawning, now opening her minute rosebud lips and turning her head as if searching to suckle. 'Oh, thank God, now Nurse Rumford will make sure all is well with you and your mummy. Don't worry, little one, I won't desert you, your mummy or Finn.'

Four

Greg Barnicoat knew at once the house was empty. Although he was met by Corky waddling round from the back, Greg knew Dorrie wasn't home. He had such a strong connection with his sister, although their physical characteristics were different. Dorrie favoured their dainty red-haired mother and Greg their strong-boned, statuesque father. 'Hello, old chap, where she's gone then? Where's Dorrie? I suppose she's left me a message. What's this? You want to show me something? Lead on then.'

'Well, well.' Greg pressed down the corners of his moustache. Corky's legendary nose had headed him straight to the three-tiered pagoda. Greg and Dorrie and their siblings had played out many Oriental dressing-up games in the folly. Genuine Eastern lanterns had been strung from the wooden decorative jutting eaves and citronella candles lit on summer evening to chase away troublesome insects. The pagoda had a cast-iron spire, on which Greg and his brothers had laughingly threatened to impale Dorrie and their sister Diana if the girls refused to allow them the lead in their joint games. The cat and dog squabbles had been won by the boys and the girls in equal numbers. The pagoda was a great source of comfort to Greg after enduring the horrors of Flanders trenches, and witnessing in the recent war the loss of so many vital young men under his command in North Africa. And there was the never-ending ache of losing his wife and son. A motor-car accident while holidaying in France had deprived Greg of his five-year-old son, Gregory junior, and his beloved homely wife, Caroline. Greg would never forgive himself for not avoiding the Breton lorry, although its driver had been speeding on his side of the road. Like Dorrie, he was on familiar terms with that dreadful inner hollowness of losing his soul mate. Greg thanked God every day that he lived in a place of so many happy, carefree memories.

Greg gazed down fondly at Corky's find. 'Verity, my irrepressible niece, sleeping like a baby on the cane sofa, she must have travelled down overnight.' Verity Barnicoat was a picture of cherry-cheeked girlish innocence that belied her obstinate forwardness. It wouldn't have surprised Greg if she were sucking her thumb, her childhood habit. She had been the rowdiest and most outgoing and the prettiest of the next generation that had played in these grounds. She had unsettled the peace more than her siblings and many cousins put together, and was envied by all and resented by some because she had won the most understanding and forgiveness from the adults. Greg doted on her, she made him laugh, and like Dorrie, he was able to see through the times she was putting on a brave front. She had inherited great-grandma Trevean's poised English rose looks, which again disguised her strong will. 'By the look of all her luggage she's here for a long haul – trouble oh trouble. We'd better get her inside, Corky. Wake up, sleepyhead.'

Before Greg had deposited the bulk of Verity's luggage on the kitchen floor, she declared in the pattern of defiance Greg knew so well, 'I'm not going back to him, Uncle Greg, not ever. Julius Urquart and I are over. For good!' Greg's eldest brother Perkin, a high court judge residing in south London, while comfortable with his two sons, one sadly lost at Tobruk, had never really known what to do with his wayward daughter, but Greg and Dorrie had loved Verity's free spirit and Verity had spent many a school holiday with them. Some summers, Eastertides, and even Christmases they had happily seen the house bursting with nieces and nephews. It had gone a long way to soothe their emptiness at losing their own children. Now they had half a dozen great-nieces and nephews.

'I rather gathered that, darling. I had noticed you've removed your engagement ring.'

'I didn't just remove it, Uncle Greg, I threw it at him. I hate him!'

'I'm sure you don't.'

'Believe me I do. He acted the polite affable young man when I brought him down to introduce him to you and Aunt Dorrie, but you don't really know what he is like. The man is an affront to womankind! You'd said that we were rather chalk and cheese. I should have taken note of that. Anyway, where is Aunt Dorrie?'

'Oh yes, she's sure to have left me a note. Just a sec, it'll be on the hall table.' Greg took his tall stocky frame off to the passage and on to the hall. 'Ah, here it is,' he said, on the way back. 'What does she say? "Dear Greg, medical help needed at Merrivale, not an accident. Have phoned for Nurse Rumford. Don't know how long I'll be, nothing for you to worry about. Love Dor." Mmm, a mother and her teenaged son live there, one of them must be poorly. Only saw the boy this morning, from a distance, but he seemed in fine fettle then, crestfallen, possibly weighed down by worries. They're very secretive.'

'Someone actually lives in that horrid old place?' Verity plonked herself down at the broad table, covered with starched damask linen, fully expecting her uncle to make some tea and dig out something tasty to eat. Her Aunt Dorrie wasn't much of a cook and Greg did most of the meals, something he excelled at and enjoyed. He also loved to pamper Verity. He was the father she wished she had, rather than the serious, uncommunicative Perkin Barnicoat. He would be utterly relieved she had come down to Cornwall. He was furious she had ended her engagement, having heartily approved of the correct and highly successful industrialist, war-decorated Colonel Julius Urquart. 'Has Merrivale been done up?'

'Not even as much as a new brick,' Greg said, pushing the giant copper kettle on to the hob. 'The owner, some faceless individual, can't remember any facts about him, must be renting it to someone of desperate means, or so it's believed. Like I said they keep themselves to themselves, but seem respectable.'

Verity shrugged, losing interest. 'Where have you just come from, Uncle?'

'From the pub – but enough about that. Do you want to tell me what the problem is, my little darling, or wait for your Aunt Dorrie?'

First her shoulders began to shake then her head drooped and Verity crumpled into floods of tears. Greg went to her and she jumped up to be comforted in his wonderfully strong arms. 'My little darling – Father's never called me anything like that. I'm so glad I'm here.'

Greg held her tight. 'And I'm so glad you've come to me, and your aunt. You know you can stay as long as you like.' He let her sob and sniffle until she was ready to sit down again.

'So Julius has really hurt you?' he asked soothingly, while wanting to put his hands round the man's neck and throttle him for upsetting his precious Verity.

'Everyone and everything has, Uncle Greg.' She gave one last sniffle into her handkerchief then the old feisty gleam returned into her daring green eyes. 'Especially Julius, heaven help him if I ever hear from him again.'

'Still the same wonderful old place, I love being in Nanviscoe,' Verity said, closing her arms round herself as if she was being comfortingly hugged. 'Everything is always the same.'

Dorrie hooked her arm through Verity's. The couple could not look more different. Apart from the age difference, Verity was a tall curvy brunette, with colourful and tasteful make-up on her angular face, with the self-assurance of a woman who had forged her own way in the world, and without a hint of Dorrie's dainty homeliness. Verity's dress, although far from new, had a cinched-in waist and matching jacket and looked crisp and chic. While Dorrie had gentle blue eyes Verity's blazed like emeralds. Verity's lace up leather walking shoes were quite new, whereas Dorrie's were as old as the hills and had seen many repairs by jack-of-all-trades Denny Vercoe. 'I don't think I could bear to be away from the place now. Where to first, my dear? The Stores or the teashop or would you like to call on anyone in particular? Everyone will be so delighted to see you. It's been a while since you were down.'

It was Verity's first outing since she had fled to Sunny Corner four days ago, and Dorrie's first time since the Templeton baby's birth. They had emerged from Newton Road and were facing the church. St Nanth's rested in the calm of solidity and spiritual continuity, its slate roof and square tower framed today by crystal blue sky and friendly hovering white clouds. It was roughly in the middle of the village, up on slightly raised ground, and the road meandered round it in a higgledy-piggledy oval shape. Facing the west door, set well back in its own grounds, was the Victorian built primary school. The separate playgrounds for the boys and girls were empty, all was quiet and Verity speculated: 'The poor little souls must have their heads down over their arithmetic.'

She went on, 'I'd really like to go to By The Way and see the Vercoe clan. I know they're a bunch of scruffs but they're such a hoot. People think Denny can be a bit of a brute but he just doesn't suffer fools gladly, and why should he not retaliate when his family is insulted? I've always found him reasonable and kind, and I do like his bulky build, handlebar moustache and thicket of wild hair. He reminds me of past times. It should be remembered he and Jean lost two sons in the war. But let's start at Newton's Stores where I'll get all the news from old Soames and the lippy Delia. I suppose she's still treating her poor cousin Lorna like a dogsbody. Then we can retreat to Faith's Fare and you can tell me the truth of what is said in uncoloured versions. Gird up your ears, dear Auntie, the Newtons chatter at the same time.'

They stepped on to the narrow granite slab pavement. As always when passing this side of the churchyard Dorrie looked towards where her little Veronica and Piers lay side by side among the dreaming headstones. She was one of the luckier war widows, to have got her husband's body back for burial. The little family had been holidaying at Sunny Corner from their Hampshire home when Veronica had suddenly and cruelly been taken from them. Dorrie and Piers had intended to retire in Nanviscoe and the vicar had agreed to Veronica's local interment. Inscribed on the church cross were the twenty-eight Nanviscoe sons who had sacrificed all in the two world wars.

Dorrie felt movingly proud that Nanviscoe's newest inhabitant bore her daughter's name as her second name.

'Mum says she doesn't want the bother of naming the baby,' Finn had miserably told Dorrie when she had arrived the next day to give her promised continued help. He had been sitting downstairs on the only armchair, a sagging clumpy affair, giving the baby a feed. 'Nurse Rumford says it's post-natal depression but I think it's deeper than that. She scares me, Mrs Resterick. She won't eat and only sips at a cup of tea. She's lost somewhere, in her mind I mean.'

'I understand, Finn.' Dorrie smiled, her head on the side while Finn handled the baby as if he was experienced in infant care. 'But that's exactly how depression can affect you. Well, you've certainly mastered the art of bottle feeding, you're a natural. Well done.'

Finn gazed down at his tiny sister's downy face, and Dorrie was struck at how much love for the baby she saw in his strong, tired features. He was a different boy to yesterday, when he had panicked and worried over everything, afraid his mother would suddenly die and how he would cope alone and without an income. Dorrie and Nurse Rumford had been required to reassure him over and over again that he did not have to manage alone. 'The villagers are very kind on the whole and when word gets round, as it inevitably does, many will offer you help. Please do the sensible thing, Finn, and accept the help and don't think of it as patronizing.' The truth of her assertion had been proved moments before when she had found a bag of baby clothes left anonymously on the doorstep. Nurse Rumford must have been seen coming and going on more than one occasion and the right conclusion had been arrived at. Dorrie had guessed the mystery donor might be Jean Vercoe, who was Denny's wife, and a caring soul. Finn had said he was grateful for the thoughtful gift, and Dorrie had seen him relax a little more.

'Nurse Rumford showed me what to do. She's been a brick and so have you. She returned again in the evening and stayed the night and saw me through all the feeds and nappy changes. She's going to show me how to bath the baby today. I'm as scared as hell about that.'

'Don't worry, dear, I'm sure you'll manage excellently. Now have you had any breakfast? We keep our own hens and I've brought some fresh eggs and a few bits from my larder. Shall I cook you a meal and then see if I can tempt your mother to take a few bites of something?'

'Oh, yes please,' Finn replied enthusiastically, his sight rooted on his sister. 'I'm ravenous. You might have to battle with the range. It's temperamental. I've managed to slip out and scavenge some more firewood. I'm trying to keep this chilly place warm for Mum and the baby.' He had grown serious. 'Look, I can't go on just referring to this little mite as "the baby". She needs a name, and if Mum won't name her then I will.'

'Have you come up with anything?' Dorrie put her apron on and produced an apple from a bagful for Finn to eat now. She bought enough apples and other fruit from The Orchards each autumn to last through the winter and spring.

'Yes, I have actually. Eloise, the name of my first girlfriend. She was beautiful. I hated it when her parents moved away. She promised to keep in touch and we've exchanged the odd letter. I shan't write to her again. I'm too ashamed to be living here and the reason behind it. I think you know all about us, Mrs Resterick.'

'I do, Finn, but we needn't mention it again. It's your business alone. Eloise is a lovely name.' Dorrie cooed over the baby as Finn gently wiped milk from her chin with a bib. 'So you've had a girlfriend already. How lovely.'

'Thanks, Mrs R, you're brilliant. I can't thank you enough for what you've done. Would you like to suggest a second name for Eloise?'

Dorrie had protested but Finn had insisted. 'Mum won't mind, I'm sure.'

So that was how part of Dorrie's precious daughter seemed a little bit alive to her again in Eloise Veronica Templeton. 'My darling,' Dorrie whispered, sending her daughter all her love across the road. 'Tell your daddy how much I love you both.'

Faith's Fare was a large sturdy hut built on the site of the long demolished tithe barn. It was run by the women of the village and had received its name from the suggestion of the redoubtable Mrs Mitchelmore, who owned the largest, although not the grandest, house in the parish. The whole thing had been Mrs Mitchelmore's idea to provide a place every day, except Sundays of course, for the locals to gather in and bolster one another up throughout the bleak days of the war. The WVS, of which Dorrie had been a member, had operated from there, among other things, rolling bandages and making up parcels for prisoners of war. 'Faith' was because it was by faith that the tea, coffee, milk and scones, buns and cake would be donated from all manner of means and the villagers, rich and poor alike, had never failed to come through. Now it was being run in the same manner, with unwanted things being sold in one corner called the Thrift Niche and the proceeds going to servicemen's charities, all at Mrs Mitchelmore's insistence, overriding any other suggestion.

First, however, Newton's Stores had to be passed by and Verity let out a gasp of horror. 'Oh no! Auntie, read the headlines on the billboard.'

JAILED COUNCIL MAN'S WIFE IN BABY DRAMA.
DELIVERED BY NEIGHBOUR.

The headlines from a local rag shouted out to Dorrie. 'Damn,' she hissed crossly. 'So someone's been digging around in the

Templetons' lives. Not Nurse Rumford, of course. Delia Newton herself, I'll warrant my last ration coupon on it. She's used a lot of ink and precious paper on these unusually large headlines. If my name is in the newspaper . . . Right, let me see to this first, Verity, and then we'll go next door for tea.'

'After you then, Auntie.' Verity grinned in gleeful anticipation as she followed Dorrie over the worn-down granite threshold of the Stores. Dorrie's head was up high and her blue eyes were threaded with sparks – what Greg called 'her sergeant-major look'. When Dorrie had said 'see to this' she really meant 'see to *her*', the denigrating Delia Newton, daughter of a civil servant and not born in the parish. She thought herself as refined, declaring her marriage to Soames Newton, second cousin to Farmer Jack Newton, as love across the class divide, which was ridiculous as the Newtons were once squires of the parish, yet she delighted in boasting that the general shabbiness of the shop premises were due to her thriftiness at not spending unnecessarily while the rationing was still on. The door, incorporated with stained-glass panels at the top, was open to let in the fresh air and kept in place by an old iron weight. When the door was opened by a customer a bell shot out an irritating *ping-pinggg*, and the villagers swore that the bell's introductory speech had annually sharpened with each of the twenty-four years of Delia's supercilious reign behind the scuffed mahogany counter.

Verity loved the Stores' interior, so evocative of bygone eras with its Edwardian decorated cash register, the carved shelves, the dozens of tiny drawers containing powders and items that even now she had no idea what they were. When the generously proportioned Soames Newton was alone she'd ask him and learn about one more mystery, but just the one at a time for he tended to rabbit on about whatever it was for ages. Portly and heavy breathing in an amusing snuffling way (amusing to others because it greatly annoyed his snooty wife), Verity quite liked him. He appeared to let his wife boss him about but in reality he did not, for it was obvious he was adept at switching himself off from her demands and complaints.

'Ah, Mrs Resterick.' The reedy-voiced Delia swept up the hinged part of the counter so she could emerge from behind it and pounce on her customer. 'Miss Barnicoat too, how wonderful to see you again. It's been a bit of a while, hasn't it, but I suppose you've been busy with your forthcoming nuptials. Come down to tell your aunt and uncle all about the arrangements, have you? Are you having a big do? Your uncle told me you mix with royalty. Will there be any dukes and countesses at your wedding? May I see your engagement ring?' She stared down at Verity's white-gloved hand.

'No, to all your questions.' Verity's answer was uncharacteristically blunt, and Dorrie was dismayed that the hurt Julius Urquart had caused her cut even deeper than Verity had spoken of. 'My engagement was a big mistake, so now you know, don't you? Happy?' Spinning on her heel Verity stalked out of the Stores.

For once Delia's wilful prying had backfired. Verity's response had stunned her and her cheeks turned pickled red. 'Oh dear! I–I . . .' Then she rallied and bristled. 'Well, really! I was only being civil. So it's not true she mixes with royalty. I knew that was a lie, I said to my husband and Mrs Mitchelmore as much. They'll—'

'Excuse me, Mrs Newton,' Dorrie uttered firmly and headed for the doorway.

'Don't you want to buy the *North Cornwall Gazette*?' Delia demanded airily, quickly on Dorrie's heels.

Over her shoulder, Dorrie stared at the other woman. Delia was ten years younger than she was but her pursed features had consequently aged her with many more wrinkles. Delia had never been an easy person although she had been pretty once, but that was now lost under pockets of saggy skin. She sided with the Reverend Wentworth Lytton against the idea of a village hall. The general agreement in Nanviscoe was that they were both outdated and mean. Delia agreed with all the ageing vicar's views, it was how she felt important and she constantly rubbed it in to the locals that Soames was the vicar's warden and as such was a gentleman to be highly respected.

'You know very well we have all our papers delivered from your very stores. Don't be disrespectful. Good morning.'

'What did you come in for then? Just to hang about?' Delia threw after her in accusation. She never failed to attempt to pull others down. People declared if there were another grocery shop and post office in the village they would patronize it and let the Newtons 'go hang'.

'I shall return bye and bye,' Dorrie said loftily. Delia Newton was the one person she liked to put in her place. She couldn't see Delia's face but knew she would be quilling with turkey-faced indignation.

Dorrie caught Verity up hurrying for the churchyard. There was a secluded wooden seat under the trees round at the north side of the church and the pair headed there. They sat and Dorrie held Verity's hand. 'You told Greg and me the facts, that you and Julius disagreed over when to have children, that he refused to go ahead with the wedding unless you agreed to have them straight away. I think it's very reasonable that you wanted to wait a year or two after typing your way through the war and then the resettling programmes in a stuffy Whitehall office; that you preferred to build up your new home and travel before starting a family. You said Julius's attitude hurt you and that you felt rejected and you're very angry, but what else is there, darling? What did you mean when you said to Greg that he's an affront to womankind?'

Verity gripped Dorrie's hand fiercely but she wasn't crying. It was outrage alone that was running though her like an unquiet engine.

'He was totally hateful.' She spat the words as if her hate was a tangible thing. 'He humiliated me, Aunt Dor. He said I wasn't normal; that breeding children was what marriage was all about, and what else did I expect when I'd one day be a baronet's wife, that I would from the start have access to his money, and the finest house and the best social position. That I'd only have to drop a few sprogs and then I could do what I liked, providing I kept it concealed.' Then Verity was trembling and gazing at Dorrie in a bewildered way, and Dorrie was horrified to read fear in her. 'When I mentioned love, he laughed in my face. "Don't be bloody foolish," he said. I'd always suspected he didn't really love me but considered me rather as a good catch. I thought he'd come out with the old chestnut that he wanted a separate life outside our home and keep a mistress, and perhaps allow me to take a lover, but what he actually said was, the bloody rotten swine, "How could you expect someone to love you?" He crushed me to pieces, Aunt Dor. I felt like I was in splinters. There's nothing wrong with me, is there?'

Still Verity did not cry but all the while her eyes swelled in size as if the core of her very self was fast being eaten away. Dorrie pulled her in close. 'Oh, darling, of course there's nothing even the slightest bit wrong with you. It's him, don't you see? He wanted you – and what man wouldn't, you're beautiful in every way – but he wasn't prepared to allow you your spirit, your zest for life, or even to have your own thoughts. It's clear to me the man's a beast and a bully. He would have systematically drained you until there was nothing left of our wonderful Verity. He'd have turned you into one of those nervy slavish wives. You truly would have been crushed, Verity, darling. You must be thankful that you've had a very lucky escape.'

'I am, Aunt Dor, believe me. The thing is, I mean, haven't you noticed Mother and Father haven't rung to ask me how I am? I fibbed to you and Uncle Greg that I rang them to say I'd arrived safely. They've disowned me. I mean really, really disowned me. Father was raving mad when I told them the engagement was off and Mother said I was the biggest disappointment of their lives. When I refused to apologize to Julius and try to win him back they were even more furious. Father insisted that I at least apologize to Sir Thomas and Lady Urquart but I adamantly refused. Father and Mother wouldn't listen to my side of things, to see that I had done nothing wrong. So they told me to leave, and that they'd washed their hands of me for good.'

Verity's trembles became feverish and her voice was edged in fury. 'All they care about is their damned position. I hate them for it. What sort of parents are they? You or Uncle Greg would not do such a thing to your child. They said they would never forgive me for letting them down. Well the feeling is mutual. I hate them with all my heart and I'll never ever forgive them!'

Five

Belle Lawry could not prevent a shiver jerking along her spine as she walked up the rough path to Merrivale. The place was unbelievably bleak and dark, the stuff of eerie dreams. Her son Sam, presently working with her husband Charlie, had played here with his friends during the property's empty years and been frightened by the apparent hauntings. 'I swear on my life, Mum, some of us saw this huge looming shadow and Jenna Vercoe swears she heard a voice.' Sam, until then a dedicated scoffer of all things supernatural, had looked warily over both shoulders as if the spooks had followed him home. 'There's something bad lingering there. We shan't go there again.' But he and the others had gone back, playing games of dare but always soon scarpering away with more scary tales.

Charlie had laughed at Sam. 'It's all in your imagination, you're all frightening yourselves.'

'I don't know so much,' Belle had reacted by chewing her lower lip. 'There's many a thing under sun and moon that can't be simply explained away. I've read accounts of people seeing their loved ones, even though they were off fighting in both wars, and then learning their son or husband had been killed at the exact same time they'd seen them. They're spiritual messages. There's nothing stronger than the bond of love. And there's always evil lurking about . . .'

'Oh, don't tell me you think all those rumours are true, my little darling, dearest.' The ever jocular, tactile Charlie had grabbed Belle and squeezed her affectionately. 'You've got your serious face on. Whoo-ooo. Let's go up there and have a seance.'

'Don't even joke about it, Charlie,' Belle had returned sternly, but she was happy to stay in Charlie's embrace, her favourite place to be since their courting days seventeen years ago. Their love had been instant and passionate, and quickly followed by a hurried wedding and Sam's birth. 'There's God and there's good and evil forces. It's not at all fanciful to believe that the evil and madness that provoked those dreadful murders is still lurking there. I hope one day the place is demolished.'

When news reached Belle that Merrivale was inhabited again, by a mystery woman and her son, of Sam's age, Belle had felt sorry for them. Dorrie Resterick had paid them a visit and received no reply, although she was sure someone had been at home. No one else had bothered to go to Merrivale, not even the vicar, but he maddened most of the parishioners by his stance that people knew where to find him if they wanted him.

Then unexpectedly, the boy from Merrivale had turned up at The Orchards looking for work. At the time Belle had been at the village school, teaching the children country dancing in readiness for the annual village Summer Fair, which would be held at nearby Petherton, the semi-grand home of the doughty and gritty Mrs Mitchelmore. During the war, the much-married, bottle-blonde Honoria Sanders, the younger sister of Mrs Mitchelmore, had offered to take over the burden of the Summer Fair and hold it at her more modern home, Sawle House, to give Mrs Mitchelmore more time to concentrate on all her happily self-imposed war work.

Mrs Mitchelmore had bristled with indignation. 'Burden? I've never found anything in my life a burden, as you know. Whatever I've had to tackle I've come out the other end on the top, as you know. Don't parade around like Lady Muck. You're no use here at Faith's Fare. You take twice as long as the other ladies in rolling bandages, and a serviceman's sock will never be finished in your hands because you don't know one end of a knitting needle from the other. You're a spectacle in the WVS uniform, all bursting chest and wiggling posterior. Hop it. The Summer Fair has always been and always will be held at Petherton. Do I make myself clear?'

Honoria was not one to allow anything or anyone to dull her indomitable spirits. 'Absolutely, old girl.' She had pouted her full scarlet lips, her voice low and purring. 'I'm not leaving the WVS today, not ever. Besides, I've supplied wool to my staff – reduced, I might add, to two middle-aged women now, I am not waited on hand and foot – and they are eagerly knitting away for the Forces, and for servicewomen too, we mustn't forget them, must we? Your boring old Sedgewick allowed Petherton to get run down. It's been dog-eared for years. Sawle House is larger than Petherton and is in fine fettle. Most of the lawn has gone for crops but it offers far more space and comfort than your grounds possibly could. Perhaps the villagers should be asked if they would like a break from tradition from where the fair is held. Don't you think it would be for the best?'

'Over my dead body! It would let Sedgewick down; he would turn in his grave.'

'Maybe he would, but be careful, Esther, dear.' Honoria had ended the spat with the same words she employed more than once to her sister.

Belle had speculated to Dorrie what those words might mean, but Dorrie always replied, 'Just sibling rivalry, I'm sure, my dear.'

'But we don't know much about their background, do we? They both turned up in the village when Mr Sedgewick returned from London with Esther as his wife, years ago, but the women have never really talked about their past.'

'We know enough, wouldn't you agree? Mrs Mitchelmore gets things done and Honoria is free-handed. They're a great benefit to the village.'

Dorrie was the most perceptive person Belle knew but annoyingly she wouldn't be drawn into forming speculative gossip.

The only time Mrs Mitchelmore was addressed as Esther was by Mrs Sanders, who was Honoria to all her friends – and she had a lot of friends, Belle among them, because she was generous-hearted and unpretentious. Unlike her sister, Honoria never issued a bad word about anyone. Someone hearing about the sisters for the first time might think Mrs Mitchelmore was masculine and gauche. The truth was she was slim and cut a strong figure, in a leonine way.

Belle had learned from Charlie that he had been forced reluctantly to turn Finn Templeton away. 'I felt really bad but we are already employing more workers than we can comfortably afford. So are all the farms until they take on casuals for harvest. I said I'd keep my ear to the ground for him but I'm not hopeful. Ex-military men usually come first, as they should.' It turned out that Mrs Templeton had given birth to a baby girl that very day. Dorrie had telephoned with the news, and had since mentioned that Mrs Templeton was not recovering well from the birth.

Approaching the drab and desolate cottage, Belle felt guilty for not coming here before. The Templetons might favour their privacy, but since the baby's birth others had sent them foodstuffs, garden produce and thoughtful little gifts. Young Finn Templeton had sought work from Belle's husband, and she somehow felt she had let him down.

From his bedroom window Finn watched the young woman with a jaunty step heading towards the back garden – another kind local, carrying a laden shopping bag. The locals knew to drop things off at the back door and only one or two had tried to inveigle an invitation inside. Finn had made polite excuses not to allow anyone in, although each time he'd said his mother was sleeping it was the truth. Fiona rarely troubled to keep herself awake for more than half an hour at a time. Finn feared she would keep to her bed way beyond the ten-day lying-in period. Leaving Eloise dozing in her cradle, loaned from Sunny Corner's attic, as were other nursery items, he quietly hurried downstairs and outside to the back garden.

The woman was coming closer and he could see her clearly. In an instant Finn's heart splintered into a thousand pieces and reformed and he felt reborn. Amazingly he saw everything with greater clarity. He heard birds trilling, cooing and chittering in the trees where before he had only heard the dark heavy boughs heaving in complaint. Whoever this woman was she was utterly gorgeous, lithe and sensuous, honed like a goddess with eyes of iridescent brown and gypsy black hair that swirled about the soft feminine contours of her peachy face. Suddenly his life didn't seem so daunting any more. It was fate her coming here, meant to be, meant for him.

She raised a friendly hand to him. 'Hello there.'

Finn usually eyed newcomers warily and shuffled his feet but this time his hand shot out and he waved back. 'Hello, good morning, my mother and the baby are asleep but you're welcome to come in.' The words were out of his mouth before he'd managed a second thought.

He stared greedily at the beautiful stranger and roved his eyes all over her. The more he looked the more he wanted to see all of her. She was a creature of dreams and already he had devoured enough of her to sketch her exact likeness on paper when she left. He didn't want her to leave, however, and wished he could keep her here as long as possible. She had ignited and inflamed something primeval and divine in him and already he could not bear to let her go.

Belle reached out her hand. 'Hello Finn, I'm Belle Lawry, wife to Charlie from The Orchards. I'm pleased to meet you. I hope you don't me calling on you.'

'Certainly not, Mrs Lawry.' Finn was surprised he had found his voice but he had no idea how he'd sounded. He simply concentrated on the warm hand clasping his, her living touch, her pulsing flesh, until she pulled her hand away. Suddenly the nightmare and despair and his humiliating fallen position were worth it to meet this awesome woman. He was crushed to learn she was married but then of course she would be; a woman of her supremacy would soon have been snapped up. He was elated to know she lived not far away yet he damned the fact he wouldn't be able to see her nearly every day at The Orchards. He smiled his deepest smile, his spirit singing heavenly themes, for she was here and he had invited her inside and would have her all to himself. 'It's very good of you to call, Mrs Lawry. Please step in. I've managed to get hold of some coffee, would you like a cup?'

'That would be very nice, Finn.'

He shivered deliciously, loving the way she said his name, gently emphasizing it a little. He fell in step with her on the patio and he smelled her refreshing lemony scent. She was wearing a cotton poppy-print skirt, quite faded, and a plain short-sleeved blouse. His eyes roamed over her superbly toned limbs, her graceful neck and shoulders and neat waist and shapely breasts. Belle was the perfect woman. She was paradise.

'But I don't want to use up your rations, Finn. After all you must find it hard to get to Newton Stores. I have a cousin in Canada and he kindly sends us parcels of food, so I've brought with me some coffee and a few other things, which I hope you'll accept, Finn.'

'I'd be glad to and I'm very grateful. You are very kind, Mrs Lawry.' If only he could call her Belle. She wouldn't belong to Charlie Lawry when she was here, and he had already worked out a way of inviting her to come again.

'My gosh, it's looking very nice in here, not at all what I

expected after all the time the place had been left to go to pot,' Belle exclaimed, once inside the kitchen. 'Everything is sparkling.' She used all her senses to glean if there was anything eerie but felt nothing menacingly peculiar, not in the kitchen anyway. It wouldn't be right to mention the prospect of ghosts and the murders to Finn. He probably had too many everyday concerns to deal with anyway to give a moment's thought to such things.

'That's thanks to Mrs Resterick and Miss Barnicoat. Together they showed me how to put plenty of elbow grease into the cleaning. They've spent hours here scrubbing and dusting and cooking and it was good having their company. Mr Greg kindly brought over some things, especially for the baby. Don't know how I would have managed without them. Mrs R has been a brick. She's been like a doting aunt to me, and Eloise too. I told her I'd like to provide some things for Eloise myself, and Mrs R told me that Denny Vercoe, the craft worker, also deals in all sorts of stuff and if you haven't got the cash he's happy to barter. Mrs R said I could pop Eloise in with her when I go out. I'd best not leave her here alone with Mum just yet.' Finn deliberately paused.

'I'd be pleased to help out with the baby, Finn,' Belle offered straight away. She admired and liked Finn very much. He obviously doted on his baby sister.

Yes! Finn yelled out inside his head, with rapture. He could manipulate her offer to suit him. 'Really? I'll be glad to take you up on that,' he replied, unable to keep the enthusiasm out of his tone. 'Nurse Rumford has been a wonderful help too, although she's getting nowhere with Mum, I'm afraid. I expect you've heard she has this post-natal depression thing. I'm grateful to the neighbours who have been so good to us, you included, Mrs Belle.' There, he had said it, turned her title into something much more familiar and she didn't seem to mind. This way he had got rid of her husband's claim on Belle. His Belle. He wanted her to become his Belle.

'You're very welcome, Finn. While the kettle's on, may I see Eloise? I've got a son, Sam, he's the same age as you and I'm sure you'll become friends. Sam's like his dad, friendly and easy-going. I would have loved to have a little girl but it wasn't to be.'

Finn didn't like her having a son who might get in the way.

'I'll bring Eloise down. Come through to the front room. I'm afraid it's not very grand.'

Finn couldn't tear his sight off Belle, who in turn was avidly examining the shabby state of the long wide room, which ran under the main bedroom and the bathroom. The furnishings were meagre.

Belle was saddened for Finn and his family. There was the evidence in the hanging shelves and a candle box of fresh wood dust outside tiny boreholes indicating live woodworm. A crocheted blanket of multicoloured squares and some chintz cushions lifted the barrenness a little, with a linen runner on the sideboard. Holiday snaps of Finn and his mother in various foreign locations were set there, with two highly detailed drawings depicting Tolkien-like creatures signed by Finn. On the mantel over the gaping brick fireplace was a bracket clock, which Belle recognized as coming from Sunny Corner, and two dark wood carved giraffes that she had seen on the shelves in the thrift niche. A white milk jug with a chipped rim was filled with wild flowers and sat on the ledge of a boarded-up window.

Finn read her emotion and loved her all the more for it. 'Pretty bleak, isn't it? Our landlord had to go away on family business. He offered us his house in Wadebridge but Mum wanted to go somewhere isolated. She got her wish here. The landlord will be back soon hopefully and he's promised to do something about the worst of the place. Mrs R said we could do with a working party in the house and outside, that Mr Greg would be glad to organize some willing villagers to hack down the gardens and remove some of the tree branches. It would make the place much lighter, but Mum said she couldn't bear that yet. God knows when she will be up to anything. Take a seat, Mrs Belle. I'll get Eloise.'

He reached the creaking landing and Fiona's voice came to him strained and muffled for she tended to hold the bedcovers over her face. 'Finn . . .'

He went in to her and made a face at her manky sweaty smells, the same as when he had brought some porridge to her the day Eloise was born. 'Yes, Mum?'

Fiona's puffy face peeped out of the crumpled sheet. 'Is someone downstairs? I thought Mrs Resterick wasn't coming until later and the nurse isn't due yet, is she?'

'It's Mrs Belle Lawry from The Orchards, where I went hoping to get a job. She's very, very nice and she's brought us some coffee, milk, a loaf and things made from her own produce. Cheer up, Mum, the people of Nanviscoe have saved us a whole week's rations and we don't need to spend a farthing this week.'

'Finn!' Belle called up the stairs. 'Can you come down at once? Don't bring the baby. It looks like a reporter is heading this way.'

'Oh no!' Fiona screeched, hiding under the bedcovers. 'Don't let them in, Finn. Send them away. Oh, the shame of it.'

'Shush, Mum, keep totally quiet. I sensed from the tone of Mrs Belle's voice that she has an idea.'

Belle hauled Finn out of the cottage and round to the front garden. 'You're called Sam, right? Leave this to me.' Next instant Belle was dragging Finn by the arm away from the place and speaking stridently. 'Come away, Sam! I told you those people scooted off the instant the news broke in the papers. It's too spooky to stay here. We should never have accepted your father's dare to come. It's a horrid place!'

Finn went with her willingly, loving her touches, but he didn't like her putting him on a par with her son. He burnt with jealousy that Belle had two men who had the right to claim so much of her.

His heart leaped when she suddenly let out a frightened shriek, and for one stupid second he believed she had actually seen a ghost. Then he saw the grey-suited, high-hatted woman holding a notepad and pencil lose the eager look on her nondescript face. The reporter said, under a network of frowns, 'The Templetons have left here? But according to the woman in the shop the village is rallying round them.'

'Good morning. We're the nearest neighbours and my husband saw them leaving in a taxicab last evening.' Belle released Finn's arm and he put his hand over that warm tingling place. 'He'd met the boy briefly, you see, and the boy shouted out the window that they were going for good. Apparently their landlord has found them better accommodation. I was glad to hear it, for this is a dreadful, cold place; it's rundown and practically uninhabitable and there are many people who swear that it's haunted. I've never had the nerve to come here before and I certainly won't be coming again.'

The woman snapped her notebook shut. 'Do you know where they went?'

'They didn't say, so my husband said. They were very private people. We never met them, hardly anyone did. My husband keeps bees, would you like to hear about them? It would make a very good story and it would be great publicity for his honey. I know the whole history of—'

'No, thank you,' the reporter said smartly. 'I have another assignment and I must get on.' She left briskly, wobbling on her high heels out to the lane, where her black car could just be seen through the scramble of trees.

'Well, that got rid of her,' Belle laughed, wiping her hands to convey she had got rid of a pest.

Finn gazed at her from huge admiring eyes. 'That's the neatest thing I've ever seen. You're blooming marvellous!'

Six

In the lane outside Merrivale a car was parked. Dorrie was concerned that the reporter, whom Belle had told her about, was back, perhaps with a photographer this time. The Templetons did not need the sort of complications caused by lurid columns in the newspapers which might lead to malicious gossip. Some locals had voiced their opinion that the Templetons did not deserve any help, that there were more deserving cases than them. 'They wouldn't have cared about the likes of us when they were in the money,' a few had observed.

Delia Newton had declared haughtily to Dorrie, 'The wife must have known what her husband was up to. She's got what she deserves. And it might be a case of like father, like son; that boy probably shouldn't be trusted. It's just as well they keep themselves to themselves. We don't want their sort in Nanviscoe, it's a respectable place.'

'Yes,' Dorrie had retorted. 'It's full of respectable, charitable and un-judgmental people who wouldn't dream of throwing the first stone.'

To that Delia had made what Greg called her 'squashed muffin face' and had continued serving Dorrie in frosty silence.

'Hello, Finn,' Dorrie called out cheerily as she entered the kitchen, ready to see off any persistent members of the press.

'Finn isn't here.'

She stood stock still. A man was lounging at the table, apparently thoroughly at home, turning a gold cigarette case and matching lighter over and over in his fingers. Finn wouldn't have got on good terms with a reporter. He stood up out of respect to Dorrie's entry and laid on an amiable smile, but Dorrie knew a charmer when she saw one. In his late thirties, slick in style, in a gleaming white shirt and dark tie, his sports jacket over the chair back, he exuded control and sophistication. 'Mr Carthewy, I take it?'

'You've guessed correctly,' he replied in a careless but interested way, offering his big tidy hand across the table. A gold signet ring gleamed on his right ring finger. 'And you must be the indispensable Mrs R. I'm very pleased to meet you. Finn and Fiona have told me how good you've been to them. Please accept my gratitude for all you've done here, and pass it on to your brother and the neighbours. It was unfortunate I had to attend to family business at Fiona's most desperate time of need. I couldn't convince her to accept more help from me. My secretary would have been willing to check regularly on her but Fiona wouldn't hear of it, even though I'd assured her Miss Marks is the epitome of discretion.'

'I'm pleased to meet you, Mr Carthewy. Finn's out, you say?'

'He's not long left to go over to By The Way, to see about getting a few things for the baby. I convinced him to allow me to hold the fort until you arrive. The baby shouldn't wake for a while. I offered to buy everything the little one needs but Finn insisted it was his place to provide for her. I admire him for that. I'm pleased he's not a grasping crook like his father. Aidan Templeton-Barr is rotten right through, but Fiona still can't see it or won't hear a word against him. I've managed to talk Fiona into getting out of bed and she's getting dressed. I'm here to persuade her to move to somewhere more comfortable. I'd almost forgotten I'd inherited this place, didn't even know it existed until the lawyers tracked me down. In case you're wondering why I'm so intent on helping Fiona I'll be thoroughly honest, it's quite simply because I'm in love with her. We were about to get engaged until Aidan stole her away from me. I've never stopped loving Fiona. I married a few years later but my wife divorced me, couldn't stand being second best to Fiona, she said; I couldn't blame her. I'd do anything for Fiona and her children. Haven't got any children myself. Finn doesn't quite trust me. I understand that, but I'm not trying to take over. I hope he'll see that, and you too, Mrs Resterick.'

'I think I do believe you, Mr Carthewy, that was a very impassioned speech. Fiona, Finn and the baby are very lucky to have you as their port in a storm.' Dorrie was to learn that Guy had served in a tank regiment during the war and been mentioned in dispatches.

The pair heard slow shuffling sounds followed by puffing and blowing and then Fiona appeared stooped over in the doorway. Grey-faced, she was in her dressing gown and slippers but had made an attempt to brush her lank hair. Guy rushed to her and supported her with caring hands. 'Let's get you resting on the settee.' Dorrie followed them into the front room.

'I don't want to go anywhere else, Guy,' Fiona whined. 'This cottage is basic but we're surviving, and Finn's hoping to get a job and he's good with the baby. Mrs Resterick – thank you for coming again – Mrs Resterick assures us we're not putting her out. We can manage here, Guy.'

'I can see Finn's not doing too badly with the help he's receiving but you're not managing at all, Fiona,' Guy said gently, easing her to sit down. He took the crochet blanket and tucked it round her as if she were a child. She was certainly childlike and looked utterly lost. 'This place will be horrendously draughty and cold in winter. The baby will suffer. You'll never become well in this environment.'

'I'll never get well anywhere unless Aidan drops his silence with me. He hasn't even answered my letters about Eloise's birth.' Fiona began to sob into the blanket. 'I don't know what I've done wrong. I wish he'd tell me. Guy, would you do something for me? I know it's a great deal to ask, but would you visit Aidan in Dartmoor Prison, speak to him and try to get him to understand that I'm waiting for him? Please!'

Dorrie noticed how her desperate begging made Guy gulp and shudder, and she saw his reluctance to comply with her request. 'I'll get in touch with the authorities and ask for a visitor's pass, Fiona, but on one condition, that you'll allow me to turn this cottage into a decent place for you to live in. Do you agree?'

'Well I . . . All right, agreed, but please, Guy, I couldn't stand a lot of disruption.'

'You won't need to. While I was in Bude sorting out new nursing care for my senile grandmother, I thought a lot about what to do with Merrivale. If you'd agreed to move out I was going to sell it cheap in its present state. I was sure Farmer Newton would have been glad to acquire it. But if you wish to stay, I'll get the place done up slowly, as your health and strength permits. I'll have to employ painters so I might as well pay Finn to do it for me, so there would be practically no disruption for you, Fiona.'

Relief plain on her sallow face, Fiona sank back on the settee. Weary again, her eyelids were flickering for sleep but she listened gratefully.

Greg was smiling, into his stride now. 'And you must have new curtains and stuff. I'm sure Mrs Resterick can advise on a local seamstress, eh, Mrs R?'

'Indeed I can. Jean and Jenna Vercoe of By The Way, where Finn has gone, can run up anything on a sewing machine. All the work and workers that you might need can be found in Nanviscoe. My brother Greg is handy with a saw and a plane, he's always glad to help anyone out, and an old boy Hector Evans would enjoy tackling the garden, with a bit of manual help. Verity, my niece, will also be glad to pitch in again. Denny Vercoe can turn his hand to plumbing and heavy work, tree felling too, if you want.'

'That would be good, eh, Fiona? Make the place lighter and brighter and provide firewood. And I'm willing to put on a pair of overalls and act as labourer to the experts. All you have to do is rest and get well again.'

'Don't know how to thank you both,' Fiona yawned, struggling to get up on her weak legs. Again Greg rushed to help her. 'Do you mind if I go back to bed? You've both made me take heart. If Aidan knows he's got somewhere nice to come home to where his family are waiting for him he'll think differently and get in touch with me, won't he? He must be so unhappy and scared. He's probably been too ashamed over what he's done.'

Dorrie took Fiona upstairs and came back down with Eloise, who was fretting with a windy tummy. She held the baby to her shoulder and gently patted her back. It was wonderful, the smell of a baby and the feel of a baby, and with Eloise wrapped in one of Veronica's shawls it took Dorrie back to wonderful old memories.

Guy was pacing the room, tossing his head like a wild stallion, hands on his hips, obviously boiling with rage. 'I can't help it, Mrs Resterick, I could kill that bloody husband of Fiona's. He's never been scared of anything in his life and he'd certainly feel no shame. I'm sure he stashed some money away when he knew the game was up. He treated Fiona like dirt, put her down in public, and made lewd comparisons between her and his litany of tarts.' He raked his hands through his hair and appealed to Dorrie, 'How can I make her see the truth? That Aidan Templeton-Barr doesn't care a jot about her, Finn or the baby? Finn realizes the truth.'

'I'm afraid there's nothing anyone can do about that until Fiona is ready to face the facts herself,' Dorrie said softly.

Guy shook his head. 'I know and I hate it. Some women are drawn to bad men. They'll endure every sort of humiliation dealt out to them yet they still love their men. I suppose I can only carry on supporting Fiona for the moment and see what happens.'

'That would be for the best, Mr Carthewy,' Dorrie replied softly. She liked Guy heartily; he reminded her of Piers, kindness and forbearing to the last but not a pushover. She was sure Guy would protect Fiona with his life. 'Actually, I've just had an idea which might ease Mrs Templeton along the way to a quicker recovery. Tell me what you think. If you agree with me, then after she's had a rest and Finn has come back we'll put it to them both.'

Seven

By The Way, the Vercoe home, was easy to locate, nestling a thousand yards down the lane of the same name, behind the north side of the village church. Finn first passed the redundant forge where Denny Vercoe's father had been the last blacksmith. When motorized vehicles caught on for farming and private use there had not been enough work to justify keeping the forge occupational. Equestrian needs were now seen to by neighbouring villages. Finn felt Nanviscoe was missing something by the silencing of blasts from the furnace and the rhythmic clangs of the hammer. Apparently, Denny used the forge as a store. He was jack-of-all-trades and worked as a dealer in a diverse variety of goods.

Finn listened to the persistent happy chirps and tweets of the birds, something he had not noticed when living in town. He had marvelled at how still and calm little Eloise seemed in his arms when he was outside with her, as if she was aware of nature's calls too. Across the fields he saw rabbits hopping about and wondered if Denny Vercoe, known for taking bounty where it abounded, was out with a shotgun to bag his family a meal. He had seven children in a wide range of ages, according to Mrs R – a lot of mouths to feed.

'Damn it, hope you're not out, Vercoe,' Finn muttered, shifting, as he was apt to, all too easily into a dark mood. 'I want to get back to Eloise quickly.' He trusted Mrs R not to be late arriving at Merrivale but he hated the thought of Guy Carthewy being there. Carthewy had the right to be inside his property, and while Finn was grateful for his charity and goodwill, he feared Carthewy's influence on his mother. After days of Finn and Nurse Rumford trying to coax his mother out of bed it had only taken Carthewy five minutes to get her to agree to do so. It was plain as the nose on his face that Carthewy was hankering after Fiona, that he would promise her anything to make her happy, and Finn feared she would plead with him to get in touch with his father on her behalf, and this might lead to his sly and calculating father using Carthewy to springboard him back into some element of the business world and the same sordid pattern being repeated.

Under his arm Finn had a large parcel of things he hoped to barter with Denny Vercoe for a second-hand, good-quality pram for Eloise so he could take her down to The Orchards to see Belle, who was never out of his mind and hopes.

On either side of the Vercoe home rambling one-storey extensions had been built. The original house seemed squashed in between and the walls were begging for fresh coats of whitewash. Moss and mud splashes clung to them. Dotted about in slapdash disorder were countless sheds made from scraps of wood and corrugated iron. The pigsty housed a small herd of pink and grey pigs with strong snouts feasting on mangolds, and swarms of tumbling piglets. There was a long strongly built chicken and bantam run and behind the wire a strutting rooster of different species were keeping a respectful distance from each other. A ragbag of cats was sprawled up on a shed roof as if they had been busy ratting all night and needed their rest. The place was open and sunny and gave off a lazy, contented air, with just an old apple tree and a hawthorn tree to offer shade. There was nothing creepy or despairing about this property and Finn felt comfortable as he closed in on it. Parts of rusting vehicles and machinery fronted the buildings. Weeds and nettles grew everywhere. A wooden sign stuck out of the hedge bearing the place's name: BY THE WAY. Finn thought it a good name for the pleasing shambles.

On the driver's seat of a wheelless rust heap was a small tan curly-coated dog, with a tall tuft sticking up on the top of its square head. In case the mutt was territorial and the old van was its sentry box, Finn strode the last few feet cautiously, but it was a friendly little creature and while creating a high-pitched din it jumped out of the cab and came tearing energetically towards Finn and then rolled over on its back to display submission.

Finn hunkered down to it and tickled its wiry tummy, wary of fleas, worried about carrying any back to Eloise. 'Daft little thing, aren't you?'

A woman appeared in the doorway at the side of the house. She had a lot of backside and frontage, all jouncing about under a full well-worn paisley apron, a waist-length cardigan apparently made from unpicked former knits, a dress that appeared to have once been curtain material, no stockings and dusty, clumpy shoes. Mrs R's declaration that the Vercoe women were adept seamstresses had not provided this woman with any fashion sense. She wore thick-rimmed glasses and had masses of dark-honey hair. She was hefting a washing basket – flasket, she would call it – containing a mountain of wet laundry.

'Morning to 'ee, my bird,' she grinned, and the pleasantry caused her to lose her frumpy image. Finn was drawn to her motherly persona and wished his own mother were more like this woman. 'I wondered what started the dog off. Quiet girl, quiet, Tufty!' Obediently, Tufty trotted off back to her scrapyard kennel. 'That's better. We can hear ourselves think now. Something I can do for 'ee, my handsome?'

'I'm here to see Mr Vercoe,' Finn said politely.

'Aw, he's somewhere about here. Be in for his crib in a minute. Go on inside and wait for him, while I hang this lot out. Can't keep to one washday with my brood. My eldest daughter Jenna's in the kitchen. Go in and talk to her, through this door. Don't be shy, we're a friendly lot here.'

'Thank you, Mrs Vercoe,' Finn replied, smiling for he was sure he was going to feel at home here. Miss Verity had talked about her happy reunion with the Vercoes, calling them the salt of the earth, and adding it was a pity the earth wasn't filled with people just like them.

While Jean Vercoe went round the back of the house, Finn sauntered over the high threshold straight into the large kitchen, one of the house's extensions. His lingering smile drained away. From bending over a treadle sewing machine beside one of the wide windows a girl of about fifteen years looked up at him. He was met with the beady stare of Jenna Vercoe, a girl he realized he'd come across before on the high street of Wadebridge, a girl and her friends that he and his schoolmates had openly jeered at for coming from an inferior background. 'Not even good enough to be oiks!' Finn had smirked, entering the verbal abuse. His behaviour had been cruel and immature and now it made him cringe.

'Oh . . .' Finn could have faced her better if she hurled scathing remarks at him about his enormous comedown, but Jenna Vercoe merely gazed at him as if he was something no one desired to find on the bottom of their shoe. 'Um, your mother told me to come straight in and . . . and wait for your father. I've come to see him,' Finn ended lamely.

Jenna took her time repositioning a loose cover of thick beige material under the machine needle. Crammed on the floor about her feet were baskets of cloth oddments. A box of rag dolls was waiting to be dressed and receive their facial features. Without looking at him again, but giving an uninterested shrug, she said in her soft Cornish accent, something Finn had ridiculed her for, 'Sit and wait then.'

Aggression he could cope with but he hated being made to feel a fool. A worm of uncertainty dragged down uncomfortably in his stomach and he went to up her. 'I, um, owe you an apology for the time we met before.'

She flew to her feet, startling Finn. 'I don't want your apology. It would mean nothing to either of us.'

Finn's brows shot up to his scalp. It was like being challenged by a wild cat, a wild cat with blazing dark eyes, yet he noticed she had a pretty nose and delicate ears. He was further forward with girls than most of his peers. He had looked them over with a male's appreciative eyes from the age of twelve, and at his sixteenth birthday dinner party, an older woman guest, strategically invited by his father because her husband might make a useful business contact, had got him out into the dark garden and instructed him on how to lose his virginity. The flames of need had flared in him again when he met Belle, but that was more than lust. He needed to see her again like he needed breath in his body. Once he got a pram for Eloise – please God let it be here today he got a pram – he would soon stride out with her to The Orchards. The confidence gained from his sexual encounter had fed his natural arrogance, but gazing at Jenna now, he sensed behind her understandable anger at him that his jibes had hurt her. Her hostility with him was his just due. 'It might not mean anything to you, Jenna, but I really am sorry. It's one good thing that's come out of my family's fall from grace, that I see myself for the ignorant, big-headed sod that I was.'

'Good,' she said simply. 'I'd rather get on with my work but it's not my family's way to be inhospitable. Sit down. I'll start on the crib. Like fennel tea? We keep proper tea only for weekends and special occasions.'

'Mrs Resterick has brought over some herb brews for my mother and me, so that's fine, thanks. Your job is a seamstress?'

'Yes, since I left school last year at fourteen. No possibility of college for me,' Jenna remarked, with an edge of regret.

Finn nodded in empathy. 'Nor me now.' He studied the banquet-sized oilcloth covered table to decide the best place for him to sit.

'Sit anywhere, we don't charge,' Jenna said drily. 'Father sits at the head; park yourself on the next chair so you can talk.'

'I've come about getting a pram for my baby sister, Eloise,' Finn tried, thinking that surely this would soften Jenna. He didn't want her to tell her father about his insulting rudeness and be hauled out by the dealer who, by all accounts, was always ready to protect his family with his bellowing roar and, if need be, his fists. 'I understand there are some young children here.'

'There is, my youngest brothers, twins Frank and Jake, are down for their morning nap. How's your mother? I've heard you're doing a good job caring for the baby,' Jenna said, and Finn felt she was interested but not in a nosey way.

'And you've brothers and sisters at school?'

'Maia, Meg, Susie and Adrian.' Jenna put a plate of rock buns on the table and stared at Finn. 'And . . .?'

'I wasn't going to dodge your questions, Jenna. My mother is getting better very, very slowly but Eloise is fine, a little small still, but Nurse Rumford says she's strong and will thrive. I was terrified the first night I looked after her on my own. I sat up all night in low candlelight and tried to stay awake but I nodded off. I heard Eloise murmur and woke up and looked into her cradle.' Finn couldn't bring himself to admit she had first slept in a drawer. 'She wasn't there and panic went through me like a bolt of lightning. Then I felt something move on my shoulder. It was Eloise. I'd forgotten she'd been fretting and I'd picked her up and cuddled her. She's practically weightless and it was lucky I didn't drop her in relief. I never thought I'd be changing nappies and not find it disgusting at my age,' he finished with a proud laugh.

Jenna faced him squarely. 'Well, I'm not sure if I like you yet but I admire what you're doing. Most people round here do.'

'Thanks.' Finn felt a little more at ease. He hoped to redeem himself fully with Jenna. She had not fired personal questions at him so she wasn't a gossip. It would be good to have a friend on the same level, understanding babies, and knowing what it was like to be unable to fulfil your potential. 'Do you know if your father has a pram for sale, Jenna?'

'I'm sure he'll be able to fix you up. Ah, here he comes now, and Sam Lawry's with him. Have you met Sam yet?'

The last person in the world Finn wanted to meet was Sam Lawry. He didn't want to be reminded that Belle was a mother and a married woman. It made her more inaccessible to him. But five minutes later he was seated round the table with the other youth, who was annoyingly chatty, intelligent and the sort who fitted in everywhere. He was tow-haired, presumably inheriting this from his father, but his eyes shone with the clear brownness of Belle's beautiful eyes. Finn resented him for his very existence. And there was the full compliment of the Vercoes who were currently at home. Presiding in the carver chair at the head of the vast table was bull-necked, heavy-footed Denny, with the build of a heavyweight boxer and a full brownish, red-streaked moustache, dominating the room like a lion. His thick lips had a perpetual jovial smile and he joked endlessly, having welcomed Finn to 'my humble little abode' with a thudding handshake. However, his heavily hooded eyes were so piercing that Finn sensed Denny could swiftly turn to bellowing anger.

Finn and Sam were ushered by Denny to sit next to him on either side of the table. 'The male end!' Denny had jested loudly, slapping down his palm and making the mugs and teaspoons shudder and chink. 'Tuck into the buns, you boys,' he chuckled, as loudly as a waterfall. 'Food's on the table to be eaten, not to be longed for. The Lord'll provide the next meal, and if He doesn't well it don't hurt to go with an hungry belly every now and 'gain, eh?'

Jenna was sitting down the other end with Jean, who was gaily breastfeeding the twins, roughly a year old. Finn begrudged Sam his comfortable acceptance of Mrs Vercoe's large pendulous bare breasts, whipped out from under her clothing. Finn kept his eyes rooted to Denny's end of the table.

'Right, let's get to business, Finn. You want a pram and you've brought something to barter with. I've got just the very one for you, only got un last week as part of a house contents sale. Built before the war but in bran' spanking condition, barely a scratch or dent on un. I could get ten bob for un. What's in your parcel?'

Finn had to clear his throat – horribly embarrassed that Sam Lawry was witnessing his bartering with someone else's junk. 'My landlord said I could take the small odds and ends lying about Merrivale, candlesticks and stuff.' He mumbled, red-faced at the end, 'Hope it's enough. I've cleaned and polished everything.'

'Should be, I'd say,' Denny said, rubbing his meaty hairy paws in relish. 'Old Elvira White kept a good house in her day. Tip it out on the table. There could be silver in them candlesticks,' he roared in mirth, accenting like a Wild West prospector. Sam and Jean laughed with him. Finn snatched a glance at Jenna. She was sipping her fennel tea, looking over the mug's rim at him with sympathy. Finn felt some relief that it seemed he had made a friend of Jenna, but he hated Sam for laughing at his expense, even though it was not unkind laughter.

Placing his parcel down in the space Denny had made for it, Finn untied the string and carefully lifted back the brown paper flaps. Some of the items he had brought were wrapped in lining paper from an odd roll he had found in a cupboard. Together he and Denny revealed the lot.

'Wow, some of this stuff is lovely,' Sam whistled through his teeth.

Finn narrowed his eyes and thought Sam had sounded like a girl. *Keep your bloody nose out*, he seethed inwardly.

Denny picked up the pair of candlesticks and studied them. 'Silver alright, hallmarked.' He turned over two porcelain trinket boxes, some odd silver spoons, a heavy glass ashtray, and a pince-nez. He perched the pince-nez on his long nose and looked like a peculiar owl. Jenna giggled. 'I remember the old dear wearing these,' Denny sniggered. 'Mean old cow, she was, wouldn't give you the smell of her farts!'

Everyone fell about laughing, and even Finn at last fully relaxed. 'The lot is worth more than ten bob, wouldn't you say, Mr Vercoe?' Finn ventured. He was sure his bundle was worth a lot more but Eloise must have a pram, it was a necessity, and he did not want to antagonize his host.

Denny put the weight of his hand on Finn's shoulder and squeezed it friendly-style. 'Much more than that, boy. I give a fair price and it's not pride on my part to say Denny Vercoe can be trusted to his last word. Come with me to the shed. I'll show you the pram and you might like to look over some of my other goods; got more in the old forge. If nothing else takes your fancy then the rest of our deal will be in good hard cash. I'll bring the pram over to your place in my van, wouldn't want you pushing it home and looking like a sissy!'

Twenty minutes later Finn left By The Way, pleased with the deal he had made with Denny, privately between the two of them, but miffed that Sam Lawry had declared he was going home and would walk with him to the crossroads. Although confident Mrs R would have duly arrived and taken charge of Eloise, Finn was eager to get home, hoping to find Guy Carthewy had left. It was obvious he was in love with Fiona, and Finn was worried Carthewy would try to fast-track his mother into a relationship with him, using security as bait. Fiona could not cope with more confusion. Finn strode along with his hands stuffed in his pockets, only speaking after Sam did.

'It's nice to have someone my own age nearby in the village.'

'Is it?'

'Well, there's a few other chaps but they've more or less gone their own way. Some have gone into apprenticeships, one or two have moved away. I've gone into the family business, of course. Same as Jenna has, following her mother's trade.'

'Really.'

'Are you wondering why I was at the Vercoes?'

Finn shrugged and kicked a stone into the grass verge. 'No.'

'I'm sweet on Jenna.' Sam suddenly stepped in front of Finn making him halt and blink in surprise. 'She's lovely. You're a good-looking bloke. I'm not going to have a rival for her, am I?'

'What?' Finn was stunned but didn't react by bawling at Sam Lawry to get out of his way; instead he found himself grinning. 'Don't be bloody daft, you prat, I've got too much on my mind right now to bother with girls. Not that I haven't had a lot of experience with them,' he wasn't above boasting. He cherished the memory of Belle. *Besides, it's your mother I want.*

'Great, we can be friends then, if you want to be.' Sam dropped back at Finn's side. 'I'm sorry my dad didn't have a job for you but you're always welcome to drop into The Orchards.'

'OK, I will, but while my mother's recovering I'll be bringing my baby sister. Mrs Belle called on us and said to bring Eloise along at any time.'

'Great, can I come to your place?'

'Sure.' Finn could gain news about Belle from Sam.

Sam kept glancing at Finn.

'What?'

'You've had girlfriends then? Kissed them?'

'Yes, and I've spent time with an older woman.' Finn winked at Sam.

'You mean . . . you did *it* with her . . . everything?'

'Yes,' Finn replied, his head held high, grinning broadly.

'Wow, lucky bugger.' A pause. 'What was it like?'

'Well, as my late grandfather used to say, if God made anything better He kept it for Himself.'

They were in the village, heading in the direction of Petherton and then the school. Finn took this way to avoid the Stores and teashop where nosy people might be lingering.

'Hey, you boy! Not you, Samuel Lawry. The Templeton boy! Come here!' From the entrance of Petherton, its iron gates patriotically removed years ago for the war effort, her feet astride like a man would stand, was the superior figure in tweeds and brogues of a middle-aged woman. She marched at the boys.

'It's the indomitable Mrs Mitchelmore, the old cow,' Sam whispered. 'Be civil to her or she'll be round to your mother demanding she teach you some manners.'

'Yes madam?' Finn said politely, but he did not move forward to meet the woman, keeping aloof. The woman would be attractive if she wasn't squared off in physical appearance. In her hand were a notepad and a scrap of pencil. Her voice had a thundering, swift quality and much about her was penetrating and hawkish. She smelled strongly of rose and violet scent. 'Can I help you?'

'Absolutely not, it's the other way round, that's why I've taken the time and trouble to address you. I'm Mrs Esther Mitchelmore, lady of the manor, so to speak, and chairwoman of all the local charitable committees hereabouts. Don't stand on your pride,

Master Templeton. That wasn't the attitude that won the British Isles the war, and I can't be doing with it. What do you and your mother and the infant need? Speak up, I haven't got all day, I'm a very busy woman. Shan't be calling on you wanting to socialize. I respect others' penchant for privacy. Take this pad and pencil and I shall see to the best of my ability, and availability of course, that you get it, via Mrs Resterick. I'm sure that should suit you.'

The notepad and pencil was pushed into Finn's hand and he stared at it, quite flummoxed for the moment. He and his mother were strangers, from a disgraced background, yet the village on the whole had showed them unreserved generosity.

Sam nudged his elbow and hissed into his ear. 'Write something for goodness' sake. Humour her or she'll get persistent.'

'What did you say, Samuel Lawry?' Mrs Mitchelmore demanded fiercely.

Sam responded with charm and a touch of fake fawning. 'I was reminding Finn that although he has just bought a lot of baby stuff and household things, Mrs Mitchelmore, he did mention he would be next requiring some towels and dishcloths.'

'Consider it done, Master Templeton. Before the day is out, a parcel will be dispatched to Sunny Corner to be passed on to your mother. Oh, and with the addition of some stationery, in case she hasn't got any, an essential for a woman of breeding, as I understand Mrs Templeton is. Now tell me why you are called Finn, short for Philip, something of the sort?'

'My name isn't shortened from anything. My parents simply liked the sound of Finn. Thank you for your kindness, Mrs Mitchelmore.' Finn's impatience was rising with the termagant. *You bloody patronizing bitch.*

'Did they really? I've heard more peculiar names,' she snorted then waved Finn away. 'Run along now. I'm sure your mother is anxious for your return.'

Finn walked on hurriedly expelling an angry sigh.

Sam had to chase after him. 'Don't take any notice of her, she's a strange old girl but she did get things done during the war. Was a great comfort, it's said, to those who lost loved ones. She's constantly at war with Delia Newton from the Stores; that woman is a mare and a half. She tries to stop everything that's beneficial to the village, she and the vicar, the lazy old sod. You probably won't be interested in this, but there's a meeting pending to be held at our house about getting a village hall built. My dad, Mrs Mitchelmore and Mr Barnicoat, and a chap called Evans, are determined to drive it through. There'll be ructions once Mrs Mitchelmore and dreary bitchy Delia Newton get started. Makes for good entertainment though,' Sam chuckled.

Finn was quietly thoughtful. 'I suppose Mrs Belle will act as hostess, with Mrs R and some other ladies. It looks like Nanviscoe is going to be my family's home for some time, so I suppose I might as well make the effort to get to know some more people. Everyone knows our circumstances yet most people have been good to us. The nasty ones can go to hell. I'll try to make it to the meeting.'

'Well, I can keep you informed, and you can come over to The Orchards at any time.'

'Oh, I will, Sam, most definitely.'

Eight

It was Wednesday morning and that meant a certain gathering of women at Faith's Fare. Esther Mitchelmore and Delia Newton were on duty in the Thrift Niche, and Belle Lawry and Agnes Pentecost were in attendance at the refreshment counter. The two sections of the hut were not partitioned: the cafe customers were sat at one of the three gingham-covered tables donated by Esther from her home and could freely socialize with the bargain hunters. Banter or gossip was often exchanged in deliberately loud voices so facts and speculation and downright nastiness soon circulated round the village.

At a table by the window (the glass scavenged from a greenhouse panel), waiting for cups of tea and home-made ginger biscuits were Dorrie, Verity and Jean Vercoe. Baby Eloise, on her first outing into the village, was cradled in her shawl in Dorrie's arms. Jean had left her big pram, so rarely out of use, outside and had a twin son propped on her lap. The three women were cooing over Eloise. 'She's such a contented baby,' Dorrie told Jean proudly.

'I can see that. One or the other of these little blighters has me up most nights. Anyway, I think you're an angel, Mrs Resterick, taking the whole family in under your roof while Merrivale is done up.'

A snort of something akin to disdain issued from Delia's snooty nose. She was dusting the shelves of donated ornaments, ordered to do so by Esther, who was as usual taking charge of everything in her inarguable manner.

Verity glared at Delia. 'You wouldn't know she was in the house, Mrs Vercoe. It's a joy to me to share in looking after her while Finn is busy working at Merrivale. It's more comfortable for Mrs Templeton and she's progressing slowly but steadily.'

'I'm sure,' Jean said, jiggling her legs up and down to make the chubby twins chuckle. 'You've always enjoyed having a houseful, haven't you, Mrs Resterick? Me too, couldn't stand it for a minute if my place was quiet.' She too shot darts of contempt at the pursed-mouthed Delia. 'Some round here wouldn't put themselves out for others, and some of them pack themselves into the front pews every Sunday. Faith without good deeds isn't faith at all. They know it; it's time they took note of it.'

Belle brought over the tray of refreshments. 'Sam says Merrivale has been completely replastered, the woodwork repaired and the roof is now being re-tiled. I've seen for myself the outlook is altogether much lighter now the trees have been thinned out. The stream that runs through the bottom of the garden has been cleared and runs down to Shady Lane again. The gloominess seems all taken away. I've also seen Mr Carthewy labouring away and up to his knees and elbows in dirt. He's given some hard-pressed men the opportunity of earning something extra, and good for him. Finn says that by and by he'll get his mother to sit by the stream. Good idea, I told him, there's nothing as soothing as the sound of pure running water. He also says he's no longer daunted about the prospect of living there again.'

Running a gleaming white dishcloth over the scrap of cafe counter, Mrs Pentecost, short, nimble, thin and bony, in her seventies with long-lashed eyes always ready to smile, chipped in. 'Rebecca says the little one is thriving. She was pleased as punch when you suggested the family move into Sunny Corner while Merrivale is being worked on. That poor woman would never recover with all manner of bangs and thumps going on around her. She'd have had no privacy, and all that dust would have been very bad for the baby. Rebecca says Mr Greg dotes on her and it amuses Rebecca when he talks to little Eloise as if she can understand him.'

'Allow me to hold Eloise while you drink your tea, Mrs Resterick,' Belle offered. Smilingly Dorrie relinquished her charge.

'Bring the child over here,' Esther ordered. She was filling in the inventory book of things for sale in the niche. People were used to Esther's bossiness and only a few took exception to it. 'I haven't had a good look at her yet.'

Piqued over the reproving remarks Jean had aimed at her, Delia uttered under her breath, 'You can bet Guy Carthewy isn't lashing out all his time and money for nothing. It's wicked.' Then she stiffly turned her back and set her feather duster vigorously over a block paperweight. She hummed a tune in an indistinguishable drone to ensure she stayed excluded from the clucky gathering. Delia had three grown-up sons all 'doing well in the city' and all 'far too busy to travel down so far to see Mr Newton and I.' Thrice a year for a week, in turn, the Newtons visited their sons, and Nanviscoe bathed in the respite.

'Mmmm, she is a pretty baby.' Esther nodded approvingly. 'Such deeply coloured eyes. I would have so loved to have had children, but it wasn't to be.'

Honoria Sanders breezed in, clouding the air with a heavy tropical perfume and swinging her fox furs. The gold and diamonds on her fingers created prisms and stabs of sparkling light. Pearls circled her neck. 'I'm delighted I never had any little sprogs, some of us aren't cut out to be mothers, eh, Esther? But this child is *very* sweet, bless her heart. Is her mother here? I can see the answer is no. I hope she's still recovering. Ah, Mrs R, I take it you're in charge of the tiny mite. Must give you some silver for her. Here's half a crown.'

'Thank you for your generosity, Mrs Sanders,' Dorrie said, grinning, for one couldn't fail to delight in Honoria's scintillating company.

Honoria chattered on. 'Hello, Mrs Newton, I see you're hiding away in there. Is that because the meeting about the hall didn't go your and the Rev. Lytton's way? We all know the vicar's reason; he's a lazy so-and-so who doesn't even want a new church hall built because he wants only to spend time writing his memoirs. He never was much cop at vicaring, hardly knew how to offer a crumb of comfort to the bereaved before or during the war, nor since. But why you, eh? I didn't attend the meeting but I've heard all about your objections – encourage loitering and rowdiness, a poor excuse indeed! There's no one in Nanviscoe with the slightest interest in doing that; people are too intent on simply surviving.' Honoria was in full flow and dramatizing her themes with flaunting circles of her silk gloved hands. 'It's time someone brought up the real reason and time you faced your pettiness, woman. Your resentment lies from long ago over Mrs Vercoe's eldest sister Anita being chosen as school May Queen instead of you. I wasn't residing at Sawle House then, of course, but I've heard the tale many a time. Your mother hinted to the former headmaster that she would make a generous donation for a new lavatory block for the school, while she had a dress made up for you. The vicar approved the appointment. But the headmaster wasn't to be bribed, and his vote along with the vote of Mrs Mitchelmore's late husband was cast for the prettiest and most honest eligible girl, Anita. And ever since then you have seethed and resented the fact that Anita's reign was considered one of the best in Nanviscoe, haven't you, shallow woman that you are? A village hall will be built, and sooner rather than later, for I have decided to give one hundred pounds towards the building costs so time and effort doesn't have to be wasted on raising funds. With similar generosity pledged by my good sister here and Mr Jack Newton, Nanviscoe will have a hall fit to entertain the King and Queen in.'

A clamour of grateful and excited voices broke out but they were brutally interrupted. Delia threw down the paperweight and it thumped, denting the wooden floorboard, and clattered and spun noisily. 'So I am to be mocked, am I? Held in the poorest regard in public and then no doubt to be scorned later in every household? No one has ever liked me. I've always been an object of ridicule and my work and ideas for the village always pushed aside in favour of anyone else's, even the tramp and the gypsies that pass through Nanviscoe. Two weeks ago, that criminal's son now living in our midst cut off my speech at the meeting under the oh-so-saintly Lawrys' roof. The Templeton boy raised his hand and all attention was turned to him. What right did he have to be there? Come on, tell me that. He's not one of us. Why did he dare to show his face when he and his mother chose at first to shun us? His words were, "May I say in view of all the kindness and acceptance my mother and I and my new sister have received I think a hall would be a brilliant thing. It's the very thing where people can meet and enjoy mutual interests." How dare he speak up when his own father is in jail for fraud while serving as a public servant! It's too much that the boy's opinion is sought and mine, a woman whose husband was born and bred in Nanviscoe, counts for nothing.

'Well, build your damned village hall, let criminals and rogues infiltrate and corrupt you, but I'll never, ever forgive you, any of you, for the contempt you've shown me, and you'll all be sorry. I'll make you sorry in a way you'll never forget!'

Nine

For the first time in weeks Fiona scrambled out of bed with some energy and feeling hopeful and excited. She glanced at the little square-faced clock on the bedside cabinet. It was seven thirty. Guy was motoring up to Dartmoor Prison today after receiving a pass to visit Aidan. Guy was taking with him at his own expense cigarettes and toiletries for Aidan. Aidan, a man of movie heart-throb looks, hated not to be well groomed. Guy was also taking long loving letters from Fiona containing glowing details of the lovely, spacious house she and Finn were guests in, and how beautiful Aidan's new baby daughter was. Fiona had added that Eloise had not been christened yet and he could change her name or add others to it, as he liked. Guy had also taken photos of Eloise. Worried about her still haggard looks, Fiona was sending a snap of herself taken soon after she had met Aidan, as a vivacious teen besotted and adoring of him. Finn had adamantly refused to have his photo taken.

'Please, Finn, do it for me. Your father will be proud to see the muscles you've developed while working on Merrivale. I've written to him all about the renovations and changes under way, and how good the locals have been to us, that most of them have welcomed us against all the odds. It will make him feel like it's his home to come out to. When he finishes reading all my letters he will feel he knows Dorrie, Greg and Verity.'

Finn had just arrived back at Sunny Corner after eight hours' work with Greg, sanding and varnishing floors. He was dusty and dirty and smelled strongly of the clear varnish they had used. He'd reported that Hector Evans had been digging over some of the back garden and Denny Vercoe had sawn the felled branches into logs.

Fiona had tried to be patient with Finn, for she could see he was weary and his limbs were aching and he only wanted to clean up and spend some time with Eloise. Later he would stroll down to The Orchards and spend an hour or so with his new friend

Sam Lawry. Fiona was heartened at how quickly Finn had made a friend of his own age and had fitted into Nanviscoe life. He had even attended a meeting about some proposed new building.

'I've told you a hundred times I don't want anything to do with him ever again. He's no good. He'll certainly be interested in Miss Verity,' Finn had bit back. 'He's always made a beeline for attractive young women.'

'What does that mean?' Fiona had wailed, slipping into the depression that was always a ready companion to her.

'Wake up, Mum, what do you think it means? He's shunned us completely since he was sent down. He didn't respond to the news of Eloise's birth, he doesn't care about her. He's probably only agreed to see Guy to tell him to tell you to get it into your head that he's finished with his family.'

Fiona had put her hands over her ears. 'Don't say that! You don't really know how Aidan's feeling. I think he's ashamed of everything and can't bear to face us. He probably thinks we'd be better off without him.'

'That last part is true. Without him around coming up with scams and schemes – and face it, Mum, get-rich schemes are all he ever talked about – we'll have the chance of making a life for ourselves in the cottage. Can't you see how lucky we are, having Guy and Mrs R and the others putting themselves out for us? How many people left in the lurch get that sort of help? I'll get a proper job, I'll find something, I'll work like a navvy to support us and pay rent to Guy, and then we can work on repaying all these people's kindness. My father doesn't want the responsibility of his new baby but Eloise is your responsibility, Mum. You've got to stop thinking about yourself and what you've lost and get well and start taking care of your baby. The three of us have been given a fresh start and you're the one who needs to pull her weight to give us the best chance for it to work.'

'You're wrong about your father, Finn, you'll see,' Fiona had confronted him angrily, and then purposefully put on a wan expression begging for understanding. 'I'm sorry things have been so hard for you. I am grateful to you and to everyone else. I'm sure when Aidan sees what everyone has done for us he will be grateful too and it will give him the impetus to change his ways and settle down quietly with us. I'm not totally blind to his faults.

I know about his other women, but he's a very handsome man and floozies always throw themselves at successful men. I believe prison will change him for the better. He's been too ambitious in the past but after suffering all the deprivations of prison life he'll come out with the right frame of mind to make a fresh start with us. I wish you would write to him, Finn. Any man would hate to know his son is against him.'

'I'm sorry I can't share your optimism, Mum. Let's see what happens when Guy talks to him.'

So sure was Fiona of her belief in Aidan that she rallied her hopes. She was actually singing while she trotted along to the bathroom. She liked everything about Sunny Corner, its light and fresh location, the house's gentle countrified style, the sheltered peaceful garden. The plumbing worked perfectly, which had not been the case in her former more modern home, and the porcelain bath with its big brass taps was comfort and luxury. After she had run a few inches of warm soothing water she threw in a handful of rose-scented crystals from a packet Verity had given her. She had spoken little to her hosts' modish, sometimes sad, but more often confident niece and resolved to get to know Verity better. She was quite a few years younger than Fiona and something of a 'princess' type, but Verity was on the same footing, being without her man, and she would be a good friend to have. She heard Eloise begin to whimper in the next room, Finn's room, and a layer of deadened skin was peeled back from Fiona's heart as she felt a tug of need to go to her baby, yet she couldn't manage to make her feet work to do so. Her little girl was waking up and in need of a nappy change, a feed and to be dressed for the day. She whispered very softly, 'Eloise, don't cry . . .'

Then she heard Dorrie's familiar light tread mounting the stairs and going in to see Eloise. 'Hello, darling,' Dorrie cooed. 'Ready to come downstairs with me and Corky?'

As Fiona heard Dorrie carrying her baby downstairs away from her she felt a stinging surge of jealousy. People, especially those in this lovely house, were so kind and only God knew how she would have coped without them, but they were behaving as if she had no place in her baby's life. But of course, that was her own doing, something she couldn't help, and these same kind people understood and were arranging things to give her lots of peace and quiet to help her to recover from the last traumatic months.

Every now and then Dorrie or Nurse Rumford would encourage her to hold Eloise when she was beautifully wrapped in a shawl and sleeping soundly, and Fiona's only reaction was to touch Eloise's tiny face or delicate fingers. Yet, just now, she had felt the urge to go to her baby. That was a good sign. She was moving forward at last. Yesterday, while reclining in Sunny Corner's garden, she had accepted that her old life was gone and she was thankful for it. Without the same conditions and situations to come back to Aidan would not fall back into his old ways, always plotting how to make fast money. He had brought himself down and Fiona was glad about that too; he would no longer be able to swagger about, always wanting to be seen as the best, the top dog. The hardships of prison life might make him see how futile his old ways were, and how much he'd once had and lost. Surely he wouldn't want to risk all that again. This dreadful downfall might be the best thing to have happened. Aidan would be proud of Finn's sterling efforts and hard work.

Looking into a mirror on the bathroom wall Fiona winced at her grey wasted reflection. 'The state of me!' she gasped, horrified, seeing the reality of how her months of hopelessness had rendered her. 'Aidan wouldn't be proud of me looking like this. I've let him down.' Her husband had fallen in love with her for her classical beauty and flair, showing his pride in how she had run his house and her hostess skills by flourishing expensive gifts. She was an excellent cook, something she had enjoyed even when struggling with the rationing.

She couldn't go on moping and letting her looks keep sliding downhill; she must change for Aidan's sake. He was a man who required a lot of love-making and he had made much of her feminine curves, but he couldn't be expected to desire her if she looked like a skinny drab. Aidan had eyes for beautiful women, and Fiona had overlooked his affairs. All she asked was that he always came back to her. By the description she had heard of the local women Fiona had little to worry about in regard to Aidan's wandering ways, except for Verity, but it was unlikely she would still be here at the time of Aidan's release. However, there was the naturally gorgeous Belle Lawry to think about. When the neighbour's wife called here it was easy to see that Finn was infatuated with her. Fiona mustn't allow any woman to outmatch her. She wouldn't aim for her chic image of old but would work to acquire the healthy vivacious country kind of beauty.

She would soak herself in the bath and call on her old expertise to make the most of herself. She would get out her hair curlers. She would ask Verity if she had a little spare make-up and cold cream. It was a lovely mild sunny day and she would cuddle her baby as she relaxed. And she would ask Dorrie if she could make the luncheon, her special vegetable omelette. There was no shortage of eggs from Dorrie's hens. She chuckled as she pictured Dorrie's delight. What a dear little woman she was. And Finn would be thrilled when he got back from the cottage with Greg, both dusty and gritty and ravenous for an hour's break.

Merrivale, our new home, Fiona thought optimistically, and this was going to be a good day, the best in ages, she just knew it. She would take a look at the curtain materials, a good choice thanks to Guy's connections and generosity, brought over by the seamstress Jean Vercoe. The podgy mother was awaiting decisions, and Fiona would make them rather than leaving the responsibility to Dorrie. To top off this lovely day, when Guy returned with messages or even a letter from Aidan her new life would really begin. Aidan loved her, she had never doubted it no matter what he had done, and when he was reassured that she loved him as much as ever, he would reach out to her again.

Guy arrived at Sunny Corner late in the evening. Dorrie showed him into the sitting room. 'You speak to Fiona and Finn alone, Mr Carthewy. The rest of us will clear out and bring in coffee when you're ready. We have saved some dinner for you. I'm sure you must be hungry after your long drive.'

In the study-cum-library, Dorrie turned to Greg and Verity. 'What do you make of his expression? It was a raft of emotions. Will Fiona be receiving the news she's been longing for, I wonder?'

Guy stood awkward and stiffly on the Oriental rug, massaging the tiredness squeezing his eyes.

'Do sit down next to me, Guy.' Fiona patted the red and cream striped, squab-cushioned sofa. 'You are quite worn out. Please don't beat about the bush. Tell us what Aidan said. Have you brought anything from him?' She glanced smugly at Finn. Her belief in her husband had been growing all day. After cuddling Eloise and tending to her all afternoon following cooking her much appreciated lunch, she was in no doubt Aidan would find his daughter as beautiful and as irresistible as she now did.

Guy sighed, working his shoulders to unravel some of the tension. He was also furious over Aidan Templeton-Barr's blasé attitude towards him. After being bodily searched and his gifts for the criminal pulled apart, he had waited among some shady-looking male characters and foul-mouthed, or weeping, or downtrodden women for the afternoon visiting time to begin. The atmosphere was rank with sweat, disinfectant and despair, broken intermittently by an ironic joke. He had sat and waited again where he had been stationed across the iron grid to face Aidan. He had tapped his fingertips together and blew out his frustration as the minutes had ticked by and then some more. Bloody cheek of the man; he had agreed to see Guy, and at the very least he should have the decency to face him on time. Then he wondered if Aidan was well – perhaps he had been beaten up. That wasn't unlikely; he had a big brash mouth on him.

Finally a warder came to him. 'Templeton-Barr is refusing to come out of his cell. He says to give you this and that you might as well clear off. Sorry you had a waste of time, sir, but that's what most of the inmates are, a waste of time.'

'Aidan didn't want to see me. All I've got for you, Fiona, is this.' Guy put his hand into his inside breast pocket. He handed over a prison-issue envelope. It had been censored and resealed by the prison, but Guy wouldn't have dreamed of reading it. He had seen how Aidan had addressed the envelope, to Mrs *Fiona* Templeton, not Mrs Aidan Templeton-Barr. Guy was gratified that he was getting the result he wanted, but he was anxious about how Fiona was going to react to her impending heartache. It was so good to see her dressed elegantly again and wearing a little make-up but he feared she would be about to take to her bed again and sink into a deeper despair than before.

Fiona had read her name on the letter and was sitting up rigidly.

'What does the letter say, Mum?' Finn asked. He had a good idea by her stricken face and Guy's embarrassed fidgeting. He clenched his fists, bracing himself for a fresh, fiercer bout of weeping and wailing from his mother.

Fiona tore open the envelope and let it fall to the floor. She held the prison notepaper before her eyes and scanned it, then said in a disembodied voice, 'You want to know what it says? What I should have known it would. I'll read it to you.'

Finn wasn't sure he wanted to hear it now, remembering his father had once been a good father to him really. There had been boys at his school who had been beaten, ignored or cruelly ridiculed by their fathers. There had been orphaned or fatherless boys, and one with a stepfather who bitterly resented him and had made his life hell.

Fiona began to read, one hoarse word at a time. '"Fiona, I thought you might have taken the hint by my long silence and broken off with me. You haven't, so I'll put this to you straight. It's over between us. You were a good and loyal wife to me but it's not enough for me to want to return to you. I met someone else months before my arrest and she is waiting for me. We will be setting up home in a secret location. I feel bad about the mess I left you in but you have Carthewy looking out for you now. Be sensible and take advantage of it. There is no point in me seeing the baby, but I'll treasure the snaps of her. Finn has made it plain that he's finished with me, so it is best I make a clean break from all of you. I am glad to know you have help from your new friends. Lean on them. Make your future with them. There will be no point in you writing to me again, accept that you would only be flogging a dead horse. I wish you well. A."'

Her eyes seething, Fiona crumpled the letter and threw it down. Finn was glad. Guy was glad. They were both thinking it good she was angry with Aidan. It would help crush her yearning for him, help heal her heartbreak. Without looking at Guy, she said tightly, 'Thank you for making that wasted journey, Guy.'

She got up and went robot-like to Finn. 'Well, you must be happy. You got exactly what you wanted. Aidan would never have wanted to come back to me with his son showing him such disrespect as to shun him.'

Swinging back her hand she smashed it violently across Finn's cheek making his head lurch to the side. 'I hate you for it and I'll never, ever forgive you!'

Ten

Verity thanked the driver of the rattling old coach, stuffy in the hot murky day, as she got off at the stop just past the Olde Plough. She had been to Wadebridge where she had been window-shopping, just for something to do. She had to be careful with her money. She had enough to last the summer then she must look for a job. She might find a secretary's post or something in the town that she could travel to daily. One thing she was certain about, while still weighed down under the hurt of her parents' unjust rejection and with her confidence taken a battering over Julius Urquart's mocking remarks: she needed the security of living with her doting aunt and uncle. The soothing experience of living in what she now considered her home was wearing off a little, however, and doubts as to whether she could make something of her future were sticking uneasily in her mind. She also had less to occupy herself with now the Templetons had moved back into Merrivale.

Fiona had insisted on returning there before all the finishing touches were done, saying she would not impose on Dorrie and Greg any longer than need be. After her husband's cruelly blunt letter, everyone had expected her to plunge again into the dark murk of depression, but while there were times Fiona had cried wretchedly for hours, she had risen every morning and dressed well from her small collection of stylish clothes. She shunned make-up and pinned her hair back in a simple bun. She was, in Greg's words, 'Valiantly soldiering on, and good for her.' She tended to Eloise quietly and with little emotion, willingly relinquishing her to others, but she took her for long walks along the lanes in her pram, avoiding the village. Until she had moved out of Sunny Corner she had shared in the cooking and housework and in the evenings read a wide selection from the eclectic study-library. Guy had now supplied her with a bookcase crammed with books of every subject.

Having agreed to Guy's generous suggestion that she become

Merrivale's housekeeper and receive a wage for the care of his (further clever suggestion) country retreat, she had selected the curtain material and bed linen for the cottage and made a list of the furniture she thought would suit its more charming new look. Fiona insisted her wage would be modest, enough to live on without her relying on Finn to bring money in. 'He must lead his own life,' she had remarked without emotion. 'I won't be responsible for dragging him down.'

Finn was still working on Merrivale and he spent his earnings on Eloise and things for his room. Sometimes he helped with the labouring of the village hall. When it was reported he had been in Newton Stores ordering art pencils and a sketch pad, Esther Mitchelmore had stumped up for him a box of artist's requisites, including an easel, palettes, oils and watercolours and brushes. 'Here boy, with the silly name,' she had called, and thrust the box at him while arriving on the building site, in a siren suit, to 'put her hand's turn' in on the building. 'My late husband fancied himself a bit of a dabbler but he was not very good at it. You're welcome to it. I'll give you your first commission, landscapes of Nanviscoe for the village hall. They'll only be on display if I consider them good enough, of course.' She had smartly killed off Finn's effusive thanks. 'One thank you is sufficient. No good to me gathering dust. When this building is up and running, call at Petherton; I have a job for a pair of strong arms like yours, clearing out my cellars.'

The awful thing was, although Fiona had apologized to Finn for hitting him so fiercely, marking his cheek for days, they were barely communicating, avoiding looking each other in the eye. Neither would reveal what they were thinking despite Dorrie's gentle probing. Dorrie was worried. 'This isn't good for them or the baby. Eloise isn't quite so settled now. Babies pick up on a bad atmosphere. Merrivale has lost its old gloom but Fiona and Finn will create a new one. It's such a shame. Aidan Templeton-Barr has a lot to answer for.'

'They have Guy,' Greg had pointed out. 'He's a constant in their lives, and so are we. Fiona and Finn are going through a time of painful adjustment. With all our help they'll come through.'

Fiona may have given up moping in her bed all day but someone else had taken to hers: Delia Newton. The day she had yelled out in Faith's Fare she would make the women there sorry for making jibes at her – wholly warranted jibes, the village as one had agreed – she had stormed home in hysterical tears and summoned the doctor. Soames had announced she was suffering a complete nervous breakdown, but by the cheery way he was now running the shop on his own he didn't seem particularly concerned about his wife. Delia's put-upon cousin, Lorna Barbary, had the unfortunate task of scurrying about to Delia's whims and demands, no doubt, and listening to her constant whingeing. Few customers in the shop bothered to ask how Delia was faring and those who did were told by a shoulder-shrugging Soames, 'Just the same. Now what can I get you?'

Verity had heard nothing from Julius Urquart and was glad about it. If she ever saw his smug horsey face again she thought she might sink an axe in it. Sometimes she even thought she understood the need to murder, and she would go on to ponder the reason why a paid killer had been sent to slaughter Neville Stevens and Mary Rawling. The Stevens family had moved out of Nanviscoe but Mary Rawling's widowed mother remained, mostly shut away in her tiny cottage further along By The Way lane. Verity had been struck at how her forays along the lane always stopped at the Vercoes. Did Mrs Rawling feel shunned, isolated and forgotten? Even Aunt Dorrie, who never left anyone out of her field of kindness, rarely mentioned her. As far as Verity was aware, if Mrs Rawling wasn't seen out for a while no one bothered to wonder why. That wasn't right, and Verity resolved to talk to Dorrie about it. If strangers like the Templetons could readily be given committed help then why not a villager whose family had dwelt there for generations?

Verity set off for home, using a hand to fan her face and the bare skin above her dusty pink, short-sleeve V-neck cotton blouse. She longed to take off her ankle socks and canvas shoes and cool down her overheated feet. Once in Newton Road, she would soon pass the hall building, its foundation stone laid last month by Honoria Sanders. She would take a look at it and say good afternoon to the workers, a different batch with various skills. The road had a slight incline and the hall was being erected behind a hedge topped with elm trees. A break had been made in the hedge and the road was muddy with tractor tracks and cart ruts bringing building supplies. There were water splashes from the buckets and cans that had been filled at the village pump that stood near the school, and taken to the site by whatever means were available each day, usually wheelbarrows and handcarts.

Carefully negotiating the entrance in case a vehicle was about to be driven out, she found a miscellany of villagers hard and happily at work. The older men were wearing caps or hats as their habit dictated.

'Hey there, darling!' Greg called out and waved, halting in sawing a long length of timber.

'Don't stop for me, Uncle Greg,' Verity called back. 'I've just come to take a quick look.'

Finn was pouring water into a pool he had made in a pile of sand and cement and he began mixing it with a Cornish shovel to the right consistency for laying block. His movements were deft. He impressed everyone that a boy from a posh background was up to menial jobs, working at back-breaking speed and never complaining. He had accumulated a following of dreamy-eyed girls. Now the long summer holiday had begun they brought him drinks of lemonade, sherbet and tea, willingly sacrificing their precious sweet ration by offering him squares of chocolate and toffees. The fact that Finn kindly refused to take their offerings made them idolize him all the more. But Finn was apt to gaze far into space and stay silently in his own thoughts, and the men ribbed him that he was 'sweet on some young maid'. Finn did not bother to deny it and flatly refused to be drawn on it, and Verity and Dorrie wondered if the girl concerned was Jenna Vercoe, although Finn took little notice of her and actually seemed to feed her in Sam Lawry's direction, but that could be a ruse.

Verity exchanged greetings with Finn and the other workers. Hector Evans, an erudite, sharp-witted little man racing up to his sixty-eighth birthday, stooped and pale from his decades spent down the coal pits of his birthplace, was laying blocks for the front wall with methodical skill. It had been his dream to settle in the Cornish countryside on his retirement, and as he had never married or smoked and was a light drinker, he had managed to save for the move to rent one of Jack Newton's cottages. His good heart and generous hand had seen him accepted as a Nanviscan. He had a miner's troublesome cough and joked that bronchitis or pneumonia could 'put me in me box as quick as lightning'. 'Hello, *cariad*, you're a lovely sight to gladden an old man's eyes, as usual,' he said, his wise hooded eyes twinkling. Verity loved to listen to his soft, melodic Welsh lilt.

'And it's lovely to see you again, Mr Evans,' she laughed in return. At that moment Verity knew for certain that she belonged in this village. Her parents didn't want her but her aunt and uncle did, as did all the other inhabitants, with perhaps the exception of Delia Newton.

Mr Walters, the middle-aged headmaster, was also there with his sleeves rolled up above his bony elbows, and with him was a willing line of his older pupils scything and hacking down a hedge and some younger ones clearing up after them. Verity knew that the children, including all the rough-and-tumble Vercoe youngsters, were excited about the village hall and eager for the sweets Mr Walters shared out to them.

'Ah, more help on the way.' Greg pointed to the entrance behind Verity.

Glancing round, she saw Belle Lawry clutching four large Thermos flasks against her shapely chest with effortless grace in her posture. Belle must have come from Faith's Fare. Her shining jet-black hair was swept back with combs at her temples and the rest swayed luxuriously on her graceful shoulders. 'The ravishing gypsy girl,' Greg called her, adding, 'I could see her living contentedly in the wild.' Turning back, Verity saw Finn become board-still and stare at Belle with total admiration and longing. Verity smiled to herself. So it was Belle who he had a crush on. Then she was alarmed to see Finn's face fall in undisguised disappointment and anger. Verity glanced round again. Charlie had joined Belle and he had slipped an arm round his wife's trim waist. *Oh dear*, Verity thought, *possible complications*.

'I've brought another willing pair of hands for a couple of hours,' Charlie said, holding up his hefty mitts. Toned in the body and well muscled in the shoulders, his features reflected his cheerful nature. His tow hair was thick and wavy, his masculine attraction set for the rest of his life. His adoration for Belle shouted out of every inch of him. 'Sam will do a stint tomorrow morning. Weather's set fair for a couple days then we're in for some rain, so the forecaster on the wireless said, but we can see that for ourselves. I hear Mrs Mitchelmore wants all work to stop here at the end of next week and all hands to be put to setting up for the Summer Fair.'

'That's right. I don't suppose we'll have any choice but to obey the Mistress of the Manor,' Greg laughed.

Verity took her leave and continued the walk to Sunny Corner, believing that if Finn didn't keep his feelings for Belle in check he would make a dreadful fool of himself.

A minute later she heard the familiar roar of a fast engine: Jack Newton's Triumph Roadster. It paid to be cautious when he was bombing along the lanes and she squeezed in tightly with her back against the hedge.

Driving with the top down, he slowed down and stopped next to her without his usual flamboyant skid of stones and dust. 'Hop in, Verity, I'll drop you home.' He flashed the whitest teeth in the locality.

Since arriving at her aunt and uncle's she had only seen him at the meeting at The Orchards. He had winked at her and she had smiled back. She liked the farmer, who had allowed her as a child to ride his ponies and play in his farmyard. She had sighed wistfully over him with her teenaged girl cousins for his outrageously handsome rugged looks and powerful physique. A few years on it had struck her that he was only ten years older than she. She laughed aside his wanton ways with a never-ending string of women, and in fact admired him, as her aunt and uncle did, for employing more ex-servicemen than his farm needed, saying they deserved every help and opportunity, the men who made the real sacrifices and endured, in his words, 'the most bloody awful experiences' while he had been refused entry to military service and been forced to work the land during the war. He considered he had had it cushy and felt guilty about it, the mark of a good man. Verity was curious about his personal life. His marriage had been ill fated; after a few months his reclusive young bride had hung herself in his gardens. He never mentioned it and there was hell to pay if anyone else did. Dorrie, one of the two locals who had met Lucinda Newton, had confided that she had seemed to live life on a different plane to everyone else. In the end it seemed the mysterious young woman had not been suited to life at all. Jack Newton now lived partly as a gentleman farmer and spent his copious spare time driving fast cars, shooting game, playing golf around the county and pursuing women.

'Thank you, Mr Newton,' Verity replied. 'I'll be grateful to get home and freshen up.'

With his deep-set eyes he slowly looked her up and down. 'I can see you're overheated but you are prettily pink. Call me Jack. We're on the same par.'

Verity was flattered he no longer saw her as a child and had now taken notice of her. It broke the chains Julius Urquart had clamped on her soul. Why shouldn't men want her? She did not need to flirt to attract men. While in Wadebridge many a man had lifted his hat to her and glanced back at her, and a father and son cleaning shop windows had both wolf whistled at her.

'I've just taken a peek at the hall. It's going up nicely apace. Aunt Dorrie and I are going to help Jean and Jenna Vercoe to run up the curtains for the windows and the stage. There's been a generous donation of blackout material. Jean is going to add some appliqué to brighten them so it won't seem so dark.'

'The hall is the best thing ever for the village,' Jack said, slowing at a bend as if suddenly mindful of his passenger's safety. 'And with my second cousin's ridiculous wife playing melodramatics it's great not to have opposition. The vicar won't bother to continue with his objections without Delia stirring him up.'

'You think Delia is crying wolf? Aunt Dorrie sent her some flowers and Delia thanked her with a shakily written note. We were beginning to feel sorry for her and rather guilty for upsetting her that day.'

'Don't ever feel sorry for that woman!' Jack's handsome features radiated loathing with a passion, but it made him look empty and sad. Verity sensed he was recalling a personal slight to him. 'She's an out-and-out bitch. She's feigning illness to make the rest of you suffer. She's very good at that. Sorry.' He shook his head to dislodge the negative rage, and smiled warmly again. 'She has that effect on me. I was sorry to hear your engagement failed.'

'I'm not sorry at all,' Verity replied. 'I would have had a miserable life. Lucky escape and all that, it's in the past. Now I'm looking towards the future.' She wondered if his harsh statements perhaps referred to the bitter, jealous Delia making life miserable for his tragic late wife. Delia delighted in that sort of thing; one only had to look at how she treated her own cousin, Lorna, a drab woman of humble circumstances, taken into Delia's kitchen and wash house when Lorna had become homeless after her parents' deaths.

'Any idea what you'd like to do, Verity? I know you've done important office work.'

They were driving up to the crossroads. 'I don't mind really as long as it's a bit of a challenge.'

'A challenge? I can't exactly promise you that, Verity, but I might have the very thing for you.'

Eleven

'Have you got any brown sugar, Miss Barbery?'

'Sorry, not a chance I'm afraid, Mrs Resterick,' Lorna Barbery replied, glancing round apologetically at all the relatively empty shelves. Dummy items represented the foods the whole country would love to have back in plenty, but sadly post-war rationing was even tighter than during the duration.

'Oh, what a shame, but I didn't really expect any different,' Dorrie said cheerfully. 'We'll have to settle for making rock buns again. Mr Newton must be finding you a godsend, having you to fill in behind the counter when he has a little break. I must say, if you don't mind, that you're looking very well and perky today?'

Lorna was of early middle age and clumpy in the body, and normally a flushed and breathless individual, but now she was holding herself up straight and was assertively calm. Villagers gladly remarked there was a pleasant atmosphere in the shop now that acid-tongued 'old woman Newton' and taken to her bed. 'And let's hope she stays there for a long while, stuck up old cow,' or something of the like was often added on to the end. Delia had harassed Lorna, belittling her when she was out of earshot. Lorna wore her habitual print apron and tea-coloured, much-darned lisle stockings and thick-heeled brown shoes, her dull thin hair rolled up at the ends and secured with hair grips, yet she looked sparky and younger.

'Any change in poor Mrs Newton's condition?' Dorrie inquired, successfully asking for bicarbonate of soda. 'I was wondering if she'd like a short visit, someone to talk to, in the hope of cheering her up. Did she read the books I handed in for her?'

'I'm afraid it's a resounding no to all your questions.' Lorna lowered her small voice to typical sickbed tones. 'It's very kind of you to think of her, Mrs Resterick, but things seem more and more hopeless. Nothing that Mr Newton or I do or the doctor prescribes or suggests lifts her out of her melancholy. All she wants to do is sleep. She doesn't eat enough to keep a sparrow alive and she's getting quite weak. Ah, here comes Nurse Rumford to give her a blanket bath. Excuse me a moment while I show her through.'

Thirty-one-year-old Rebecca Rumford was tall with a softly moulded figure and a comforting, optimistic manner. Her dark hair was scrupulously pinned up under her white long-tailed cap and she donned thick black stockings all year long. She looked and was utterly agreeable, which was how she usually got her patients to cooperate with her ministrations. She said breezily, 'Good morning, ladies. The wind is picking up, the weather is on the change but it won't hurt the gardens to have a drop of rain. Now, how are the pair of you?'

The two women replied that they were very well.

'Wonderful, keep up the good work.' She passed through behind the counter while Lorna held up the partition. 'Mrs Resterick, I passed Miss Verity on my bicycle yesterday morning while she was on her way to Three Meadows Farm to start her new occupation. She was so excited about it. How did she get on with her first day?'

'Oh, excellently, Nurse Rumford. Farmer Newton couldn't have given her a better task,' Dorrie answered, smiling at the memory of Verity's enthusiasm when she arrived home at teatime.

'May I ask what Miss Verity's new job is?' Lorna asked shyly. 'Mr Soames is always interested in anything that happens on his cousin's farm.'

'Mr Jack has hired her to sift through decades of the estate's business papers and then afterwards to go on to Meadows House and do something there.'

'How nice,' Lorna said, then blushed and gave a silly schoolgirl's giggle. 'I know Mr Jack has a certain reputation, but I do so like him. He's always been kind to me and makes me smile. The other day when I was in Wadebridge picking up some things for Mrs Newton, Mr Jack saw me waiting at the bus stop and he kindly gave me a lift in his sports car all the way here to the front door. It was such a novel, thrilling experience, and he asked me how I was and said I was doing a wonderful thing for Mrs Newton in her hour of need. He even asked how she was even though sadly she's never ever had a good word for him.

She's never looked for anyone's redeeming features,' she ended with more than a trace of hurt.

Dorrie and Rebecca Rumford exchanged understanding looks. Lorna was an old maid, rather afraid, it seemed, of men, but Jack Newton's style of chivalry had clearly charmed her.

'I'll just go through and say hello to Mr Soames and then attend to Mrs Newton,' Rebecca said, after pressing a soft hand to Lorna's skinny shoulder.

When Dorrie left shortly afterwards with her shopping she frowned into space. She was pleased about Verity's new job but worried that Jack Newton might try to press his beguiling masculinity on her. With Verity on the rebound from a crushed heart it could have very undesirable consequences.

In her careful way, Lorna crept upstairs with Delia's lunch tray and into the double bedroom, which meandered through the living quarters to lie directly over the shop. At first Delia had overheard much of the goings-on below and created a fuss about what each customer had bought, or not bought, what they said, and how they had said it. She had complained bitterly about the inappropriately cheerful voices and laughter. Her demands on Lorna, sending her to dash pell-mell to bring her up precisely made cups of tea and meals, to change the bed linen in a certain way – the same with ironing it – and to do the dusting, the polishing and the sweeping of home and shop, and even how to beat and brush the doormats, had gradually tailed off because Delia had grown so sleepy.

'You're not doing yourself any good at all, Mrs Newton,' Nurse Rumford had gently chided her this morning. Lorna had listened from downstairs after Soames relieved her at the counter. 'Too much sleep and lying about has made you lethargic. During the blanket bath your limbs were limp and you were a little uncooperative. Keep this up and you'll start losing your muscle tone and will find it hard to use your legs. The doctor has cut down the dose of your sleeping tablets. I'll talk to him about halving it again. Now, before you go I'll walk you to the bathroom. I shall ask Miss Barbary to take away the commode and you may only have it at night.'

The trip to the bathroom had been quite a performance.

'Come along now, Mrs Newton. Try to put your feet into your slippers. No, no, no, sit up straight or you'll fall off the edge of the bed.'

Lorna had smirked, knowing from the nurse's vexed tone that she, like everyone else in Nanviscoe, believed that Delia was exaggerating her symptoms, symptoms of depression that had never been there in the first place. She had lived all her life in the tyranny of jealousy and snobbery, which she had dumped gleefully on others. The women in Faith's Fare had pushed her down firmly into her place and her malice had charged her to seek revenge, but rather than make people feel sorry for her they couldn't really give a damn, which was true justice. Now Lorna treated herself by gloating over the shrew that had treated her with such cruel disdain.

'You'll never get yourself a man, Lorna. You're too gauche. You walk like an oaf. Your hair is thin and dull, your eyes are squinty, and your eyebrows are too bushy, your figure is dumpy and as for your hands, ugh, they're ugly. You're hairy all over, double ugh! I've seen you in a bathing costume, believe me any man would be horrified to see your pale lumpy flesh, and as for the way your nose goes bright red in winter! You can't dance. You can't do anything clever. You haven't even got a nice smile. You've nothing to attract a man; no money and no position. You're only good enough to work in service and then only as a scullery maid. It's the fate of being an old maid for you and you'll just have to accept it.'

The jibes and insults Lorna had suffered had tormented her like nothing else had, not even when she was thirteen years old and the smelly old man next door had touched her in a very private and forbidden place. He had given her a threepenny piece not to tell anyone. Lorna had not told on him, but after spending the money on sherbet dabs she had been careful to keep away from the old bastard. When Lorna had cried to her late mother about Delia's taunts, Mrs Barbary had patted her head. 'Remember, my handsome, sticks and stones may break your bones but names can never harm you.' It wasn't much help to Lorna but she had held on to her mother's other saying: 'Just remember that the tide don't go out unless it comes back in again.' She clung to the belief that one day Delia would get her just deserts. Now that day had come, and Lorna wasn't going to spare her.

She plonked the tray down on the bed table. 'Wake up, sleepy-head, can't believe you've dropped off again already,' she said in a fake kindly voice. 'I've made a nice spam sandwich for you and put in a little chutney. You're partial to a bit of chutney.'

Lying on her back in the middle of the bed, her mouth wide open while she breathed adenoidally, Delia barely moved a muscle; one eyelid only flickered a little. It was no surprise to Lorna. She got the reduced dose of sleeping tablets down Delia's throat every night – accompanied by a full dose of one of her own. Since staying under this roof Lorna had needed occasionally to drug herself out of her lonely torment, but since Delia's self-imposed bed rest she didn't need sedatives at all, and she revelled in Delia's comedown. Soames had moved into the back bedroom and since Delia's more dozy days he only looked in on her first thing in the morning, but in case he just happened to pop upstairs, Lorna kept up her soothing nursemaid tones.

Suddenly, Delia stirred and lifted herself up on her forearms, shaking and trembling. 'I need the commode!' she shrieked. She sensed that much but comprehended little otherwise; her eyes stayed glazed.

'Now, now, the nurse said you were to shuffle along to the bathroom. We must get you moving again,' Lorna said officiously, enjoying herself. She dragged away the bed table and pulled back the bedcovers. It was very satisfying not to have to bother to be gentle. 'Swing round and I'll put your slippers on.'

'I can't. Oh no, it's too late,' Delia wailed, horribly awake now.

As a strong-smelling dark yellow stain pooled around Delia's lower regions, even though Lorna knew she would have to clean it up – and Delia too – Lorna laughed softly, gloating.

'I'll report this to the doctor the moment I've got you sorted out, poor thing. I will insist they take your illness seriously. You could have something really dreadful wrong with you.'

'Oh, do you think so?' Delia sobbed clearly in fear, her wan face hot with shame.

'It reminds me of a young family man I once knew. One minute he was as strong as an ox then some strange malady overtook him and he went swiftly downhill. Can't remember what was wrong with him but he was dead and buried inside two months. Now don't you worry, Delia. I'll soon have you sorted.'

It took nearly an hour before Lorna got Delia's floppy naked body washed and into a clean nightdress. While Delia shivered slumped on the easy chair that Soames had carried upstairs for the early days of her infirmity, Lorna added a quilted bed jacket and a plaid wool shawl round her quivering shoulders.

'Thank you, Lorna,' Delia addressed her humbly for the first time. 'I'm sorry you have to do this.'

'Oh, I don't mind,' Lorna replied cheerfully, tackling the soiled bed linen. Thankfully Nurse Rumford always advised a rubber sheet for a sick room, so the mattress had been spared. 'You couldn't help it.' Never was there a truer word, Lorna revelled to herself. Delia's humiliation would be complete when the neighbours saw the extra bed linen hanging on the washing line this week.

'Is the shop busy?' Delia mumbled, trying to stay awake.

'Quite busy, I think. While Soames was taking his crib, I served Mrs Resterick.'

'Did she ask after me?'

Delia halted at unfolding the clean bottom sheet and her eyes bored into Delia. 'No, not at all.'

'Oh, does anyone ask after me now?' Delia kept her heavy head up with a hand.

'No, no one, I'm afraid.'

'Oh . . .' Tears filled the edges of Delia's droopy eyes. 'I haven't seen Soames for days. Seems I've been forgotten, that no one cares about me.'

'Yes, Delia.' Lorna licked her lips with delight and went up to Delia and hissed into her ear. 'I'm afraid it does. You're quite forgotten and no cares about you any more.'

Twelve

Taking her new position seriously, Fiona dragged herself out of bed early each morning and got dressed to make Finn's breakfast and prepare his crib box of sandwiches and her home-made cake. Neither spoke much over the kitchen table, both glumly polite, like strangers. Over a single cup of tea Fiona would plan her day's cleaning and cooking. Finn would eat quickly and go up to his room to give Eloise her first bottle and nappy change and dress her for the day. Fiona would hear him talking and laughing to Eloise, amusing her with toys and rattles, but Fiona was too raw inside to be warmed by it, to feel the pride in her son that others constantly remarked she must have in him. All she was glad about was that the baby, secure in Finn's devotion, always drifted off to sleep and stayed down for the next two to three hours so she could get on. She and Finn were talking now. If he went to the hall building-works she would ask him how he'd got on and he'd tell her. He would ask her how Eloise was throughout the day and how Fiona's day had been. They were talking, politely, warily, and just about giving each other a smile.

Finn would bid her a quick goodbye, his tin crib box tucked inside a long-handled cloth bag Dorrie had made for him, reminding Fiona if anyone happened to be calling there that day, usually Dorrie or Belle. Then Fiona put all her energies into her duties. Keeping Merrivale pristine, without a thing out of place, and tending the burgeoning gardens was her means of keeping sane. It had turned into an obsession, she knew that; she cleaned in corners and reached up to high places she had done only the day before, but it was how she coped, how she kept hysteria at bay, how she got through the days and more importantly the gnawingly lonely nights. It was all she could do for Finn and Eloise for her emotions were shut down, dead. Learning so brutally that Aidan no longer wanted her, and because she still loved him despite of it, she didn't really want to be alive at all. If she didn't have to consider Finn and the baby . . .

If Eloise woke before her next feed was due then Fiona would take her to the room she was working in, prop her up with cushions and surround her with toys leaving Eloise to amuse herself, or be distracted by watching Fiona's movements. Fiona never spoke to Eloise, hardly looked at her. If downstairs, she would switch on the wireless and that was the way Eloise heard human voices when they were alone. When Eloise needed a feed, although she knew it wasn't a good thing to do, she would lay the baby on her side and prop her bottle up on the cushions and Eloise would suck at the teat until she was finished. Fiona then winded her and changed her nappy and once Eloise was sleepy she'd take her up to Finn's room for the afternoon, or better still, sometimes Dorrie or Belle would take her out in the pram. Unless he had business to see to, Guy turned up every weekend. Fiona cooked for him and it was nice for a while to chat to him, and smoke with him outside: she couldn't bear ash in the house and there was Eloise to consider. Guy didn't mind her rules. Thoughtfully, he never stayed overnight to prevent scandalous gossip.

Fiona took muted pleasure in the things she had chosen for Merrivale. The floral, brocaded sitting-room suite was new and wonderfully comfortable. A lot of the things were new and some were carefully selected from auction rooms, all in warm, light-coloured wood. Some of the furnishings had come from Guy's house, treasures of his grandmother, small porcelain pieces, a Georgian wall clock, a whatnot, platters for the kitchen dresser. New glass replaced the boards at the broken windows. The kitchen and bathroom plumbing were fully modernized. The fourth bedroom had been prettily designed as a nursery, but Finn, protective of Eloise, wanted her in with him until she was a little older. 'I don't want her feeling unwanted and lonely,' he said. Fiona knew this was a barb at her lack of bonding with Eloise, something he was fervent to compensate for himself.

She was dusting and polishing the fully furnished guest bedroom even though neither Guy nor any one else was ever likely to sleep there, and she sighed, irritated to hear Eloise begin to fret. 'Wait. Go back to sleep. It's not time yet.' She ran the feather duster over the top of the wardrobe, the curtain rail, the pair of wild herb paintings and her baby's low cries became increasingly pitiful wails. 'Must be wind,' she thought impatiently. 'I'll see to it then get on in the bathroom.'

Pushing back Finn's bedroom door, which he kept ajar so Fiona wouldn't miss Eloise's cries, she marched up to the cradle, picked up her baby without glancing at her face, put her loosely against her shoulder and rubbed and patted her back. While doing so Fiona looked out the window to the side of the cottage and down on the newly turned earth, planted by Hector Evans with late cabbages, onions and potatoes. They would need watering again this evening, she ruminated. Guy had placed a water butt for this purpose, filled by the rain that had intermittently spoiled all or part of the last few days. Eloise gave a couple of loud burps and her crying eased away. Eloise smelled sweet but Fiona checked her nappy for wetness. It was slightly damp. It could wait a bit longer to be changed. Laying Eloise back down Fiona put a little soft lamb on her chest and put her tiny warm hands over it. 'Play with that then go back to sleep.' Again she did this without looking at her daughter's face. She felt nothing for Eloise. All she wanted for her was to stay safe.

Finn always threw the covers over his bed and Fiona waited each morning until Eloise needed attention before she made the bed properly. Fiona planned to slip away hoping the baby would drift back to sleep. On top of the bed Finn had left his sketchbook. It had been months since she had taken interest in Finn's favourite pastime, his skill that he had hoped would become his livelihood after further study. She froze on the spot, and for the first time acknowledged that Aidan's rejection of her was also a rejection of Finn, who had subsequently lost his future, his dream. Fiona accepted his resentment for her slapping him; she had put her own feelings before his whereas mothers were supposed to be sacrificial and put themselves last in the family. While Eloise fidgeted in the cot she took Finn's sketchbook to her own room, gleaming and heavy with polish, and sat down on the bed. She wanted to see if Finn's drawings gave a clue as to what was on his mind. She dreaded to find a page with her appearing hangdog or mean, or a caricature (Finn excelled at those) of her cleaning in a whirlwind or as a witch perhaps. However, the pictures seemed to be all of Eloise. Eloise kicking her legs and grabbing her tiny feet. There was Eloise with her rattle in her pram. Lying on a blanket in a field surrounded by buttercups and butterflies. Being held by Dorrie at Sunny Corner, and Jean Vercoe at By The Way. Fiona gasped in wonder at an amazing ethereal study of Eloise being held by Belle Lawry, with Belle's hair encircling them both and Belle gazing lovingly at Eloise as if she was her mother. Fiona felt pangs of jealousy. She had carried Eloise inside her body and given birth to her. There were the gorgeous details of Eloise's first smiles. Jealousy again, for Fiona had not noticed her baby smiling into her eyes. At the last drawing Fiona felt as if an icy hand had clenched her heart. It depicted Eloise with her little face puckered up about to cry.

It hurt Fiona. Her baby was about to cry with discomfort, pain or fear and before now she had not cared a jot. Slamming into her mind came a rhyme from a skipping game Fiona had taken part in as a child:

Poor little baby, no wonder you cry
Your daddy doesn't love you and your mother's going to die.
But God will send an angel
With wings long and fair
To take you up to heaven
To join your mummy there.

Fiona jumped to her feet. 'My poor baby, I promise I won't leave you.' She paced the floor, wringing her hands, striding from the paisley rug to the polished floorboards and back again and again. '*Your daddy doesn't love you . . .*' Suddenly she was the angriest she had been in her life. Fury and offence frothed up inside her and spilled out into a strangled scream of pure rage. She clenched her fists, made movements like shredding a cushion, then as if throttling someone's neck. Aidan's damned neck! 'That's right,' she seethed at the ripped and mangled image in her mind. 'Your daddy doesn't love you, Eloise. He doesn't love Finn and he doesn't love me. He probably never did. I was just the sort of pretty, adoring, compliant wife he wanted, a good hostess, willing in the bedroom, grateful for my good fortune in life and living for his approval and compliments. Yet all the while he was laughing at me, making a fool of me, squirming because I couldn't let him go. He'll make a new life with this tart he's got and won't give us another thought. Well, he'll squirm all right if he ever gets down on his luck and tries to wheedle his way back into our lives. His beastly rotten charm won't work on me again.'

She punched at that image and could almost see her wrath for real. 'I hate you, do you hear? Rot in hell.'

Her energy whooshing out of her she flopped down flat on the bed, the back of her hand over her brow, sweating and panting. 'Why did I spend so much time moping for that worthless man? Finn was right about him all along. I should have listened to Finn. I've caused him so much worry. No wonder he'd rather spend time with Dorrie and Sam Lawry and the Vercoes. I've got a lot to make up to him.'

Poor little baby . . . 'My darling little girl,' she whispered in remorse, sitting up. 'You don't need an angel from heaven, you've got one here on earth. Dorrie Resterick.'

Standing up and straightening her dress and half apron and pushing back the locks of hair that had fallen lose from the pins during her frenzy, without caring about her rumpled bedcovers, she went straight to Finn's room. 'I'm coming, Eloise, my precious little girl. I'm going to hold you and play with you all morning and then I'm going to move your things into my room to catch up on the time I've stupidly lost with you.'

Thirteen

'What do you want?'

'The warm welcome I never get from you, Esther,' Honoria Sanders replied in her throbbing voice. Honoria was not offended; it was Esther's way to be curt and Esther didn't mind her walking straight into her house. Honoria was wearing the latest fashion, a full-skirted dress in olive green and a bolero cardigan. 'So, here we are again, the day before the off. For getting the grounds ready for the great and wonderful Summer Fair.'

Esther used little of the house; it was too big and cumbersome to be kept clean all year round and heat in the winter. She was in her sunny south-facing drawing room, on an ancient threadbare settee, her shoes kicked off and her big feet tucked up under her, drinking tea, gulping down a sandwich, a notepad and pencil on the lap of her tweed skirt. 'Yes, and I've got everything well under way as always so you can hop it. Take your murderous heels, pearls, diamond-heavy fingers, painted lips, bouncing tits and wiggling arse out of here.'

'Really, Esther,' Honoria simpered, putting a hand in a manner worthy of a Hollywood screen siren to her ample chest. 'At least I've got breasts. Remember you're a lady, so get those legs down and sit like one. I've come to ask if you've got anyone interesting lined up to open the fête? There's no one mentioned on the posters. If you're dragging your nets and coming up empty I've got a suggestion for you. Any more tea in that pot?'

In a flash Esther had her long wide feet resting down on the worn pink and cream carpet. Threadbare described just about everything in the house where tradition dictated nothing new and modern after the early years of Queen Victoria's reign. 'Help yourself, use my cup; fire away.' The sisters were never really at loggerheads. Insulting one another counted as affection between the two who were so utterly different. Having been left entirely under the care of nannies throughout their childhood they had often found that each other was all they had.

Honoria lowered herself down beside her sister and took tea without milk and sugar. 'A bit stewed but does the trick. Right, to the point, as I know you like it. An old friend of mine has got in touch, Squadron Leader Tommy Whitley, a spitfire pilot, Battle of Britain hero. He's staying in Rock for a few weeks as a house guest to the Honourable somebody-or-other. Asked if I was free to see him this weekend. I mentioned the Summer Fair and dived in with a mention that he would be perfect to perform the opening speech. He's a humble sort, but he said he'd be glad to rake up a few words if you'd like to have him. If you're already fixed up he'd be happy to be a guest of honour.'

'A war hero will be just the ticket. Villagers will love it. I'd call on an old professor acquaintance of mine but he agreed only as a last resort. Bit bumbling these days. He'll be glad to be let off. Good on you, Honny. This pilot was a lover of yours, of course?'

Honoria relinquished the teacup and opened her crocodile skin handbag and produced her lavish cigarette case. She smoked from a silver-tipped holder while Esther smoked between her fingers. 'Just for a night or two before he was thrown into the thick of it. He's such a sweetie. His wife left him for a retired MP and they buggered off to Monte Carlo. Jolly rank of her, I thought. Now he only sees his kiddies when he goes over there. He'll be staying at Sawle over the weekend.'

'And you'll be giving him pleasure for old times' sake,' Esther said, matter-of-factly. 'Give me his details. I'll dash round and add his name to the posters. News will soon get round. Give the locals something to look forward to.'

'Fine, I'm glad to be of help. Oh, I brought over whacks of stuff for the stalls. Your handyman Ellery has unloaded it on the lawn. Would love to come back later and help with the setting up but must slip home, ring Tommy, and get ready for his stay.'

'Thanks, old girl,' Esther said gratefully then added dismissively, 'you wouldn't be much damned use here anyway. Don't want the men distracted. See you on Saturday with our special guest. Don't dare be late.'

Honoria sashayed to the door. 'I was about to say cheerio but you look as if you've got something to say.'

Breathing in seriously, Esther asked, 'Do you ever regret not finding someone special, that particular someone, your soul mate? You could have had children, Honny. It was never an option for me.'

'Not in the least,' Honoria answered with emphatic cheeriness. 'I wasn't made for monogamy. Life is to be lived, in my book. As for children, couldn't have stood the hideous responsibility. Made sure I could never be knocked up. But I like to help others' children when and where I can. Events like the Summer Fair are important for the children. You have a different reason but we both love to see their happy little faces. And the village hall will be brilliant for them. Must ensure lots of things go on there for the kiddies.'

'You've had a happier life than me but I am happy really. Marrying Sedgewick, as old and as infirm as he was, was perfect for me. He had children with his first wife but they all sadly died in infancy. I would have enjoyed being a stepmother – if they'd grown up and been agreeable.'

'But it wouldn't have been wise, Esther,' Honoria said, showing sadness for her sister.

'I know, and adopting would have been too tricky . . . but I have my works, Faith's Fare and the rest. I like having you close by, Honny. I'd hate it if you moved away.'

'Well, we'll both have to one day. You couldn't possibly stay here forever and wherever you go I'll come too – to make sure everything goes right for you.'

'I don't know what I'd do without you.' Suddenly trembling, Esther leaned over and hugged herself. 'That awful thing . . . If everyone knew . . . everything.'

'Esther dear.' Honoria spoke and smiled stridently. 'Don't worry, old thing. I've protected you before and if necessary will do so again, whatever the cost.'

Fourteen

'Well, that's us done, Mrs Pentecost, we're completely sold out.' Dorrie smiled happily as she and the other woman packed up their trestle table on Petherton's lawn. 'Not a slice of cake or fruit pie, scone or biscuit left. The village tea tables will be in for a treat this weekend.'

'Most of it should be tasty despite the use of substitute ingredients for egg, sugar and spices. We're lucky here, having The Orchards to supply us with all manner of fruit.' Mrs Pentecost gathered together all the lace doilies, lent from various homes, to take home to launder. 'No elaborate offerings from Delia Newton this year. When is the silly woman going to pull herself together and get out of her bed? Never known anyone to sulk as long as her.'

'But isn't Rebecca a little worried about her?' Dorrie stacked the plates on to a massive teak tray with high rims, used in the long-ago glory days of entertaining Society at Petherton. She and Mrs Pentecost would take a turn at washing crocks inside in the gloomy, cold-all-year-round, high-ceilinged scullery, then they would be free to enjoy the other stalls and side shows, until the packing up at the end of the day. The children's country dancing was due to start in forty minutes, always a favourite of both women. 'It's the impression I get.'

'I suppose so. I think tests have been mentioned, but I still think Delia's trying to get back at us, and I'll vouchsafe she's enjoying making poor little Lorna Barbary run about for her.'

'Hello, ladies, you have done splendidly, gold stars all round, you're the most reliable of my team.' Esther pounced on them happily. She was wearing an elbow-length, pleat-fronted dress with a wide diamanté buckled belt, a summery picture hat, and had swirled her hair about her head, adding a sparkly slide, and dark pink lipstick. She looked attractive but rather cumbersome. Her rounded cheeks were flushed with excitement. 'Were you talking about the suffering lady of the bed with diverse things wrong with her? I would be surprised if Delia doesn't show up here before the end of the day in an invalid chair, in blankets and bonnet, looking for sympathy. Can't see people being fooled if she does; she won't get very much pity. It's good to see Miss Barbary has managed to snatch a few minutes away from her. Mr Soames Newton is treating her to a cream tea. She must be a godsend to him.'

Esther swept her hands in a circle to indicate the bustling scene all around them. 'One of our best years, don't you think? Busy tea tent, continual music from our home-grown talent, the brass band and the smaller groups. We have gifts, produce, the white elephant, hula hoop, Punch and Judy, fortune telling by Gypsy Rosalie – she's as much a gypsy as I am, but no matter, load of old tosh anyway. Ruffles the Chirpy Chappie Clown is going down a treat with his magic tricks. A chap from Bodmin, you know, late of the DCLI. I read about him and snapped him up, says he'll come every year. The kiddies like to look forward to their favourites. They will remember things like this all their lives. Mr Walters says he's expecting to get some good essays out of his pupils' experiences today. The painting competition was a winner. Squadron Leader Whitley was a jolly good sport to have agreed to be the judge. Talking of painting, the Templeton boy is brilliant with a brush or a pencil, did you know? Oh, of course you do, you've seen them. The posters he made for the event have caused quite a stir, all those little pictures of the promised events down in fine detail. People have asked him to draw their children, pooches and whatever. He was happy to agree, should earn him a bob or two. Talented boy that, damned shame he can't complete his education.'

Dorrie peered through the crowd and spotted Finn having a go at the coconut shy. Next to him was Belle. 'It doesn't have to be a foregone conclusion that Finn must altogether forget his dreams of becoming a graphic artist and illustrator. Greg and I having been talking about Finn, and now that Mrs Templeton is making excellent strides, we were wondering if Finn could try somewhere for a scholarship or bursary. The main objection might be from Finn himself. He's sworn he'll never leave little Eloise.'

* * *

'I'm so pleased things are back on track between you and Fiona,' Belle said, throwing her last ball at a coconut on its stand and narrowly missing again. Finn had won a tiny rag doll for Eloise.

They walked away. Finn hoped no one had noticed how often he had gravitated towards Belle today, careful not to make it always when she was alone. She was currently having a break from the white elephant stall. Sam had finally plucked up the courage to ask Jenna to be his girl, she had agreed, and Sam had paraded her on his arm. They had played a much-appreciated stint together on their guitars, Jenna singing in her clear country-style voice. The couple were gathering up used cups, saucers and plates and taking them to the scullery. Charlie was busy at The Orchards and wouldn't show up until later.

It was rapture for Finn to be so physically close to Belle; his whole self was prickling and shivering inside with feathery whispers and the need to touch her. He was a little afraid he would actually reach out and possessively take her hand. He refused to entertain the thought that Belle only saw him in a motherly way. 'Now Mum's seen my father for what he really is at last it feels like we've started a new life. The only bugbear is Guy Carthewy. Don't get me wrong, I'm grateful for all that he's done for us and it's a heck of a lot – and goodness knows how I'll repay him, but I will, no mistake – but I wish he wouldn't interfere.'

'In what way does he interfere, Finn? Gosh it's hot, let's get a beaker of juice and sit somewhere breezy. On the fountain steps.'

'OK.' Finn was delighted she had not suggested sitting in the tea tent. It was full of old biddies seeking shade, and no doubt as much gossip as they could wring out of everyone, and Belle might be sidetracked.

'Guy means well, I know,' he said when they were perched on the stone steps under a dry cherub water fountain. 'He's offered to sponsor my fees to go to college or even university. He wants the leeway to move in on Mum now she's planning to get a divorce. Guy, of course, has offered to pay all the legal expenses. But Mum is just as likely to change her mind. She really adored my rotten old man. Guy will just add to her confusion.'

Belle looked Finn in the face and he gazed blatantly back into her eyes. He had done many drawings of her, secretly hidden in a tiny wall cupboard in his room, a place once used to keep candles and lanterns. He drank Belle in, breathed her in, stealing more and more of her for his forbidden memories. The beautiful reality of her now was more than an image. It was written all over his heart and as soon as he was alone he would capture it on paper. For the millionth time he imagined kissing her lush lips. 'But some of what you've said isn't a bad thing, Finn.'

'It is to me,' he said, his voice dropping to a husky quality. 'I'm not ready to leave Eloise in anyone else's care. Mum seems to love her as a mother should, but she could easily slip back again into that awful depressed state. Eloise is my responsibility and I'll be keeping it that way for some years to come. My future doesn't count. Besides, after all the troubles of the last months I'm perfectly happy.' *I'm not ready to leave the area and hardly ever see you. I'm perfectly happy when I'm close to you like this.*

'That's good to hear, and I do believe anyone can make something of themselves no matter what their circumstances are. Now Fiona is beginning to venture out again, I'd like to invite her over to The Orchards,' Belle said. 'Do you think she would join us for Sunday tea tomorrow? Sam has invited Jenna, but we'll still be a small group.'

'She might possibly,' Finn smiled, happy to get another chance to be where Belle was. 'But Guy Carthewy is there most Sundays.'

'Well, he's welcome too. I think he and Charlie would get on fine.'

'They haven't got anything in common,' Finn said, keeping the sharpness out of his answer. *Except for both of them getting in my way.* He loathed it when Belle mentioned Charlie.

A sudden stir of excited voices made them look towards the edge of the lawn. Pushing Eloise in her pram was Fiona, and Guy was with her, looking wholly like a complete family. 'Mum's here!' Finn squawked in disbelief.

'Right then, I can ask them both to tea personally.' Belle was up and walking towards the newcomers. Finn ran after her.

Verity was the first of the crowd to reach Fiona and Guy. 'Hello!' Then she lowered her voice sensitively. 'You look wonderful, Fiona, and you've done very well to come out. What did you think of your first look at Nanviscoe and now here? Hello Guy.'

'It's all very charming.' Fiona's reply was genuine and nervous.

Her hair had reclaimed its glossy sheen, and the feather-embellished hat she wore pinned jauntily to the side of her head was sleek and chic. In a classic tea dress with peplum waist and silk stockings, her heels not too high to accommodate her long walk, she was a picture of discreet glamour, and was receiving many complimentary comments. She glanced at Guy for support. He was hovering protectively. 'I've been thinking for a while now about walking to the village. Guy convinced me I might as well plunge in and come to this event where I'll meet just about everyone at once.'

'Well, let me introduce you to some people,' Verity said. 'Here comes Belle. And Mrs Mitchelmore is on the way. You've heard all about her.' Verity watched Fiona anxiously, hoping she would cope with the exuberant greeting she would get from the lady of the manor and the influx of people wanting to see the baby, and Fiona and her generous landlord. At least she wouldn't have to contend with the bitchy Delia Newton. She need not have worried. Fiona was calling on her old hostess skills and chatted quite comfortably to all the well-wishers and nosy parkers. She thanked those she knew had been good to Finn. Guy was charm and gallantry itself and many asked about the changes to Merrivale, saying they were pleased the renovations would have laid the old ghosts to rest. Finn was all smiles to have his baby sister here. He proudly gave Eloise the rag doll. He took control of the pram and pushed Eloise about to further show her off. People were putting sixpences and shilling pieces into the smiling baby's tiny hands for good luck and fortune and Finn carefully gathered them from Eloise's clutch.

While Belle went back to the white elephant stall, Verity led Fiona and Guy to the tea tent, where she introduced the couple to everyone there. They bought tea and plain scones, butter only available on the first batch laid out. 'Seems you've just missed the vicar,' Verity said, as they sat at a table covered in snowy linen with a small vase of violas. 'The Reverend Lytton never has much to say anyway. He's an old misery. May I ask if you've thought about having Eloise christened in the church? St Nanth's is lovely inside.'

'No, I haven't thought about it at all, but I will. I'll talk to Finn. I'm sure he'll agree on the Godparents being Guy, Dorrie and yourself, Verity. Would you do us – and by that I mean Finn and me – the honour of becoming one of her Godmothers, Verity?'

'I'd be delighted, and it would be my honour. Wentworth Lytton will rush through the ceremony but it's what we all promise God that counts.'

'I've still got Finn's christening robe. I'll put on a little tea after the church. Invite Nurse Rumford and Mrs Pentecost too, and the Lawrys and the Vercoes.'

'What, all the Vercoes? The children too?' Verity laughed. 'Are you sure about that?'

'Yes, I am,' Fiona smiled. 'Jean and Jenna will keep the children in line, and it's only for one afternoon anyway. Jean and Denny have been good to me. I want to repay all for their kindness. It's time I faced up to life again. Thanks to Dorrie, Greg and yourself, Finn and I have been quickly accepted into the community. And Guy will be there, of course.' Fiona looked at her lifeline.

'You'll always be able to count on me, Fiona,' Guy said.

Verity saw the love for Fiona shining out of his pleasant eyes. Perhaps in time there would be another cause for celebration.

'Enough about us,' Fiona said, nudging Verity gaily. 'I want to learn about your Mr Newton. Is he here? I haven't as much as caught a glimpse of him yet.'

'Jack is not *my* Mr Newton.' Verity made a surprised face. 'He's my employer and I see very little of him. I enjoy my work in his farmstead office. It was in a bit of a mess but I soon cottoned on to his disordered way of doing things. He actually had everything pretty much up to date. He didn't really need my services, but he's good about finding people work. I dare say he would have found something for Finn if he had gone there instead of The Orchards that day. The staff are a cheery lot, from cowman to stable boy. From what I've gathered Jack was so horrified as a boy by his father and grandfather's harsh treatment of the workers, including regular thrashings and docking of pay, that he is set on making amends. There are only workhorses kept there now. I learned that Jack was thrown off his pony as a youth and hurt his back and hasn't ridden since. Accounts for his passion in fast cars, I suppose. Apparently, he begged the Forces to let him join up, even as a squaddie, but they all turned him down, declaring his back would soon give up on him so there was no point. Next week I'll be starting in the library of Meadows House. It needs to be put into order. His father was a great collector of books and maps, he says. Some are still packed in boxes and have never seen the light of day. I can't wait to open them!'

'Jack Newton sounds fascinating, so much more than a ladies man. I hope I get to meet him sooner rather than later,' Fiona said.

'Sounds like my kind of chap,' Guy agreed. 'Passed him on the road once or twice, drives a bit too madly, of course, but I suppose it keeps his mind off things. Can't see him being a happy man, really. May I filch the last scone?'

Fiona put the scone on his plate. 'Tuck in, you are a one to fill up,' she told Guy indulgently, then back to Verity. 'So is Jack Newton here today?'

'Oh, definitely not.' Verity dipped to a whisper. 'I forgot to mention that he hasn't attended the Summer Fair since his wife died. She hung herself. He found her body on the morning of the Fair and has never spent this particular day in the village since, even though Mrs Mitchelmore thoughtfully changed it to a week later. Lytton refused to take her funeral in the church or allow her to be interred in the churchyard, and she was buried quietly somewhere in the grounds of the house.'

'The poor man must have been devastated,' Fiona whispered too. 'It's no wonder he doesn't want to be reminded of that dreadful day.'

'Sounds like there might be some sort of mystery behind it,' Guy ruminated. 'I wonder if Mrs R has ever thought so.'

'Well if Aunt Dorrie has, she's never mentioned it,' Verity replied ponderously. 'I'll ask her about it.' It was then that Verity recalled she had meant, before her new job stole all her attention, to ask her knowledgeable aunt about Mrs Rawling, mother of the wretched murdered Mary. Mrs Rawling didn't go to any village events and seemed to have been quite forgotten. Verity resolved to find out if there was more behind it than just the poor woman's wish to be left alone.

Fifteen

'Lorna . . . Lorna are you . . . there?'

Again Delia was met with silence. She had no idea how long it was since she had awakened and lay muzzily calling for her cousin to help her to the bathroom. Where was the wretched Lorna? For that matter where was Soames? There were no sounds coming from below in the shop, no bell ringing to announce customers.

Delia was consumed by panic, the same kind of vile choking feeling she was experiencing more and more. They had abandoned her, had gone for good. That crazy lurching dream was not a dream at all, but real. Soames and Lorna had packed their bags and sneaked away leaving her alone, to wither and starve and weaken and die.

'Ohh!' She began to cry and fat tears seared down the sides of her face and ran into her ears. The two people who were supposed to be caring for her had absconded and left her to die in her own wetness, for that would be the case if she didn't soon get on the lavatory seat. She had been left to die in agony and humiliation. Lorna, the bitch, the wicked taunting bitch, had resolutely refused to let her have the commode in the bedroom until the evening and more than once Delia had suffered the horror of her own hot burning pungent urine wetting her lower regions.

Then through her mugginess Delia realized she didn't have to stay put and wait for that cruel fate, for her own evilly arranged murder to catch up with her. Her limbs might feel like lead weights – and sometimes as if she had no limbs at all – but Nurse Rumford had kept expressing to her that she did have strength in her arms and legs, that the weakness was all in her mind. The nurse spoke either patiently or briskly to her, stubbornly refusing to believe that Delia was as weak as a newborn kitten. 'You have to try, Mrs Newton. You have to change the way you think. I'll lift your legs down over the side of the bed and then Miss Barbary and I will take you by the arms and walk you up and down the landing. You can do it, try, try, try. If you persist in just lying there, in giving up, you will lose all your muscle tone and you truly will become an invalid. Ignore feelings of dizziness, even of feeling sick. You *can* walk. Come along now, trust in Miss Barbary and me and between us we'll have you up and about in no time. Think how wonderful it will be to sit in your armchair in your sitting room again.'

Nurse Rumford had been gentle and strong with her but Lorna always managed to hurt Delia and drag her to the bathroom rather than support her carefully.

'She's hurting me,' Delia would cry.

'No, I'm not, I'm doing my best,' Lorna would wail. And Nurse Rumford believed her because Lorna was sly about pinching Delia or grabbing her roughly.

'Try not to make a fuss, Mrs Newton. Be brave, be determined,' Nurse Rumford would say.

When Delia was back in bed gasping for breath after each ordeal, Nurse Rumford wrote down her notes and ignored Delia's distress. Delia would lament, 'I'm not putting it on. I feel really terrible. Let me sleep, all I want to do is sleep.'

When Nurse Rumford left, Lorna would leer down at Delia. 'Now you know what it feels like for the shoe to be on the other foot. For years you tormented me, made me feel less than a worm. You were brave and determined in those days about putting me down every chance you got. Me and others like poor Mrs Rawling. The first day she came into the shop after her daughter's murder you cruelly told her that her Mary got what she deserved, shot like a dog for fornicating. You destroyed the remains of the poor woman's dignity. You're an evil, malicious witch. Well, you're the one who is shit under my shoes now. I hate you and Soames hates you. Do us all a favour and die. Make it soon.'

Remembering every damning malicious word of Lorna's, Delia flew into a rage. From somewhere deep inside her she let out a scream. It had hardly a decibel, but her wrath rendered up enough energy to allow her to push back the covers and drag her legs down over the edge of the bed. Bit by bit, grunting like a pig with half a nostril, she got her feet down to rest on the rug. She flopped her head to her chest and waited for her faintness to clear. Reaching out shakily she got a grip on a glass of water and slowly, slowly managed to take a few sips. It was risky owing to her burning need to urinate but she was desperate for sustenance.

'Bitch!' she gasped, her slumped body heaving in the effort. Her mind wasn't hazy and she knew Lorna's insistence and jeers about her being forgetful were lies. The fact was Lorna rarely put her meals close enough for her to eat and minutes later would laugh and take the uneaten food away. 'You bitch, you're starving me, trying to kill me. We'll see about that.'

Delia had no notion that it was the day of the Summer Fair. Still believing she had been abandoned, but probably on a Sunday for a day's jaunt, she was determined to get to the bathroom and then raise the alarm to her plight. Nurse Rumford might be attending her tomorrow but Delia wasn't going to wait until then, to suffer any more of Soames' neglect and Lorna's cruelty.

Looking up she planned her way out of the bedroom by reaching out and grabbing hold of the chest of drawers, the wardrobe and the glass doorknob, she'd shuffle round the open door and get out of the room. If her legs failed her she would crawl to the bathroom on her hands and knees. Somehow she would do the necessary and get down the stairs on her bottom. Then she would haul herself up on to her knees at the nearest window and bang on the glass for help. Someone would be about sooner or later, neighbours going to and from the church or children outside playing.

It was proved that Nurse Rumford was right; she *could* use her legs. They were shaky and wobbly but inch by inch she was out of her room and lurching along the landing, with the aid of the wall and a tiny table with a potted fern on it. She had to pass the top of the stairs and then she could grab the bathroom doorknob.

She heard a clicking noise and paused to listen. She knew that noise. Someone had opened the kitchen door that connected to the passage below. A second later Lorna appeared, decked out like she had been to a wedding – but wait! She was wearing the new hat Delia had bought for the Summer Fair. Fury and indignation swept through Delia in burning waves. 'Take off my hat, you thieving bitch!' She hurled each word like a poisoned splinter down the stairs.

Lorna was pinned momentarily to the spot but then she hauled in the full confidence born out of her bitter resentment. She tossed her handbag on the gate-leg table. 'So you've managed to get out of your stinking bed, have you, you sweating, smelly hag? You'd better move double quick if you want to make it to the bathroom or you'll be fouling your prized Axminster, which you're always boasting about, and if you do I won't be cleaning it up. Instead I'll rub your bleddy snooty nose in it, just like the bitch you are.'

'You evil dirty maggot, that's what I called you as a girl, maggot! And that's what you still are, Lorna Barbary, a flea-ridden, mangy maggot.' Wrath giving her super strength, Delia gripped her hands on the top of each stair rail. 'You were the one who used to wet herself. The boys called you pissy-wissy, while you cowered in the playground blubbing into the hanky you kept in the pocket of your pissy knickers. You were a joke and you're still a joke. I see it all now, what you're up to, trying to take over my life. You must be mad if you think you can get the better of me. You've been feeding me with extra pills, haven't you? Making Soames and the nurse believe my condition is worse than it is.'

'Condition?' Lorna scoffed, while facing Delia at the foot of the stairs, with her hands on her hips. 'There's nothing wrong with you! You were just putting on all that depression stuff to get people to feel sorry for you, but it backfired. No one cares about you, in fact they despise you and that includes Soames. He often says he couldn't manage without me. And I'll tell you something, you hard-hearted bitch, I *am* going to take your place. People were saying at the Fair how nice it was not to have you there, making nasty remarks about other women's outfits, running down their kiddies just for skipping about and enjoying themselves. You're a bigot. You make people miserable. You're no use or ornament to the world, just a leach of people's souls. No wonder you get on so well with the cold-hearted vicar. You're two of a kind, neither of you has any right to step inside the church. No one would miss you if you dropped dead. Do everyone a favour and do it this very second.'

Lorna held her breath, and hoped and hoped. Delia's arms were trembling with the effort to clutch on to the stair rails and her knees were sagging. Her overall weakness was getting the better of her. *Fall, fall, fall . . .*

Lorna moved away from the stairs. Delia was unlikely to be able to hold on much longer. She was too weak to stay on her feet and hopefully she would plunge down the stairs and break her wretched neck. Lorna made sure Delia did not fall on top of her.

The darkness of her fury overrode the rest of Delia's senses, even her need to use the bathroom. Leaning forward she shrieked at fever pitch, 'I'll never let you take over my life or my husband, Lorna Barbary.' But her balance was too precarious, her limbs too weak to bear her weight and her feverish mind too stretched to keep in balance and Delia crumpled and plunged headlong down the stairs.

As Delia screamed in shock and fear, Lorna wrapped her arms round herself and laughed and laughed in a sort of mad hysteria. All her efforts had worked and her dreams for revenge on her lifelong tormentor were coming true.

Delia's plummeting weight hit the middle of the stairs with a crunching of bones and she tumbled over and over down the rest of the steps until she hit the passage runner in a twisted mass. Her neck had broken seconds before and she was dead.

Her leg flailed out and hit the tall umbrella and hat stand, which toppled over. At the same moment that Lorna turned to look down at Delia and assess her injuries, the heavy stand whacked Lorna full in the face. Her skull fractured, Lorna dropped like a millstone. Stunned and senseless, her brain bled in on her and two minutes later she too was dead.

Sixteen

'It's best sometimes to leave certain people alone and that includes Mrs Rawling, trust me.' It was the advice Dorrie had given to Verity when her niece had brought up her idea of calling in on Pauline Rawling.

'If you think it's best, Aunt Dor, then I won't,' Verity had replied. 'Mrs Rawling doesn't welcome callers, I take it?'

'Not even those with the best of intentions, dear.'

Dorrie would never forget her time on Pauline Rawling's doorstep soon after the grisly discovery of her daughter Mary and her lover Neville Stevens' bloodied bodies. Dorrie had taken a posy of white roses tied with black ribbon, and a basket of provisions, sure the bereaved mother would not feel like shopping for some time. She had already sent a letter of condolence, but she had been nervous at facing the long-term elderly widow who had lost her only child. Pauline Rawling was a curt, bluff-voiced woman, never given to socializing. It was never easy to gauge when to call on the bereaved if you were not close to them, and it was unlikely Pauline Rawling would welcome callers.

Dorrie had knocked on the front door of the shabby small cottage, waited a minute then tried again. All the curtains were drawn over including the small square of cheap glass in the top half of the door. The single curtain in the door was lifted back at the corner and Pauline Rawling's face, slightly distorted behind the flawed glass, looked out. She opened the door an inch. 'Mrs Resterick, I was more or less expecting you to show up. You're the main do-gooder in this village. Your sentiments are kind but not needed here. I can manage, thank you.'

'Well, I'm sure you can manage, Mrs Rawling,' Dorrie had said, trying not to sound embarrassed or hesitant. 'Would you at least like to accept the flowers?'

'I don't need or want the usual stuff that goes with a death. What good would they do? Won't bring Mary back. Won't alter the fact she reaped what she sowed after all she did. She was a disobedient child, a liar and a thief, who thought nothing of stealing from her own mother's purse, and she grew up to be a whore. I don't know what she was up to but she gloated that she and Stevens were soon to come into a hefty sum of money and would be clearing off and living the high life. Well, in reality she chose the low life and met an end that was her due.

'There's no use beating about the bush: she hated me and I grew to despise her. I couldn't wait for the day when she would leave me in peace. But rather than just slinking off she's left me in the never-ending misery of her disgrace and I'll never forgive her. I'll pay for her funeral when they release her body but I won't go to it. The time of the funeral won't be announced. There will be no tolling of the bell, no hymns, no flowers and no headstone. She lived like an alley cat. Now she's dead, but she'll never be forgotten because her wickedness will feed the gossips for years and years. She's cursed me for the rest of my life and for it I curse her memory. It was good of you to call, Mrs Resterick, but I won't keep you. Good day to you.'

Dorrie had left feeling chilled to the crevices of her bones. For a long time the horrific double murders had cast a macabre gloom over Nanviscoe, edged with the fear that there might yet be new victims. The horror of Pauline Rawling's coldness towards her unfortunate dead daughter had never left Dorrie. Much later, when she had found out the true reason behind the murders – Mary and Neville's bid at blackmail – Dorrie had wondered if the mother knew about it. If so, she could either be a dangerous person herself or lead anyone curious about the tragedy to the same dreadful fate.

'Promise me you'll never go to see Mrs Rawling. You're very kind to think of her, a stranger to you, but believe me, it would be a terrible intrusion in her case.'

Verity had been intrigued by her Aunt Dorrie's dour emphasis but she had promised her she would never set foot on Pauline Rawling's doorstep. As she began work for the second week in Meadows House, Verity mused that Nanviscoe had experienced quite a few tantalizingly mysterious events.

Unpacking Squire Randall Newton's boxes and crates of tomes, maps and even some artefacts from around the world was as thrilling to Verity as opening her presents as a child at Christmas. The cargo had travelled all the way from various countries in Europe, South America and the Middle East. Excitedly, when first looking over the stack of unopened treasures, Verity had thought that Hitler might have sent his cohorts to kill and steal them if he had known about them, but then she decided they were probably too small-fry for that maniac's interest. Objects worth hundreds, perhaps thousands of pounds, hidden from sight for over twenty-five years could be languishing inside all this packaging, and it was her job to bring them out to the daylight. She was transported back to her childhood when she had played explorer games with her siblings and cousins. Aunt Dorrie and Uncle Greg had joined in and she and the others had learned the exciting remarkable facts about famous pioneers, pirates and buccaneers. She must be careful not to unleash dangerous creepy-crawlies, spiders and beetles – not because she was afraid of them, but because they could leap out and strike her down with poison or a nasty skin disease. And curses! She would say a quick prayer before she opened each box in case an ancient curse had been uttered over something inside. She had laughed at herself about that, but as Aunt Dorrie might say, 'You never know . . .'

Jack had brought her here to his home the first day. 'You know the farm well, Verity, but did you ever see the house?' he had asked, after he had handed her out of his motor car. 'It was built roughly about the same time as Sunny Corner. When you come to think of it, it's strange that a Newton and a Barnicoat have never entered into marriage. The house is not very impressive but rather it strives for comfort. It's what my forebears plumped for after first establishing the land and trotting off to explore the world and enduring similar deprivations to the natives. So, no extravagant front steps, just the doorstep, granite, of course, and good and wide. Plain front porch but the windows give a good view of the stream garden. You must wander about outside at will, Verity, you'll find it very tranquil. My family, and that includes me, have never spent a lot of time here really but it's always been the perfect place to retreat to.'

'I've only caught glimpses of the house while playing or out riding. I always thought it looked cosy and sheltered among the trees and the usual exotic tall bushes found around big houses.'

Verity had clutched her hands together at her chest. 'I can't wait to see inside the house and especially inside all your father's boxes.'

'Where would Cornwall be without its gentleman's glut of rhododendrons and camellias?' Jack answered, as if thinking about it for the first time. 'My great-grandfather fretted about the lack of late-summer colour so he was responsible for the borders of hydrangea, hypericum and heathers and the rest. My favourites are the heathers, all types and colours. I've added many of them myself. As for inside, there's a downstairs cloakroom so I'll ask you to keep to the ground floor, but do make use of the drawing room for your comfort. Cathy, the maid, will bring you meals and tea trays but feel free to ring for anything you want at any time.'

So I'm not allowed to wander upstairs, Verity had thought, that is a bit mysterious. Has he anything to hide? Then she told herself not to be so daft. It was his house, his private domain. No one wanted others to intrude on their bedrooms. 'You didn't mention what you've hired me for, Jack. Aren't you at all curious about your father's finds?'

'I was years ago. I made to open a box once and my father lashed out at me and ordered me to never touch them again. Since then I've never really cared about what is in those boxes.' Jack had shrugged his shoulders, but Verity had seen that he was still upset by the incident. 'You may have heard my father was a very hard man.'

'Aunt Dorrie has mentioned Mr Randall was famous for his quick temper.'

'That's an understatement, but anyway, he died before he'd opened his stuff and I suppose it's time it was unpacked. I don't want to leave it to the next generation. I'll show you to the library in a while, but first come with me.'

Verity had pondered those words: 'the next generation'. Unless he married again and produced children Jack wouldn't be heralding in the next generation. He had a sister somewhere. Apparently, she had run away from her finishing school and had since been disinherited. Jack's younger brother had taken himself off long before the war and was said to have drunk himself to death in some foreign land. Presumably Jack was alone because of his father's brutal behaviour.

Jack had taken her to the huge impeccable kitchen, where copper pans and blue and white china were arranged like crack troops on parade, but the room was made homely by the smiley presence of his husband and wife house steward and cook, Sidney and Coral Kelland, a chatty, lumpy-bumpy couple, who had been in service in Randall Newton's day. Verity was becoming more interested in the Newton family history by the minute and she was hopeful the Kellands would tell her much about it. With them was the housemaid, Cathy Vercoe, a niece of Denny. Denny had taken orphaned Cathy in along with her sister Tilly, who was a maid at Petherton. Cathy was an agreeable young woman of straight figure, discreet and loyal. The company drank tea and ate slices of delicious sponge cake. Verity felt very welcome here and was amused by how the staff kept gazing from her to their master as if seeking to ascertain if there was anything deeper between them than an official capacity. It was obvious the Kellands held Jack in some affection as well as respect and were probably hoping their master would marry again and live a happy settled life.

After showing Verity the downstairs rooms Jack opened the double doors of the library. The smells of leather and beeswax polish hit Verity's nose. The long room of heavy-curtained windows was warm from a wood and coal fire. Dominating the room was the custom-made table and brown leather chairs. There were many smaller tables and upholstered chairs. Set down on the floor near the door, in a neat row, were containers of various sizes.

'There's eight wooden boxes and one crate. I've brought in a caddy of tools and opened them all. I don't want you hurting yourself, Verity, so be very sure to ask Kelland for any help that you need. Don't lift anything heavy. Your task will be to lay all the items in their categories on the table and to make lists. I don't require you to do anything complicated. If anything is damaged or fragile put it down one end. Take your time, there's no hurry at all. There are some cotton gloves on the shelf there. I don't want you hurting your hands or getting grubby. Anything that's really heavy or you are not sure about please just leave it where it is. Nothing is urgent. I'll pop in next week and see how you are getting on. Following that I'll have more work for you in the farm office, if you're happy to continue working for me.'

'I'm sure I'll be perfectly happy to, Jack. I think I'm going to be fascinated to get stuck in to those boxes.'

'That's obvious,' Jack said. 'Your eyes are lit up like Christmas lights.' Verity noticed he was getting restless, even uncomfortable. She went on to learn from Mrs Kelland that he never stayed in any place for long. 'I'm off to play golf with friends at Mounts Bay. Settle yourself in slowly, Verity, and thank you. Don't forget that the Kellands and Cathy will be only too happy to wait on you. They prefer it when someone is in the house.'

He left the room, and Verity had watched him as he had halted and heaved a sigh and lit a cigarette. It came to her then that despite Jack's caddish reputation he was probably actually a lonely man dragged down by bad experiences he couldn't forget, and the fast life he led might merely be his way of filling in time. That saddened her.

Now, she was expecting Jack to show up to see how her work was progressing. She had enjoyed every moment of her time spent at Meadows House, watching the piles of books and maps grow as she delivered them out of their dark solitude. Her lists were long for there were books on every subject, in every language, including Latin, by authors and illustrators of every nation and walk of life. Some were originally from Britain. Judging by the editions on the Newtons' shelves, Verity believed Randall was a seeker and collector and had lost interest in his finds after that. Why else leave his collections unpacked and nailed down? While Verity was sure Randall had been a bully, who had found most things in his life unsatisfactory and grown intent on destroying it – hence the dejection of his three children – she felt there was no mystery about him, but she was still curious about the tragic fate that had befallen Jack's young wife, Lucinda. And Verity was puzzled, like all of Nanviscoe, over another tragedy, one that had cast a gloom over the highly successful Summer Fair, the deaths of Delia Newton and Lorna Barbary. Aunt Dorrie and Uncle Greg were attending the coroner's court today to hear the official verdicts of the deaths, accidental everyone assumed, although most were only really sorry about the long-suffering Lorna's untimely end.

For now Verity contented herself with the sad death of Lucinda Newton. She had got all the facts that her aunt knew about the unfortunate woman.

'No one locally knew the poor woman and few of us even caught a glimpse of her. Jack met and married her in Italy, brought her home without announcement and she never left Meadows House unless with him in the car. Jack spoke of Lucinda warmly but offered little information about her. I went over to the house to welcome her to Nanviscoe and was shown into the conservatory. She told me she liked to be there with the vines and greenery, and preferred to be out of doors as much as possible. Apparently, she spent most of her time out in the grounds, with her little white poodle. Jack found her body hanging from a beech tree, the dog howling up at her from the ground. The poor thing pined to death soon afterwards and was buried in Lucinda's grave.'

'So what was Lucinda like, Aunt Dor? What did she look like?' Verity had demanded excitedly. 'Were she and Jack madly in love?'

'I don't think it was that sort of marriage. I think Lucinda was a troubled, fragile soul and Jack married her to protect her. He certainly doted on her. It was the one time he rarely left the house. But Lucinda liked to be alone with her dog, Polly. I think she lived mostly in her own make-believe world, a child's world. She had lots of dolls displayed about the house and looked at them often, almost as if she was talking to them. I think she found comfort in them. Sadly, I wasn't at all surprised when I learned she had killed herself. She didn't seem to belong to this world. Her looks? She was tiny and delicate and gorgeous, beautiful in an old-fashioned way, like a doll herself. She had thick ebony hair and long eyelashes and eyes that were so dark they seemed pitch black. Her voice was soft and faraway. It was like being with a real-life fairy, but one that had had her wings stolen. She spoke only of Polly, whom she cuddled and cosseted incessantly, and the plants and trees and the stream. You couldn't help being drawn to her, to want to protect her. When Cathy brought us high tea she fed all her cake to Polly and only took a sip of tea. She was a lost waif and I instinctively felt sorry for her. I sensed if she stepped outside of the grounds alone she would be very frightened.'

'Golly, she sounds the complete opposite to me.'

'She was, poor soul. Every time I called on her after that, Jack or Cathy said she wasn't available, invariably out in the gardens or resting. I really felt for Jack. I could feel his sorrow and concern for her, and his devotion. Yes, he loved her very much and he was distraught when she died, yet somehow . . . relieved for her, I felt.'

'Poor Lucinda, sounds like she had run away from something haunting her. Poor Jack too, I can understand why he plays the field now. After being attached to such an ethereal being, it would be hard to settle down with a woman in the normal way.'

'I think you've hit the nail on the head there, Verity. I know Lucinda sounds fascinating.' Dorrie had raised her brows purposefully. 'But I think it would be most inappropriate to pry into her past . . . don't you?'

'Absolutely, Aunt Dorrie,' Verity had replied, but she had meant it rather tongue in cheek.

She had not mentioned Lucinda to Cathy or the Kellands, but she had looked in every downstairs room and the conservatory for Lucinda's dolls. None were to be found, but there was a photograph of her and Jack, holding hands, among the framed Newton family parade on the piano in the drawing room. Dorrie's description of Lucinda was spot on. Lucinda was shown in a long white lace dress and pumps with a white ribbon threaded through her black hair. Only as tall as Jack's upper arm, against which she was leaning. Yes, she had been like a very beautiful child and her most outstanding feature had been her large guarded eyes.

Verity brought herself back to the present, chiding herself for once again using her employer's time to mull over his private life. After all, contemplating his wife's life and death and making mysteries out of them was snooping and it was sort of a betrayal to Jack, who had not really needed to give her a job here. She had even searched for Lucinda's grave, hoping to discover more about her character from its design and inscription. It was ghoulish and downright nosy and Jack did not deserve it. He was a good man and he had been kind to Verity.

Picking up the ledger and pencil in her gloved hands, she added the details of the final book she had taken out of the fifth box she had unpacked, which by its labels had been freighted across the seas from Cyprus. The book was ancient and well worn, as was about a third of the stuff, and Verity assumed Randall Newton had procured these curios out of fascination, perhaps finding interest only in the buying or bartering process. Many of the items had covers she thought of as having come from various animal hides and smelled pungent and she was glad of the gloves – a clean pair were provided for her every day – so she did not have to touch them. The thick tome she was holding was badly scuffed and had practically fallen apart, as was its predecessors, and she wondered if they were a job lot. The book cover was bare of inscription but Verity recognized the content as Arabic fables, and this was how she logged it in, then she laid it down carefully on the appropriate pile and wrote out a ticket for it.

Verity had meant to ask Jack what he intended to do with the stuff. While taking her first morning break, which she had in the kitchen, welcomed by the small staff, Mrs Kelland was able to tell her. 'Mr Jack is going to sell them. He's talked about it now and then, meant to get some auction house round to value it all and take it away, but he never did. We're all glad he's brought you here instead, Miss Verity. It's lovely having someone in the house. The three of us work just as hard when Mr Jack is away but it's not the same. We feel more valuable when we have someone to serve.'

Verity, who before had thrived only on lots of company, enjoyed it here in the quietness of Meadows House and strolling through the gardens and talking to the servants. Away from her old life she had put Julius Urquart and the hurt he had caused her firmly in the past. She wished she could work here forever.

The day wore on and Jack did not come. She finished for the day and said goodbye to Cathy when the maid brought her hat. Directly across from them in the spacious hall was the staircase. Of dark oak and uncarpeted, the stairs went straight up, and the landing divided to right and left and above the closed banisters were the tops of various doors, a very tantalizing sight to Verity. But she must forget the pull of those forbidden doors and break off wondering what might – just might – be secreted behind them.

Seventeen

Finn was cycling to The Orchards on a special mission, one of his own making. He was on a rattling old heap of metal and rust put together from at least four different machines and which he had assembled himself from scraps procured dirt-cheap from Denny Vercoe's yard. Guy had, inevitably, offered to buy him a new or a second-hand bicycle, but Finn had immediately refused.

'There's no need for you to keep up your grand gestures,' Finn had replied moodily. Guy jumped in too quickly and too often with his generous offers and to Finn it smacked of interfering. 'I keep giving you our gratitude for all you've done, but Mum and I can manage now, can't you get that into your thick head?'

Having collared Finn outside on the patio where he was building the bicycle, Guy had coloured up as if drenched in crimson paint. 'Sorry, old boy, sorry again, I know you hate me calling you that. I'm taking away the enjoyment of you doing things for yourself. I can see you're very happy doing that.'

Wiping an oily hand across his already greasy brow, Finn had muttered, 'Yes, I do know what I'm doing. Can I have a cigarette?'

'Not without your mother's permission,' Guy had replied, standing back to avoid getting his smart flannel trousers filthy.

'I'm not a bloody kid!'

'So you keep trying to prove but talking to me like that, you rude, surly little sod, says that is exactly what you are. And where was the please?' Guy stalked away.

Finn got up off his knees, taken aback for the moment. Guy had never shown him anger before. 'Hey, wait, it's my turn to say sorry, and that was a nice change from all your usual sickening ingratiating stuff.'

Guy swivelled his head round. 'Did you mean that apology?'

'Yes, guess so.' Finn shrugged his broadening shoulders as if he did not really care that much about it. 'So, can I have a smoke . . . please? I can afford to buy my own. My drawings have brought in a tidy sum and I'll soon be starting at Petherton and doing a few jobs for Mrs M. I'll pay you back.'

'I'll think about it,' Guy retorted, turning fully round. 'Finn, I'd like it if you and I got along even if we'll never be friends. But let me tell you this, I think the world of Fiona, and Eloise too, and as long as Fiona is happy to have me around I'm going to feature in the life here. So can we both try to rub along, at least?'

'Of course,' Finn had replied, nonchalant about it. Despite his resort to sarcasm and temperamental brusqueness with Guy he had done a lot of growing up since the move to Merrivale. 'I've got used to having you around. It's good that Mum knows she has you to rely on. Just lay off all the bloody fussing, eh? Give me some space. I like the independence I've gained.'

Guy had scratched the back of his neck, clearly stunned by Finn's unexpected change of stance. 'Oh, well, fair enough, we have a deal, Finn. Your mum is proud of how independent you are and, if I may so, I am too. From tomorrow I'll be spending a few days at Bude. Now my grandmother is a lot better I'm going to take her on a little holiday at Torquay, a place she loves. I won't spend any time worrying about you all here. Then I'll be back in time for Eloise's christening. Finn . . .?' Guy was reddening rapidly again and nervously licking his bottom lip.

'What?' Finn said with mock impatience. 'Go on, take another stab, but make it your last.'

'It's just . . . well, man to man, please don't take this wrong and please think about it carefully . . . If you ever want to take up your studies I'd be very happy to sponsor you.' Guy raised his hands to still any protests. 'I mean that as a friend. I know you don't intend to go off and leave Eloise and your mum any time soon but it might be something you'd want to do in the course of time.'

Finn gave small thoughtful nods. 'Thanks, I'll keep it in mind.'

Now he was freewheeling down Meadow Hill, whistling happily, his eyes shining as bright as the sun, his insides surging with delectable anticipation. He was off to The Orchards and at this time of day Sam and Charlie would be making deliveries to the wholesalers and shops, and Belle should be there alone. Last evening Finn had dropped over to show Sam some of his latest drawings and he had deliberately left his sketchbook there.

He shot across the crossroads with only a cautionary glance either side of him and was upon the entrance to Sunny Corner. Dorrie and Corky appeared on their morning constitutional and the flurry caused by Finn's foolhardy fleetness swept off Dorrie's favourite hat. 'Oh!'

Finn skidded to a halt, leapt off his machine, picked the crochet hat off the top of the hedge and presented it to Dorrie. 'Sorry, Mrs R, hope I didn't scare you too much.'

'You did rather,' Dorrie scolded him. 'More to the point, Finn, you nearly knocked poor Corky off his legs.' She patted Corky to reassure him.

'Sorry, old chap.' Finn hunkered down to Corky but the dog snorted in umbrage and tilted his head away. 'I'll be more careful in future,' Finn promised Dorrie.

'I should think so.' She smiled. Finn easily brought a smile to cheer her gentle heart; she had seen great strides in his character. 'Where are you off to as if there's a fire raging?'

'Oh, just popping along to The Orchards. I left my sketchbook there. Are you off to write some more poetry? Thank you for the lovely rabbit poem you copied out for Eloise. I've illustrated it – I didn't think you'd mind. I got a frame from the Thrift Niche, and I've hung it in her room. She's now sleeping very well in there by herself,' he ended, like a proud father. 'You must take a look at the framed poem.'

'I will, and of course I don't mind. I've seen for myself that you're a very accomplished artist. Everyone is impressed by your depictions of the village to put up in the new hall.'

'Everyone except for the vicar,' Finn said, then he put on the Reverend Lytton's breathy voice, apt to be interspersed with watery coughs. 'He approached me while I was set up with my easel across from the church and said, "Is that the best you can do, boy? Hope you're not going to portray the tower like that. It isn't bent, you know." Miserable old so-and-so, I had the tower as straight as a die.' It wasn't what Finn had uttered under his breath at the time. 'I've never seen such an ugly man as him before. He looks like something crossed between a bullfrog and a bulldog. I'm not happy that he's going to christen Eloise. He might scare her badly.'

'Don't worry. He won't really look at her and he certainly

won't be holding her. He says he has very bad rheumatism in his shoulders; they do creak a lot. I think he's rather terrified of babies. It's not surprising, I suppose, as he's an old bachelor. Well, we'd better get on our way. Corky is getting restless. Now, Finn, more haste, less speed. I don't want to see you ending up flying over those handlebars and getting a cracked head, or putting some unfortunate in a ditch.'

Dorrie walked off, thinking Finn a most handsome young man and how nice it was to see him smiling so much nowadays.

Finn shot off on his bike wishing he had a grandmother just like Mrs R. Well, he more or less did; he and Eloise had her as a worthy substitute. Dear ladies like her made the world a much better place.

Making short work of the last mile to his quarry, Finn veered off for a roadside thatched-roof, chocolate-box, rustic dwelling, its gleaming white front perfectly graced by criss-cross log fencing covered with rambling roses. This was a wholly enchanting place to Finn, for a queen among women lived here. If Mrs R saw Belle the way Finn did she would dash off a poem that would set the world alight with awe and wonder on love, the romantic and the intimate.

Ringing his tinny sounding bell to announce his arrival, and to bring Belle out from the hot houses if she was in one of them, he walked his bike round to the back and leaned it carefully against the wall. It would be a crime to make a scratch or leave a dirty mark on this paradisiacal home. His heart did joyful somersaults when Belle popped her gorgeous dark head through one of the open windows.

'Finn! Good morning. You're a surprise this time of the day. Come along in. Is everything all right?'

Each of her words reached his ears as if drifting on golden threads of welcome and care, and her surprise at seeing him was obviously a welcome one. 'Everything is fine. I've just slipped over because I think I left my sketchbook here and I'll need it later.'

'Oh, of course, it's in a safe place in the sitting room.'

He joined her inside. The room smelled deliciously of hot toast, waiting to be eaten at the end of the table nearest to the range, which was laid with breakfast things for one. 'I like to get on first thing then take a late breakfast alone when I've got time to get my thoughts together. Sit down, Finn.' Belle took a brightly painted mug off a hook under a shelf and put it on the table. 'I'll freshen up the pot and get you a plate and knife. Help yourself to toast and marmalade. I've made more than enough for myself.'

'Wow, thanks a lot, Mrs Belle, it's very kind of you.' He always looked for a way to compliment her, then hoping to impress her, said, 'I rode here on the bike I made myself from bits and pieces. It goes like the wind, so fast in fact I gave dear Mrs R a bit of a fright.'

'Sam said you were working on a bike,' Belle said when they were seated. Finn was as close as he could get to her. He took a long secret sniff of her perfume, a gentle whisper of lemony jasmine, which he now loved so much. He had asked her recently what it was called, adding that his mother might like it as a present sometime.

'It's called Wings of Love,' she had replied. 'Charlie bought it for me on our fifth anniversary and I've worn it ever since. I don't really think the title is right for a son to give his mother. I'll always be glad to advise you any time on suitable gifts for Fiona.'

'That would be brilliant,' he had replied enthusiastically. He lay in his bed that night picturing a shopping trip into town with Belle, having her all to himself. Standing close to her looking in shop windows, taking coffee with her in a quiet side-street cafe. Then he had taken them to a desert island, with him in just a pair of shorts and Belle in a soft floral sleeveless dress. The sand was warm and golden-white, the sky pale and calm and the sea impossibly blue with balmy cresting surf. In his daydream, he did not waste time in running towards Belle on the shore. They took each other in eager arms and whispering words of love had gently fallen down on a soft blanket on the sand, amid lush green tropical leaves, where they kissed and made love again and again. And there they would stay forever, with Eloise, and watch her grow up. No one else existed.

When he got the chance he would cycle to Wadebridge and find out how much Wings of Love cost then he would save up and buy some to secretly sniff and pretend Belle was with him.

Slowly, he spread marmalade on a slice of toast. 'This is a treat.'

'You're welcome,' Belle smiled.

Her smile melted his entire insides and he felt light and insubstantial. He smiled back, kept smiling. Today she was in a home-made pale blue blouse with a cardigan casually thrown on top. To Finn, she looked blissfully feminine, sexy and steamy. His eyes trawled down to her decently covered breasts, for a moment only, so the ravenous glint he knew must be there in his eyes would not betray him. In his imagination he had touched and kissed those breasts. He had kissed her lips, her eyes, and the tip of her nose, her neck and shoulders. He had trailed his mouth all over her, even to her forbidden places. He could almost taste her now.

He panicked. He should not be doing this. Another moment and it would be more than his eyes that would betray him. If he offended or disgusted Belle she would never allow him near her again. If she told Charlie, the blasted nuisance who was always winking at her and was far too tactile with her, even as her husband, Charlie would thump his lights out. And Finn wanted to stay with Belle and just enjoy the experience of being alone with her – he got little chance to be. Trying not to let his hand shake in his ardour he took a gulp of tea. He had to think of something conversational.

'So the verdict on the two women from the Stores was accidental death?'

'Yes, a tragedy for both women. Mrs Mitchelmore was most put out, says it quite spoiled the Summer Fair, but that's an uncharitable way to look at it. I wish you the best of British, Finn, having to poke about in her cellars. Shouldn't think she's got much in the way of fine wines or concealed treasures she can send to auction to help her keep up that ugly old place. To get back to the deaths, it's assumed Delia struggled out of bed for the bathroom. Lorna arrived home, Delia's footing failed her and she plunged down the stairs, then in a terrible trick of fate her hand or something sent the umbrella stand to crash down on poor Lorna's head. I feel sorry for Soames Newton. It must have been a dreadful shock to have discovered the bodies of his wife and her cousin slumped at the foot of the stairs.'

'I shouldn't think he'll be too long getting over it,' Finn said, recalling Delia Newton's obnoxious manner.

'Well, he's certainly got the women flocking round to help him, cleaning and cooking meals. I held the fort in the shop for him on the day of the inquest. I quite enjoyed it. Anyway, you came for your sketchbook. Hope you don't mind, Finn, but Charlie and I took a peek through it last night. We were very impressed by everything you've done, the delightful ones of Eloise surrounded by fairies and cuddly animals, the fairy-tale buildings and scenery. We loved your drawings of scenes from famous books. The Dickensian characters from *Great Expectations* were easily recognizable. You got bitter old Miss Havisham in her tattered wedding dress exactly how I've always pictured her. Have you ever thought of becoming an illustrator for books? I should think you'd do very well in children's books. Charlie said to suggest to you that you send off a collection of your work and see what happens. There are a few children's books in Thrift Niche. You could take down the addresses of the publishers from them.'

From being thrilled that Belle loved his work (he had discounted Charlie sharing the experience with her) Finn now went rigid. *Charlie said . . .* Charlie was his rival, his enemy in his way to Belle. Charlie should keep his nose out of Finn's life.

'Finn, what do you think about what I've said?' Belle asked.

Finn heard the uncertainty in Belle's voice. 'It's a very good idea, thank you, Belle,' he answered rapidly, hating that he had made her feel uncomfortable. 'And yes, I have run it through my mind.'

'I'll look out Sam's old childhood books and jot down the addresses,' Belle said. With breakfast over she stood and started clearing the table. 'I'm afraid I'm going to have to shoo you out now. I've still got a busy day ahead. More in the house to do and meals to prepare, and then it's outside to help with the mass of pruning and insect control. It's my job to stake the tomatoes and spray them with compost tea. I'll fetch your sketchbook.'

Finn said a cheerful goodbye but as he cycled away from The Orchards he was thoroughly disgruntled. Of all the words Belle had said to him what kept blowing coldly through his mind was *I'm afraid I'm going to have to shoo you out.* It was the way one would speak to a child, a young person. Belle did not see him as a man, not yet, and it threatened to tear his heart to splinters. He was a man, an experienced sexual being, and somehow he was going to show this side of himself to Belle.

Eighteen

Jack arrived home late at night. He crept in but he wasn't surprised to be very quickly waited upon by Sidney Kelland. His house steward was conscious of every creak and scuffle of the house. He had heard his master, jumped out of bed on the second-floor servants' quarters, pulled on his dressing gown and slippers and presented himself at the foot of the stairs.

'Can I get you anything, sir?' Kelland asked in a voice steeped in genuine respect and helpfulness. 'It's good to see you again, sir.'

'Thank you, Kelland,' Jack replied simply. 'You go back to bed. I'll just get myself a nightcap. Tell Mrs Kelland I'll be taking a late breakfast.'

'Yes sir. Goodnight, sir.'

'Just one thing before you go up, Kelland. How is Miss Barnicoat getting on?'

'I watched her carefully, Mr Newton. She's kept to your rules and asked questions only in relation to her work, and kindly asked every day about the health of the staff. Mrs Kelland and I and Cathy have all enjoyed her presence. She likes to take her morning tea with us round the kitchen table.'

'Good, good.' Jack nodded his head. 'Back up to your slumbers, Kelland, and I'll see you in the morning.'

Going off to the capacious drawing room, Jack poured himself vodka and tonic water. He was aware of the lingering lightness of Verity's summery perfume and nodded in satisfaction. As he always did when in this room he went to the piano and picked up the photograph of Lucinda and himself. 'Hello, my love,' he whispered, his voice hoarse and husky, his heart immediately choked with pain, sorrow and regret.

He downed his drink and went outside into the moonlit night. Leaving the formal gardens he followed an unmarked and meandering path known only to him and the Kellands. He passed through bushes and trees, something he could do even on a pitch-black night, turning off to other paths until at last he came to the small natural clearing, once his childhood retreat. On the spot where he had built a camp, with blankets, books, a lantern and teddy bear to escape the reality of his father's harshness, Lucinda and her beloved Polly were now buried. He had made it a beautiful grave for a beautiful girl, his child-bride.

Dipping down and sitting with his back against a beech tree, Jack gazed damp-eyed at the grey-stone grave, closed in by green-painted picket fencing. The only words on the headstone were 'Lucinda and Polly'. It was all Jack had felt was needed. He never brought flowers. Flowers withered and died and Lucinda had hated dead things. 'How are you, dear girl? Have you been happily playing with Polly? The angels are looking after you. They must love you so much. You're so like an angel yourself. They must understand why you did all you did. You know I do. I only wish . . . but that doesn't matter now.'

His mind slipped back to when he had first come across Lucinda, on an early morning in a quiet piazza in Florence. She had stood out for many reasons, the most compelling her rare and innocent young beauty. Dressed in old-fashioned ankle-length white lace with a pink sash, a bonnet and dainty slippers, she had been clutching a tiny white poodle and had looked lost and frightened. Jack had been gripped by an immense desire to help and protect this ethereal stranger.

He had lifted off his hat and addressed her carefully. 'Good morning, miss, may I be of assistance to you?'

'You are English,' she had chimed in relief. 'I am also, from Hertfordshire. I was brought here years ago by my guardian, after my parents were killed in a train crash. I'm looking for a respectable hotel to stay in. Do you know of one?'

'Well, I'm staying at the Hotel Alessandra. I can recommend it. The rooms and service are excellent. My name is Jack Newton, by the way. I'm pleased to meet you.'

She had given him a sweet curtsy and Jack's fascination with her had grown. 'I'm Miss Lucinda Aster, and this Polly. Is the hotel far from here, Mr Newton? I feel apprehensive out here in the streets. I've walked a long way and I'm rather tired. I would so love a nap.'

A nap? It was obvious Miss Lucinda Aster had been kept as a little girl, and just as evident now Jack had taken a closer look at her were the holes in her slippers and the dust on the hem of her dress. She truly did look overcome with weariness and discomfort. 'It's just a couple of streets away, actually. I'm here sightseeing.' Street sweepers and early risers were staring curiously at Lucinda and Jack felt she was vulnerable and therefore at risk of meeting misfortune, even danger. She needed a protector. 'Would you like to take my arm, Miss Aster?'

Her careworn frown disappeared and she nodded. Jack had realized how shy she was and what an effort it had been for her to reply to him. She trusted him, and he felt his heart wrapping around her. He could be a charlatan, a terrible threat to her, yet in her limited experience, because there was no doubt she was totally unworldly, she trusted him. Many emotions had hit Jack, and he wanted to be this girl's shield and minder at all costs. His father had habitually jeered that he would never amount to much, yet something in his character had told this innocent he could be thoroughly trusted and counted upon.

'I'm so glad I got you away from your misery, Lucinda,' Jack whispered through the damp night. 'And that you found peace and a delight in life for so many months, until things overwhelmed you and you took the only way out you felt you could. You're always on my mind. I just wish I could have done more to save you. Rest in peace, my angel.'

Nineteen

Ladybirds in top hats, butterflies with long tapering tails, a mole in neck ruffles, rabbits dressed as clowns, flowers with smiling faces and multicoloured petals, a faraway castle flying an impossibly long shimmering flag. These were just some of the fairy-tale depictions Finn had added to the copy of Dorrie's rabbit nursery rhyme.

'I can't admire it enough, Mrs R, your wonderfully cute poem and Finn's brilliantly clever illustrations,' Guy said enthusiastically. He was back from Bude, and he and Fiona were at Sunny Corner with Dorrie and Greg for afternoon tea. Eloise was asleep in her pram, the hood up to keep the sun off her delicate healthy pink skin. Guy looked happy and relaxed, and Dorrie knew it was because he was with Fiona. They almost seemed a couple in spite of the fact that Fiona would have to wait a long while to be divorced. It was a perfect sunny day and they were out in the front garden, under the magnolia tree, in lounging chairs around a circular table covered with crisp white linen. Having started off with iced drinks they were now on the treat taken from Dorrie's precious cache of Earl Grey. 'Ever thought of clubbing your talents together and trying to get a book published? I'm sure you could come up with many more wonderful rhyming stories for kids, and your hilarious and ironic adult poetry would be just the thing too. Finn could quite ably illustrate both. The charm and fantasy of it would be just the ticket after the bleakness of the war years. People are ready for something new on all counts. The country is going wild over Princess Elizabeth's forthcoming wedding. The new films are avidly popular. Why not get in there in another medium?'

'Oh, I don't know if I want to do such a thing myself,' Dorrie said, more than doubtful. Also a little worried. She liked her simple life and did not want anything like personal accomplishment shaking it up, but to help Finn take a step out in life . . . She passed around the cheese straws, squirming inside for Greg had that familiar look of getting fired up about something. He could be a stubborn so-and-so when the bit was between his teeth.

'That's a jolly good idea! It's a wonder I've never thought of you publishing your stuff, old girl. Collaborating with Finn could be the very thing for him, start him off on a good career.'

It set Dorrie thinking. If Finn could get a foothold in the market there were all manner of avenues he could approach after that. 'Well, I suppose it would be fun to get some of my poetry into book form for posterity, but I wonder if Finn would care to work alongside an old dear?'

'Finn doesn't think of you like that!' Fiona jumped in quickly, allowing a little amused laugh. 'No one does. You've got more vitality than the rest of the village put together. He loves your rabbit poem and the other sort of verses you've written.'

'Finn regards you as an aunt and a friend,' Guy encouraged.

'Yes, Dor. You've said he's drawn Billy Bunnytop to a T. You could sit round a table and compare ideas but I should think if you simply give Finn some selected poems he'll dash off the ideal stuff. He's got a perfect instinct for what is needed. He got all the village buildings off pat. Haven't heard a single suggestion of his work needing a tweak or two, not even from Mrs Mitchelmore, and that's saying a lot. People love the portraits he's done of their family members. He's a dab hand at animals too. I'm in wonder of the drawing he did of dear old Corky as a gift to us. Pretty lifelike, got all Corky's mannerisms. From your description of the late Lucinda Newton, she would have made a perfect lost princess for Finn's paint brushes.'

And so, as always happens in conversations, the subject was changed. Fiona said, 'I've started to become interested in the locals. Jack Newton has come to mind, with Verity now working for him. His young wife was something of a mystery, I understand. Has Verity found out anything about her?'

'No,' Dorrie replied with the pride she felt in her niece. 'In this instance it would be snooping and Verity has kept strictly to the job she's employed to do.'

'So there is a mystery?' Fiona said, pausing in picking up her cup.

'Not at all,' Dorrie replied firmly. 'Jack's wife was a shy young soul, that's all.'

'But she killed herself, Dor,' Greg reminded his sister in the way Dorrie found maddening. He was a hound on the scent again. 'Strangely enough, Hector and I were only saying the other day about her—'

'You and Hector Evans are a couple of determined gossips,' Dorrie chided. 'Better-fit you just got on with helping in finishing off the hall when you're there.'

'We weren't at the hall at the time,' Greg retorted in the smarmy superior tone of one indulging in sibling rivalry. He resented Dorrie getting high-handed with him in company. 'We were in the pub *actually*, having a drink with the landlord, Johnny Westlake. The three of us had been working our socks off plastering the hall's inside walls. Johnny Westlake is a born and bred Nanviscan like me, and we've got the right to wonder about those who come among us.'

'Only Mrs Newton did not choose to come among us. She wanted to retain her privacy, and Jack ensured she did, and that doesn't make her life and sad demise anyone else's business. The village can look forward to great things ahead thanks to your efforts in getting the hall built, Greg, concentrate on that.'

She had smartly put him in his place and Greg was flummoxed to find a word that would dig him out of his hole of embarrassment. 'Where are the ginger biscuits?' he demanded grumpily while stabbing his forefinger on the arm of his chair. 'I made them specially for today. You said you would put them on the table.'

'I'll trot in and fetch them,' Dorrie said sweetly. She had got into the habit of 'forgetting' to lay everything out for social occasions where Greg was included. It made the ideal excuse to escape a thorny subject he was set on analysing to dust. Affable and caring he may be, but he could be mulish in equal amount.

But in the eternal tug of the sexes, Guy came to Greg's aid. 'Can the ginger biscuits wait, Mrs R? I'm fascinated. Given Jack's proclivity for sophisticated ladies, the sort not looking to tie him down, from what I've gleaned about Lucinda she was a very strange choice to take as his wife.'

Aha! Dorrie could read Greg's mind exclaiming the word with satisfaction. Fiona was looking at Guy and nodding her agreement with him. All eyes fell expectantly on Dorrie. She considered them with a schoolmistress's withering put-down stare. 'Does it really matter?'

Faltering, the three glanced at one another hoping someone would come up with a suitable reply. Guy was the one to cough apologetically. 'I suppose not.'

Smiling pleasantly, Dorrie said, 'I'll get the ginger biscuits.'

When she returned with the plate of delicacies, the others were chatting about Finn's first time at Petherton. 'I was just saying, Dorrie,' Fiona explained, 'that Finn's having a glorious time rooting about in Mrs Mitchelmore's cellars. He comes home very dusty, makes for extra laundry.'

'Really?' Dorrie peeped into the pram. Eloise was breathing deep and evenly and wouldn't wake for a while yet. She was such a contented baby, and it was lovely to see Fiona enjoying mothering her now. Fiona had glanced in on her daughter every minute or so. 'But boys do like anything dark, creepy and mysterious, I've found.'

Offering round the plate of his famed baking, Greg muttered drolly, 'So it's all right to find Petherton mysterious then?'

'Any cellar that hasn't seen the light of day for years is bound to evoke that kind of interest.' Dorrie ignored Greg. 'Tell us how Finn gets on with the redoubtable Mrs Mitchelmore, Fiona.'

Twenty

Wearing a cap pulled down tight on his head, Finn fought through a dusty curtain of cobwebs, which glowed eerily in the light from the three lanterns he had hung on nails from the overhead beams. By rights, the spiders that had made this clinging mass should be at least as large as sparrows, with hairy legs and feelers like pike-staffs. A mouse scuttled away from his feet and seemed bigger than the usual greyish variety. Its nails made loud scratching noises and Finn fancied those nails would make deep cuts through human flesh. This happened on the first day he had ventured down the narrow creaking stairs of the larger of the two storage cellars, this one running under the kitchen and ancillary rooms. The first thing he had come face to face with was a skeleton – a real one, he was to learn, for it was a relic of a former Mitchelmore who had been interested in medicine.

He could mention all this to Mrs R and she could form a funny or perhaps a spooky poem out of it. But Mrs Mitchelmore would not approve. She guarded the privacy of her not particularly historic home, striving for the same sense of mystery, Mrs R had remarked to Finn, that the Royals kept themselves in to remain above all other folk.

Finn found Mrs Mitchelmore bossy and starchy, with a hint of kindness, but also personal reserves. While spelling out her first instructions it seemed she quickly became aware she was standing too close to him and she'd backed away.

'You are to tidy and stack, tidy and stack, that's all you need to do,' she had barked at the outset, leading him out from the scullery where he had entered the house. 'Before my husband's day everything unneeded was just pushed down into the cellars and they're in a right merry mess. Except the wine cellar; Mr Mitchelmore was most particular about the way he kept his wine. You'll find all sorts, from old clothes, unwanted furniture and a hideous rocking horse – that can come up, I'll see if it's worth restoring. Put it carefully in the corridor. When you're completely done, Finn, I'll take a look and see if there's anything noteworthy or of value. Take the rubbish outside and make a bonfire of it. Ellery will tell you where.

'Right, now to safety measures. I've propped the door open so it doesn't get accidentally shut on you. There are no windows down there so don't stay down too long at a time. Be careful you don't pull something down on yourself. There's the toolbox for you in case it's needed, and brushes, a dustpan and rags.

'I've shown you where the cloakroom is. Soap and towels have been put in there for you. Wash up at several intervals. I don't want to see you looking like a coalman.' The cellar door in question was opposite the side of the descending servants' stairs and next to the laundry room. A narrow bench ran between the two rooms. The walls towering upwards were of flaking greenish paint – shabby, but in a proud aristocratic way. 'A jug of water and tumbler will be placed on the bench for you. Have you brought a packed lunch and something for mid-morning?'

'Yes, ma'am.' Finn had patted the rucksack hanging over his shoulder. 'A flask of tea and sandwiches.'

'Good chap, your mother packed it for you, I'm sure, but tell her there was no need – Mitchelmores have never begrudged hospitality to casual workers. Food and drink will be provided for you from tomorrow. If you have any questions, then clean up and seek someone out and ask. I'll stick my nose in on you from time to time. Let me know the minute you've finished all. Well, good luck and get to it!'

Finn had found the darkest recesses of the cellar had been left empty. He could understand the servants of former times not wanting to venture so deep into the corners. The jumble of discards had been packed almost to the bottom of the stairs, the last of it, he fancied, just chucked in on top. First he had squeezed into the recess behind the stairs and swept it out, coughing and choking until he took off his shirt and wrapped it around his nose and mouth. It was hot and airless and stuffy and he sweated, in his words, 'like a hog on a spit'. Time and again he filled the giant-sized metal dustpan full of dust, splinters and masonry debris then tipped it into a box he had emptied of dog-eared papers to carry outside to the dustbins. It was a long trek down to the kitchen garden and beyond it with the burnable rubbish but his lungs gratefully inhaled the fresh air, damp today from the light misty rain.

The general maid had told him where to locate the rubbish heap. He had seen her at the Summer Fair, neat and shiny-faced in her dreary uniform of calf-length beige print dress, apron and cap, on duty and enjoying the sights she could not take part in while on duty. She had looked vaguely familiar and he realized why when she told him her name was Matilda Vercoe and she was a cousin to Jenna, and sister to Cathy who was in service at Meadows House. 'Everyone calls me Tilly except Mrs Mitchelmore. I wish I could pull out the things down there with you,' she had squealed excitedly. 'Who know what you might come across – love letters, wedding dresses, photos torn up over a long lost sweetheart.'

Finn had taken to Tilly. She reminded him of Eloise, all sweet and pert and lots of chuckles. She was sixteen years old but looked a couple of years younger. 'Can't see there would be anything of the romantic kind in this rather dour place,' Finn said to the dreamer, then whispering to her disappointed expression, 'But I'll let you know if there is.'

'Wizard,' Tilly trilled, obviously from something she had read in a storybook about posh children in a boarding school. 'I'll be bringing your crib and lunch from tomorrow.'

Every time he had scanned his gritty eyes over the piles of stuff he was to sort out he thought how Denny Vercoe would find this a treasure trove. No doubt, if Mrs Mitchelmore should find need of his services she would send word to him via Tilly. After clearing the recess Finn unearthed a badly marked hunt table and dragged it into the space he had made. There were a variety of unwanted stools and armless chairs and he placed these at either end of the hunt table. Now he had somewhere to push smaller items tidily underneath this irregular platform and he could stack larger items on top of it. He kept one sturdy stool to stand on. There were some hooks and nails along the stair rails and Finn planned to hang pictures from them. There were clearly a lot of paintings, all dreary and faded. On a long high shelf running along the length of the cellar he would replace the dust-laden odds and ends on it, all clearly rubbish, with anything ornamental he found.

Finn had brought his bicycle torch in with him so he could scrutinize items up close. He scratched at his grimy hair. Where to start? His skin leapt to find himself looking into the fearsome eyes of the dappled painted rocking horse that was peering out of stuff piled on and packed around it. He would get the wooden horse out of the cellar but first he had to remove the items blocking access to it. He loaded these on the hunt table, heavy dusty curtains, an Art Deco radio cabinet, a box of men's grooming items, a dressing-table mirror, heavy pedestals. He put an empty broken suitcase on the stairs and filled it with mouse-eaten stuff for the rubbish heap – mouldy cloth, a battered squeeze-box and much more. With these out of the way he carefully lifted up and hefted away a wheelchair, a basic contraption probably used on outings for decrepit Mitchelmores. With the cellars full of redundant stuff Finn wondered what the attics were like. He was enjoying himself; even the most inconsequential thing he pulled out of the melee was of interest. Who had owned this? Why had it been consigned to dark seclusion? Some items were broken from being thrown in here, by laziness or perhaps bad temper, the culprits perhaps being scared of the dark or spiders and making a hasty retreat.

Finally he was able to drag the rocking horse – he had named it Old Beady Eyes – away from the huddle and haul it towards the stairs. It was as heavy as it was ugly, a job for two men, but Finn did not want to ask Ellery, an old grumpy man, for help on his first morning. Ducking down he put his shoulder under the horse's belly and reached up and gripped the bridle with his hand. This was going to be dicey. If he fell or the weight of the horse was too much for him it would drag them both down, or the horse might get stuck on a stair, he could take a terrible tumble and be badly injured, but he was too stubborn to be sensible. It was a matter of honour to him to get the rocking horse, a goal mentioned by his employer, up top and on display. It would be a good time to take a break and a breather outside and have a smoke.

It was slower going than he anticipated. After the third step Old Beady Eyes was denting his shoulder and pressing down heavily on his neck. Finn was in pain, the strain was making his head throb and he imagined a blood vessel inside his skull might break. But he was not going to give up. Taking a deep breath, he charged upwards taking the next four steps in one mighty effort. If he fell now he was going to be horrendously hurt. He gasped in another breath and repeated the foolhardy risk on just one step. He was feeling light headed and sick. But he had given himself no choice but to keep going up the last three steps. The next big breath hurt his insides and he grunted and yelled in pain as he stumbled, one step at a time, until his shaking feet made the summit and he was out in the corridor.

The malicious weight of Old Beady Eyes brought him down on his knees and the horse's rounded belly cracked him on the head. '*Bastard!*' he rasped under his breath, hating the rocking horse, but he had climbed every one of the fifteen steps.

Thankfully there was no one striding along the long corridor while he panted and wiped off his sweat and pulled in his breath. The muscles of his arms shaking like thin bendy rubber, he lifted Old Beady Eyes against the wall opposite to the bench, but not touching the wall. It was too dusty. He drank the water left for him on the bench in one lusty draught.

The next time he climbed up to the corridor he found the horrid mocking rocking horse had been washed clean and in places where its paint had not been worn away it was gleaming. Each day Finn made sure he left here with a spotless face and scrubbed hands, smelling of Lifebuoy soap.

One afternoon he was on his way with armfuls of tat for the steadily growing rubbish heap and met Tilly on her way in lugging a heavy flasket of dried laundry on her hip. As always she greeted him cheerfully, as if she had known him for years. 'I popped over to Uncle Denny's yesterday. Jenna is happily walking out with your friend Sam Lawry. She's only allowed to say goodbye over the garden gate, mind. Uncle Denny has threatened him with all sorts if he tries to misbehave.'

'Good for him, I should think so too,' Finn replied, giving her a pleasant smile. She always blushed a little when he smiled at her and Finn knew she was a touch in awe of him. Once he had gazed at her intensely and this had sent her into twittering shyness. Tilly likely had a bit of a crush on him. He doubted Tilly knew much about what her expression 'tries to misbehave' meant. If only his smiles had a similar effect on Belle; if only she saw him as a masculine being. That she would speak enthusiastically about just him, rather than this idea dreamt up for him to partner Mrs R in producing an illustrated children's book. It was marvellous of Mr Greg, Guy, and his mother to have such belief in his and Mrs R's abilities, to encourage them with a new project and possible future, and it would be wonderful to work at home and spend so much more time with Eloise, but his feelings, his love and desire for Belle were uppermost in his mind.

In his free time, when he couldn't think up a reason to go to The Orchards, he fashioned sketches of Belle together with Eloise. Of his beautiful baby sister sleeping peacefully in Belle's arms and Eloise reaching up her tiny arms to Belle, and giving Belle the glory of her first smiles. And as much as he loved Eloise and Belle he resented and loathed Charlie Lawry.

Once when Finn had taken Eloise to The Orchards and was with Sam and Belle, Charlie had popped in to make a telephone call, causing tight worms of discontent to churn in Finn's gut. Those beastly worms twisted into iron-cold jealousy when the wretched man had nuzzled Belle's ear and laughed, 'We'll have to keep trying for a girl, darling. There's still plenty of time.' Finn knew it was wicked but he couldn't help himself, for his aching desire for Belle grew with every minute of every day, and he wished Charlie would meet and be seduced by a femme fatale and desert Belle. Or meet some quick and painless predestined death.

He always kept one drawing of Belle folded up deep inside his trouser pocket so when sure he was completely alone he could gaze at it and love Belle. He would touch his heart and swear there would not be another woman for him, and to wait for years for the chance to have Belle if that was how it turned out to be.

'It's the christening of your little sister this Sunday afternoon, isn't it?' Tilly cheeped. 'Uncle Denny, Jenna and the family have been invited, um . . . I–I,' she stuttered and bit her lip. 'I've got the afternoon off . . . I, um . . .'

'Come along with the other Vercoes,' Finn said at once. 'Three o'clock at the church.'

'Thanks, I will! Oh thanks, Finn. I'd better run along or I'll be in for it from the mistress if she sees me dawdling.' Tilly hurried off, trilling, 'Keep your sunny side up, up.'

Finn forgot about her immediately. He wasn't looking forward to the church bit of Eloise's christening, resenting the fact that the vicar's lazy, stand-offish reputation meant Eloise wasn't going to be given a proper, moving ceremony. But at least afterwards Belle would be at Merrivale for the spread his mother was laying on in celebration.

Twenty-One

'I see you've nearly finished in here, Verity?' Jack said.

'Just the crate to unpack, Jack.' Verity gazed at the particular item, its wood long gone grey with age. Jack had prised off the top of the crate at the outset, but now for Verity was the best part, lifting off the packing straw and discovering the first concealed piece. She would guess – book, map, artefact or something that really was priceless treasure – but there had been none of the latter so far.

'Would you like to delve into the crate, Jack?' she said gaily.

'I'm definitely not interested in its contents,' Jack said softly, but Verity traced anger in his voice. He took her gently by the arm and led her out of the library.

'Is something wrong?' she asked, perplexed.

'I'm afraid there is, Verity, but first I owe you an enormous apology. I've looked through the books and maps you've painstakingly laid out on the table and found that most of it was valueless junk that my amoral father had added as a cover for what he had really sought. I'm sorry to say, Verity, that among that tatty old stuff, in foreign languages, is pornography, nasty stuff. It doesn't surprise me that my father would sink to that. I had intended to call in an antique book expert to see if anything might have been valuable. Instead I'll have it all removed to the farmland and burnt. I'm so sorry all your hard work has been for nothing, especially as I understand you enjoyed it. I'm sorry you had to touch such unsavoury stuff. I should have checked the contents before I asked you to. I feel ashamed to have had that filth lying in the house for so many years.'

'Oh.' Verity could not think of anything else to say. She didn't care about the old books and other stuff she had logged and labelled, but she was profoundly disappointed to learn her time here at Meadows House had come abruptly to an end.

'I've given you a bit of a shock,' Jack said, ushering her into the drawing room and sitting her down on the sofa near the fireplace. 'I'll ring for tea.'

'I'm not really shocked about your father's guilty secret, Jack. The only thing that matters is that I've really enjoyed working here. The house and gardens are so peaceful and I so like the Kellands and Cathy.'

Jack suddenly gave her a stunning smile, which highlighted his powerful handsome looks. 'I'm so pleased to hear it because I want you to spend a lot more time here.'

'Really? You have something else for me to do here?'

Jack sat next to her and took her hand briefly. 'I have a special job for you to do, Verity. Tea then explanations.'

'So you want me to help you redesign the look of parts of the house,' Verity said a little later. They were now standing in front of the staircase. Would she finally be given permission to climb up and look round the first floor? Hoping so, she was curling her fingers into fists.

'I've got tired of a mobile life. I want to be more settled and spend most of my time here, but before that some things need to be changed. I didn't have the heart to do it before. I had to find someone I could totally trust to do a special job. I'm perfectly confident I can trust you, Verity.'

'Thank you, Jack,' she said, sensing her time spent here had somehow been a test that she had passed, but she didn't mind. She had enjoyed the work, very much liked the house and the staff, and very much liked Jack. She was wholly comfortable with him, there was no pretence in him and she could just be herself, unlike the fraught time she had spent with her fiancé – which seemed so long ago now. 'I'll be very happy to undertake any job for you.'

Jack took a long considering look at her. She was lovely, honest and reliable, yes, but she was also great fun and down to earth. He didn't have to wonder, conjecture, question or doubt. Verity was the one.

'I'll take you upstairs to a certain room.'

So there is a mystery upstairs, Verity thought. She was sure she knew what her test had been. Kelland, in particular, had been attentive towards her. Likely he had been ordered by Jack to watch her to see if she would pry and steal away to the forbidden part of the house. Jack knew he could trust her and Verity was proud of her own discretion. She was excited about what he was about to reveal to her, and strangely nervous too.

Jack led her to the last room along the upstairs corridor. 'This was my wife Lucinda's room. You've never asked about her, Verity. You must have been curious.'

'I have been curious but it's not really my way to snoop. I looked at her photograph in the drawing room; she was very beautiful.'

Jack nodded, his heart filling with emotion. 'She was, she was gorgeous, but she wasn't really of this world. Just being alive here on earth was a terrible trial for her. She was mentally ill, of course, something that took me ages to admit to and accept.' Jack told Verity of his first meeting with Lucinda. 'After I brought her here, which I had to, you'll understand why, I tracked down her old nanny. Lucinda's strange behaviour started the moment she passed infancy. In between short times of lucidity she would refuse to mix with other children and spoke mostly to herself and her toys. She would grow frustrated and bang her head and stamp her feet and scream for hours. The servants thought she was possessed by a demon and soon the nanny was the only one prepared to stay. Her desperate parents had her and the nanny taken away to an isolated house in the Hertfordshire countryside. Her parents were killed and her guardian then had her taken to Florence. He kept her in an attic decorated like a playroom – Lucinda, the nanny and eventually a little white dog, Polly. She was only allowed outside for one hour a day.

'As time went on the nanny was worn down by the claustrophobic conditions and begged to be allowed to return to England. The guardian reluctantly agreed. The rest I learned from the guardian himself. I called on him with the news that his lost ward was safe and sound in the hotel. He wasn't interested. It was easy to see he loathed having the responsibility of Lucinda, and he was set on putting her in an institution. I'd spent time with her. I was utterly charmed by her. It wasn't her fault she had an affliction. I offered to take over Lucinda's care. The guardian willingly accepted and signed her legally over to me. He told me I'd need to ship all her things over to her new home or she would crave them and never cope. Of course that meant a hastily arranged marriage. Lucinda had not officially been declared insane. She trusted me. She called me "My Mr Jack". I think she thought I was part of a fairy-tale and that I'd got her away from a wicked dark lord. Our ship's cabin was filled with her dolls. Lucinda was ecstatically happy; she would walk Polly on the deck believing she was living out an adventure. People were besotted with her at first but quickly thought her an oddity and then they thought she was quite mad and shunned her. I had to keep her under wraps then, as it were, make up stories so she wouldn't take fright. Poor, dear Lucinda.' He sighed deeply.

'I'm sorry, Jack.' Verity found it natural to slip her hand around his. He squeezed her hand gently, and they were bonded in his secret, more than friendship.

He produced a key from his trouser pocket and unlocked the door in front of them. 'I think you should prepare yourself for a bit of a shock.' He stepped inside the room taking Verity with him. He shut the door carefully.

'My goodness!' Verity gasped in awe. 'It's . . . it's . . .'

'Not a room for an adult or a child, is it? It's a carnival, a creepy carnival. It scares me, the peculiarity, the absurdity of it all. It was how Lucinda wanted it, her room arranged like she was in a fairy-tale, a pantomime. Her little bed in the middle of what looks like a stage. Costumes, dozens of costumes for Lucinda to dress up in, even a fairy wand and wings. And all these dolls, there are exactly two hundred and twenty of them here. And there are more. They are in the trunk.' Jack couldn't prevent himself trembling as he took Verity along to a sea captain style trunk at the foot of the bed.

Suddenly he wrapped his arms tightly around Verity as if he needed to protect her. 'I shouldn't have brought you here. What's in the trunk is shocking, horrible. It's my fault. I shouldn't have pandered to all of Lucinda's wishes but I didn't realize how disturbed she was.' Turning Verity he looked intensely into her eyes and said in desperation, 'I should take you out of here.'

'It's not what you want, Jack,' she said soothingly. 'You've brought me here because you trust me to have the strength to face what you had to face. You've brought me here because you know I'll understand.' Verity was feeling the most nervous of her life but she was ready to face what was inside the trunk, however abhorrent.

Jack had a second key in his hand. It was small and elaborate and had fake rubies on the ring top. Still clinging to Verity he stooped and falteringly unlocked the trunk, then straightened up with a lamenting sigh. Verity gave him an encouraging smile. 'Go on, Jack, lift the lid.'

'Thanks,' he whispered, and Verity felt that although he was drawing on her freely given support, he was becoming more and more drained. Stooping again he threw back the lid. Rather than look into the trunk Verity watched Jack. He had closed his eyes. She waited until he opened them and looked down. 'Oh no,' he rasped in a sickly whisper.

Verity knew he had been hoping the horror within the trunk had somehow gone, but it had not. She stared down into the trunk and her whole body gave an involuntary shudder. The trunk was filled with dolls, mostly parts of dolls, their limbs and heads ripped off with ugly force. Red paint had been splashed on them to depict blood. Eyes had been poked out or pushed inwards. Hair had been hacked off. Two dolls had their heads twisted round above string fashioned as a hangman's noose. Doll torsos had been stabbed and slashed, dabbed with red paint. The dolls' clothes had been cut, ripped and dripped with red paint. The carnage wasn't of real people but it was almost as horrifying and gruesome. 'Oh, my God, when did she start to do this?'

'Probably not long after I brought her home. I'd noticed a certain doll had disappeared and when I asked her about it Lucinda would laugh and say it had been naughty and she'd punished it. This always coincided with red paint marks found on the table. She'd say she'd been making pictures but there was no evidence of any and I began to wonder what it meant. There were no sharp things kept in her room. Then one afternoon I overheard Lucinda in a rage; she wasn't shouting or screaming but her tone chilled my soul. I came in and discovered her stabbing a doll with a nail file. I was astonished by her strength. She had gone completely wild and crazy and her eyes were glazed over. Polly was cowering in a corner and I was frightened of Lucinda too then, Verity. I feared if she saw me she would come after me and there wouldn't be a thing I could do to defend myself even against her slight build. So I hid in the room until her madness seeped away. Then with eyes blank she gathered up the butchered doll and put it in this trunk and pushed it in under the bed. Then she cleaned up the mess, not completely, leaving a touch of paint as if she was leaving a touch of evidence of the terrible thing she had done. After that she lay down on the bed and fell asleep, at once looking like an angel. I couldn't tear my eyes from her. Lucinda was vulnerable and couldn't help being ill but she was also dangerous. I would have to watch her ever more closely. Eventually Polly crept on to the bed and snuggled into her.

'I left the room and ran to the bathroom where I was sick. I've felt sick to my stomach every day since, Verity, because the very next day Lucinda went outside and hung herself, and as much as I was horrified and distraught I was glad. I didn't know how long I could go on shielding her and I was terrified she would hurt Polly or one of the staff. The Kellands and Cathy were brilliant about Lucinda and devoted to her. Cathy would join in her games. She knew instinctively how to treat Lucinda. Lucinda couldn't have borne being put in an asylum. She didn't deserve that. If she had not been locked up and kept away from all reality she might have lived some semblance of a normal life. I loved her. It was a strange love, like a father or a brother's, and I miss her, Verity. I miss the times when she was happy and laughing and running barefoot through the stream. I'm glad she's at peace now. I'll never regret knowing her and having her in my life. I miss her and feel I failed her.'

Jack broke down and wept and fell to his knees amid the outlandish nursery scene.

Verity went down beside him and wrapped her arms around him. She gathered his head on to her shoulder. 'Cry for as long as you need to, Jack. You haven't been able to grieve and now you can. Cry for Lucinda and cry for yourself. Believe me when I say you didn't let her down. You brought her freedom and saved her from a terrible end in incarceration. And you brought me here to help and I won't let you down.'

Twenty-Two

Finn insisted on holding Eloise in the dark, chilly church throughout her baptism. Soames Newton was in attendance as vicar's warden, watching the events avidly in case something happened that he could gossip about in the Stores, yet smiling broadly at all and everything, a jollier individual now he was a widower and plied with lashings of female company and attention. He had made it known he was invited by, no less, Mrs Honoria Sanders for tea today. Finn hated Soames' bobbing about, lighting candles, carrying his warden's cross in a jaunty way, croaking the responses in the service when others present in the body of Christ were asked to make them.

The creaking Reverend Wentworth Lytton mumbled and raced through the proceedings. When he muttered, 'Name this child,' and Dorrie proudly declared the baby was to be baptized Eloise Veronica, Finn, while glaring darts of displeasure at the vicar, loudly and clearly repeated, 'E-lo-ise Ve-ron-i-ca.'

Fiona dug him in the ribs. 'Shh.'

Lytton duly sprinkled the blessed water over Eloise's forehead, dripping some into her eyes, further angering Finn. Eloise obligingly cried 'the devil out' and Finn cuddled and comforted her.

Once outside in the warm and windy sunlight, the party posed in the church doorway while Guy took photographs. Verity took some photos of him with Fiona, holding the baby, and Finn. Finn smiled with joy. He had secretly accepted that Guy was likely to be his future stepfather. Guy was his friend, and Finn wanted everyone to know it, which included the few curious villagers milling about in the churchyard.

'Congratulations, Mrs Templeton,' Soames bellowed heartily, slipping between the baptism party and holding out his thick podgy hand to Fiona. 'You have a beautiful little daughter and a fine son. You've made a new life for yourself after going through some very trying circumstances – I know what that's like – and the best of British to you!'

Finn accepted a vigorous handshake from Soames, Finn thinking the shopkeeper's buoyancy would never annoy him again.

Dorrie and Greg smiled, as proud of the Templeton children as if they were their own grandchildren. Dorrie wondered what Finn would say to Lytton if he knew just before the service the vicar had asked Fiona if Guy was her child's father. Finn would be hurt and furious for sure. Fiona had hissed back at the vicar, 'I can assure you she is my husband's child so there's no need for you to be sanctimonious about it. Do you want to baptize my daughter or not?'

'I did nothing wrong by making the inquiry,' Lytton had retorted, wheezing in indignation.

'That was most unchristian of you, Mr Lytton,' Dorrie had chastised him crossly.

'Never mind him,' Guy had said sternly. 'Only Eloise and God matters in this, and the godparents' vows. Don't let him spoil the day.'

Dorrie was afraid Fiona would let the miserable vicar spoil the occasion but Fiona did not. 'We're just as good as him,' she said airily. 'I've done nothing wrong and I and my little girl have every right to enter the church.'

Finn had concentrated on Eloise so far, but now that his mother and sister, and Mrs R, were driving on ahead in Guy's car to uncover the food already laid out for the party, Finn singled out Belle. 'You look lovely,' he said, nonchalantly, for Charlie was virtually stuck to her side, holding her arm linked through his.

In a semi-pleated skirt and matching jacket and perky hat, her hair pinned up, Belle had the appearance of an understated movie star. 'It was a lovely little ceremony, Finn. One of Reverend Lytton's better ones actually. You mustn't mind him. He's old and bumbling and set in his ways. Charlie and I are going to take Mrs Pentecost and Rebecca in the van to Merrivale. I suppose you'll walk with Sam and Jenna – oh and young Tilly.'

'That's right,' Finn said. He had been going to ride his bike but remembered he should act as escort to Tilly. 'We'll be walking with the Vercoe family.' *But I'll get you alone at some point.*

With Jean pushing the twins in the pram and Denny giving the other younger children a ride on his shoulders and back, the group set off. Finn found himself striding side by side with Tilly. She made a trim little figure.

'I can't abide that vicar,' she whispered vehemently.

'Why?' Finn asked uninterestedly, thinking about how he could be near Belle again.

'He refused to bury poor young Mrs Newton in the churchyard. She was mistress for a while to my sister Cathy. She says Mrs Newton was the sweetest, most innocent person in the world. And she shouldn't be blamed for doing away with herself; she was a sick lady and couldn't have been really aware of what she was doing. Now Reverend Lytton has condemned her to wander about in limbo, forever a lost soul because she's not lying in consecrated ground.'

'Don't be daft,' Finn said. He had always scoffed at such notions.

'Oh, you believe she is in Heaven then?' Tilly had to run a few steps to keep up with him.

Thoughtfully, Finn slowed down to accommodate her. 'Your sister believes her mistress was an innocent lady. God's got nothing against the innocent. It's not in His nature. All I can say is thank goodness He's more merciful than humankind.'

Tilly suddenly put her hand through the crook of his arm. 'Oh, thank you, Finn. I'll tell Cathy, it'll be some comfort to her.'

'It will stop her looking over her shoulder,' Finn laughed, happy to keep Tilly on his arm. He enjoyed the moments she snatched to chat to him at Petherton. 'Ghouls, ghosts and the rest of it are stupid superstitious beliefs, nothing more. When you die you either go up or down and you go where God thinks it's fair. Have you ever been to Merrivale, Tilly?'

'No, run past it a few times from out in the lane and it always looked dark and scary to me. Can't wait to see all the changes your mum and Mr Carthewy have made.'

'I did a lot of the work,' Finn reminded her.

'Yes, of course, you're very talented. Finn, will you do a picture of me? I look awful in photos.'

'Yes, if you like.'

'Would you dash one off for me today while I'm all dressed up?'

'Be pleased to.'

'And . . .'

Finn glanced at her to see why she had halted and found she was blushing fiercely.

'What? Don't be afraid to say.'

'Could . . . could you, um, make me look pretty?'

Laughing kindly, Finn slipped his arm round her waist and gave her hug. Tilly was such a little sweetheart. 'That will be easy, you silly, you are the prettiest thing.'

Tilly gulped in surprise to be hauled in against his strong body and was filled with delight. She immediately fell in love with Finn.

Twenty-Three

'See what I mean, Aunt Dor?' Verity whispered to Dorrie as they passed round slices of christening cake. With none of the usual mixed fruit available dried plums from The Orchards had been added to the cake. 'About Finn rooting his eyes on Belle? Do you think we ought to say something to him?'

'Not us. I'll get your Uncle Greg to take Finn quietly aside, it will sound better coming from a man. I agree with you that there's cause for concern. Finn could make a big fool of himself and lose Sam's friendship. It would be a pity if trouble came here now everything has settled down nicely.'

Dorrie trotted to the end of the sitting room where Greg was in deep conversation with Denny. Discussing horse racing form, undoubtedly, Dorrie shook her head ruefully. Greg struck a handsome sight in country gentleman form. Denny was wearing his suit, his bulging mid-section straining his braces and waistband. 'Cake, Greg? Cake, Denny? Could I have a quick word, Greg?'

'Not now, old thing, Denny and I are on important issues. There's not a disaster pending, is there?'

'No, well I can see you two are discussing something important,' Dorrie replied airily. 'But I would like that word with you soon – old boy.'

Dorrie made it her business to watch Finn surreptitiously. Tilly Vercoe was shadowing him, transfixed by him. She obviously had a deep crush on him, and Finn was happy to chat to her, but his gaze kept straying to Belle. Belle was sitting with Eloise on her lap and tickling the baby's chin and making her chuckle and coo. Charlie was gazing dotingly at his wife. He looked up and caught the direction of Finn's dreamy eyes and frowned. Dorrie shot towards Finn.

'Did I hear you're going to do a drawing of Tilly? Why not take her out into the garden, somewhere sunny, where you'll get a good light.'

'Oh, yes, could you do it now please, Finn?' Tilly trilled. 'I have to be back on duty quite soon.'

'Sure, let me get my things and we'll slip outside.'

Dorrie heard the reluctance to leave the room in Finn's reply. He ran upstairs and was soon down again and collected Tilly. 'This way.' As Tilly eagerly followed on his heels, Finn stopped beside Belle's chair and, leaning over, he made a fuss of Eloise. Dorrie saw Charlie staring down, unimpressed, on Finn's lowered head. She sighed, for to anyone's mind Finn was unacceptably close to Belle, his cheek almost brushing her arm.

Belle was on the bed early waiting for Charlie to join her. All she was wearing was her Wings Of Love perfume. Charlie came naked into their slant-ceiling bedroom, lowering his head under the low doorway and beams, having finished in the bathroom. As he always did, he dropped his clothes and shoes to the black floorboards. Belle gazed hungrily at his muscular arms and torso, the crisp dark hairs on his chest and arms, his huge rough knowledgeable hands. She wanted him, urgently. He put his hands on the bed and came at her. She gripped his bottom lip with her teeth and pulled him to her.

'You grow more beautiful every day,' he murmured lustily, and he leapt on her.

In seconds they were striving with each other, almost fighting with each other, seeking to use their mouths and hands in new ways, almost unbearably exquisite ways. Love-making was like this for them sometimes when their heat and need was verging on the excruciating. They used every variation they knew and time went on and on.

If Sam were home instead of being with Jenna at By The Way he would have been disturbed by the variety of his parents' grunts, moans, exclamations and sighs. He might have believed they would even break their bed. He certainly wouldn't have been able to face them again without being horribly embarrassed. Belle and Charlie loved it when Sam wasn't in the house so they could let themselves be at their wildest.

The couple finished on an earth-shattering yell. It was a while before they were able to separate and fling themselves sweaty and exhausted flat on their backs. They grasped each other's hands.

'Bloody hell, that was marvellous,' Charlie got out eventually. 'Wondrous heaven, I love you so much, Belle Lawry.'

Belle turned on her side, levered her body up a little then dropped down across Charlie's oily chest. She murmured, 'Glorious heaven, I love you so much too, Charlie Lawry.'

They lay still and cooled down, their heartbeats gradually slowing to normal and their breathing easing. They were sated and relaxed. Nearly every day they made love. After such a prolonged, fierce coupling they had no need, and indeed no energy, to go again.

Charlie wrapped them cosily in the covers. 'It's strange and disappointing that we've only managed to produce Sam, not as much as a sign of another baby. Does it still worry you?'

'Not as much as before,' Belle said, snuggling in closer to him. She loved this time after love-making when Charlie would tenderly caress and stroke her, play with her hair, kiss her with long loving pecks, and ask about the deep things she might have on her mind. 'I used to be very jealous of Jean Vercoe so easily pushing out kid after kid, but I wasn't that bothered when she had the twins. When Fiona Templeton had her little girl I viewed it much the same way as Dorrie did. After all, Dorrie lost her only child. As long as I've got you and Sam I have everything I could ever want. I'd never let anything come between us and our happiness.'

'Me neither.' Charlie kissed her again, on the brow, the soft place above her nose, and held her thoughtfully.

Belle knew this special routine of his, as she did his every hint of breath and his expressions. He had something on his mind concerning what she had just said, about the thing that scared her most, her family peace, happiness and togetherness. A trickle of panic rode her naked, sweat-lagged back but her desire to protect her precious family superseded the dread. She was ready like a tigress to fight for her man and her son.

'What is it, darling?' She spoke out of love but also as a demand, raising up above him and claiming his eyes, his beautiful greyish-blue eyes, now darkened with unrest.

'You've got an admirer, darling, nothing new of course, you turn the head of every man who passes you by, but this one is different.' His tone was serious, grave.

'And you do the same to women. Different? What do you mean? Who is it?'

Charlie clamped her to him territorially. 'I'm talking about Finn.'

'Finn! Don't be silly. He's just a boy, just Sam's friend. No, never.' Belle let all the tension out of her body. This brought her femininity brushing against where Charlie was mostly a man and she wanted to make love to him, to pleasure him, to do all the work. 'Besides, it looks like he's getting together with little Tilly Vercoe, and his mind is always mostly on Eloise.'

'And you. I'm not joking and I'm certainly not imagining it. I've seen it with my own eyes, Belle. I'd wondered about it once or twice but today in Merrivale it was unmistakable. The boy is besotted with you. It's well past being a crush. He adores you, he looks at you as if he wants to ravish you. It shocked me, disgusted me, and I wanted to punch his face in there and then. If this isn't nipped in the bud there could be big problems. I'll warn the bugger off.'

'Oh, Charlie, don't do any such thing, promise me,' Belle snapped, but it wasn't Charlie she was angry with. 'I believe you. You couldn't be mistaken over something you're so positive about. I don't want you to get into trouble over a callow youth. He's not important. He's a newcomer, the son of a criminal and a neurotic woman, come to that. He's not worth letting any hassle be caused to us, or Sam. You will swear to me you'll do nothing. You nearly ended up in court over that persistent salesman back-along.'

'I'm hardly going to lay into a boy, am I? And Finn is just a boy, although he doesn't think so. I don't think he's quite wet behind the ears; he's probably had some experience with a woman, likely a girl. I'd just take him aside and tell him his longing is inappropriate and offensive and to stay away from you, from all of us.'

'I suppose I was a bit melodramatic but I can't bear the thought of you being locked up away from me for even a day. And I'd hate for Finn to feel he'd made a right fool of himself, and for Fiona to be upset now things are going so well for them both. Leave this to me. I'll speak to Finn, put him right.'

* * *

In the early hours Belle was downstairs pouring herself a large whisky. Sleep had evaded her as the facts and implications of what Charlie had told her went round and round inside her head.

'Damn you, boy,' she seethed under her breath. 'You come into this village and lap up all the help people have willingly given you. I come to your house and you look at me with lust! You wretched little bastard. Who do you think you are? You're just a lowlife nothing. How dare you look at me and imagine knowing me intimately, to want to take me away from my beloved Charlie. How could you think I could want you in that way, you're just a brat, a spoiled brat who doesn't acknowledge what his place is. You're evil, a demon. Want to wreck my life, do you, Finn Templeton? Destroy my happy family, to cast Charlie and Sam into hell? Well, I hate you for that. I could kill you.'

Twenty-Four

While Belle was fuming in her front room and thinking murderous thoughts, Finn was outside in the darkness pacing up and down the bank of the stream, trampling down the grass and moss and kicking at it.

Greg Barnicoat's confidential chat ('A word to the wise, Finn') kept thumping into his mind. Thank God his neighbour had taken him aside, to this very spot, at the end of the christening party and delivered his speech – delivered Finn from making a complete and utter ass of himself. 'I'll come straight to the point, Finn, and you must listen to me and take note. I'm speaking to you as a friend and as I would have done as an officer to the men under my command. Not for a moment must you sweep aside what I'm about to say, it's very serious.'

At first Finn had been puzzled and worried the secret meeting was something about his mother. Or that he had done something dreadfully wrong. Greg had continued like a judge peering down over his glasses. 'Verity and Dorrie have noticed that you've taken more than a shine to Belle Lawry. No, don't argue with me. They wouldn't have got the notion if it weren't so. Unfortunately, Charlie has noticed it too. You must end this infatuation immediately, Finn. Dorrie and I know the Lawrys very well. They are devoted to each other and will both be deeply offended by your interest in Belle. They will see it as a betrayal to their hand of friendship. If you persist it will cause an unholy rumpus. Belle would shun you, Sam too, but Charlie would come after you with his fists. He's done so before. He's utterly jealous where Belle is concerned. He once nearly beat a chap to within an inch of his life. I witnessed it and Charlie's rage was so great I couldn't drag him off the man. If the man hadn't wanted to keep the true reason for his severe injuries a secret, because he was married and didn't want to lose his job, Charlie would have gone to prison for a long stretch.'

'Don't go on, Mr Barnicoat,' Finn had muttered forcefully,

feeling smaller and sicker by the second. 'I understand what you're saying, really. Thanks for telling me. I won't deny my feelings . . . for . . . her. Now would you mind leaving me alone?'

'Of course, whatever you do now you must – I stress *must* – hide your feelings for Belle Lawry.' Greg had put a fatherly hand on his shoulder. 'If you need someone to talk to I'm readily available.'

Finn nodded, miserably, desolately, his guts heaving and his head threatening to implode and plunge him into a well of dark despair. Alone, he bent over double and clutched his middle. He sank to his knees and hit the ground with his head. He banged his head into the dirt of the stream bank again and again. *Fool! Stupid, stupid fool! You showed yourself, left yourself wide open. They know and after what Mr Barnicoat said they must hate you for it.*

He was desperate to break off his anguished thoughts but peace refused to rescue him. He loved Belle but now she must loathe him. He couldn't bear it. Where once there had been kindness and interest in her eyes for him there would now be contempt. To her he was a green odious child. He couldn't stand it, how he had made such a crass idiot of himself. For one terrible minute he wanted to die, throw himself into the stream, keep his face under those few inches of trickling water and let himself drown.

Then from the cottage he heard Eloise cry and he shot crazily to his feet. *My treasure!* Eloise was his everything, how the hell could he think of wanting his life to end when he had his baby sister to care for? His mother was better in her health but it wasn't written in stone that she wouldn't have a relapse. Her mind might always be shaky. Some future bad event might send her down again to the depths.

Finn kicked viciously at the ground, sending grass and dandelion leaves and flower heads to shower into the stream. He screamed silently at the miles of dirt, earth and rock under his feet. 'No! You can't have me. I won't go down to the depths.'

He needed to switch off his mind, clamp off his thoughts. He needed to sleep. He needed to rest. He was as weary as if a hundred years had fallen upon him.

Somehow he staggered into the cottage. His mother and Guy were in the kitchen, the only ones now left in the place. Fiona was holding a fretting Eloise. Guy was passing her the baby's bottle. 'Finn!' Fiona shrieked. 'What on earth is the matter? You're dirty, you're bruised, have you taken a fall? You look terrible. You're ill. I must call in the doctor.'

'I'll be all right, Mum.' He knew he was in for a panicky reaction and had an excuse ready. 'I got bitten by a horse fly; remember when I was bitten a few years ago? It's just an allergic reaction, and I tripped over a large stone. I feel sick and a bit strange. I need to lie down, that's all. You don't mind if I don't help you clear up, do you?'

'Of course we don't,' Guy said. 'There's not much left to do anyway. Are you sure you'll be all right? Want me to help you up the stairs?'

'No, you both see to Eloise. I hate to hear her getting upset. She's had a trying day, being fussed over and passed around. I just need the calamine lotion and to sleep.'

'I'll look in on you in an hour,' Fiona said.

Finn nodded and squeezed out a weak smile. He had to get away from them. By willpower alone he walked as steadily as he could into the sitting room. He grabbed a half-full bottle of sherry and crawled up the stairs. Ripping off his suit jacket and tie and kicking off his shoes, he glugged down the sherry until it was empty, coughing and snorting and gasping, the pain of his heart shredding him. He threw the bottle under the bed, yanked his curtains across to darken the room, got in under the bedspread and pulled it up over his head. Soon the drunkenness blotted out his raging torment taking him straight into sleep.

He was back on the bank of the stream. He couldn't hear the water's innocent dripping and trickling, the fire of his wrath and the stamping of his feet were blocking it and all else out. He never wanted to see Belle again. He knew now he had never really been in love with her, just the image he had made of her, what he had thought her to be. The pedestal on which he had placed her was crushed to dust, as he felt his sanity was when he woke up feeling so sick he feared he would die.

The wild beating of his heart echoed throughout his brain, round and round growing louder and louder, seeming about to split his skull open and spill his brain on his pillow. Drinking so much sherry so quickly had poisoned him. It probably wouldn't kill him but if he didn't do something about it he'd be seriously ill for days. His throat was dry as a drought. He was dangerously dehydrated. And he was going to throw up! Heaving aside the bedspread he somehow got to the bathroom. Soon after he was bent over the toilet bowl, down on his knees, his mother was there, rubbing his back, talking. He didn't know what she was saying but was sure it was the usual soothing stuff to suit the circumstances.

When at last he raised his spinning head and sat against the bathroom wall groaning with the pain in his head and his guts Fiona said she was going to telephone for the doctor.

'No,' he moaned, shivering and twitching. 'I didn't really get stung . . . got drunk too much, sorry. Need water . . . lots of it.'

'Oh, Finn, how could you have been so silly? I hope this will be a lesson to you,' Fiona tutted, vexed, yet her tone had sympathy for it was easy to see he was suffering horribly. She filled glass after glass of water for him but made him sip it slowly. 'You won't be fit to work at Petherton for a few days. I'll let Mrs Mitchelmore know.'

He wasn't going to argue with that. The last thing he wanted was to show his face anywhere for a while. Getting drunk that way was a harsh lesson to him and not the only one. He had learned not to make snap dreamy judgements about a woman no matter how beautiful she was, and that there was no such thing as love at first sight. Belle Lawry's beauty was only skin-deep. How could she be offended – as Greg Barnicoat said she would be – because another man fancied her? His infatuation had been a sexual one but what did she expect? If she didn't want to be noticed, she should dress more like a housewife, make herself a bit frumpy. She was not a deliberate temptress but she was a fake, putting herself forward as all sweetness and light. Yet she did flaunt her sexuality – she had been pregnant when she'd married her bloody smart-ass husband!

'Keep to your ready-fisted big-headed husband.' He aimed his words down the hill and past the crossroads and Sunny Corner to The Orchards. 'Don't come near me again. I'll show you both you're wrong, that Mrs R and Verity got it wrong. I'll concentrate on Tilly, a decent, natural girl, and I'll treat her with utter respect.'

Thanks to the timely intervention of his *real* friends he had avoided being made to be the biggest fool, a figure for gossip and ridicule. His reputation and pride were more important to him than some fruit-grower's wife. Finn gave an ironic laugh. He had something of his father in him after all – and he realized that wasn't a bad thing.

He had a plan, a good one that might stand him in good stead for the future. He should have plunged in straight away at the suggestion that he partner Mrs R at trying to get a book of illustrated poems published together. He would work his heart out on it. Mrs R had dropped in some selected poems but so far he had only browsed through them – that was what made him a fool, not concentrating on his future; after all his future was tied in with Eloise's and she was his priority. That meant he had to do what was best for her and although it went against the stamp of him, he must shuffle off his pride and go to Guy, ask him to sponsor him in getting a place at an art college. Finn wasn't so big-headed he didn't realize he still had a lot to learn about his chosen craft. This would delight and satisfy his mother and be good for her and in turn good for Eloise, and that was his goal, the only thing that mattered to him.

He had only a day's work left on the first cellar at Petherton, and if Mrs Mitchelmore didn't like him having some time off, then too bad. He felt guilty over his attitude. He rather liked Esther Mitchelmore with her forthrightness, and occasionally it surfaced that she had a racy, even barrack room sense of humour. He hoped she wouldn't mind waiting for him to be well again to finish tidying and cleaning the last part of the cellar and burning the rubbish – he was looking forward to putting a match to the gigantic bonfire he'd built, for Mrs M had kept little of the cellar's contents. She had turned down his suggestion that she call in Denny Vercoe and get a few bob for the rickety furniture and odds and ends, which he could mend and sell on. 'It's all part of Petherton and my husband family's past and there it shall stay,' she had declared firmly.

The only time he was going to leave home while working on the art for Mrs R's poems was if Mrs Mitchelmore still wanted him to carry on at Petherton and start on the second cellar. And to see Tilly. Sweet, innocent Tilly, when she smiled was adorable. He had a plan for her.

Twenty-Five

Esther was in the little upstairs room of the Olde Plough, sometimes used for wedding receptions, where she had called the next meeting of the village hall committee. A long, plain room, it nonetheless had a few splashes of grandeur, all gifts from ancestral Mitchelmores: a huge elongated gilded framed mirror, a mahogany hour-striking clock and an array of embroidered Biblical scenes. A couple of uninspiring bronze equestrian groups sat up out of reach on the heavy oak mantel shelf above the yawning brick fireplace. Keeping company with the bronzes were some tarnished silver cups won in local darts tournaments. The thick brocade curtains at the diamond leaded windows were also originally from Petherton, cast-offs. Once a wine colour, they had fallen via time and sunlight to a grubby brown. Now too fragile to launder they were thick with dust, as Esther had found out to her chagrin. The meeting room, she felt, was a little part of the Petherton estate and she was cross that all in all it had been allowed to languish into sloppy disorder.

The landlord and his wife, Johnny and Margaret Westlake, were loosely related to Denny Vercoe and embraced the Vercoes' lackadaisical way of life. Esther had complained about the tarnish and dust, but Johnny and Margaret, both commonplace and ebullient hosts, had laughingly told Esther to mind her own business.

'You won't be laughing when all the meetings I'm involved in are held in the new village hall in future and your drink takings are down,' Esther muttered cuttingly.

She sat down at the 'top table', having previously asked Johnny to set out two other tables at right angles to it. The people of Nanviscoe had their lives to get on with and only a few of them were capable of being a pioneering leader – Greg Barnicoat came to mind but he was too nice, didn't like offending anyone and that was a necessary part of true leadership. Esther quite enjoyed offending those she thought deserved it. Her prime target had been the late, barely missed Delia Newton. Jack Newton should be leadership material but his father's incessant cruelty had leeched anything useful out of him. Jack, when he wasn't tom-catting, set about making amends to the world for the brute Randall's existence in it. Esther secretly liked Jack. She also liked Finn Templeton, currently recovering from severe dyspepsia, but she wasn't one to admit to anyone she favoured. Jack was at last throwing off his morbid widower weeds, letting go of the lingering threads of his peculiar tragic young wife, credit to the presence in his life of the fully womanly Verity Barnicoat. Like Dorrie Resterick, Esther had met Lucinda Newton while making the usual respectful first visit. Esther had left appalled by the freakish perpetual child, who had allowed Esther to preside over the tea and cake, and she had been glad to get away and had never called back. In Esther's opinion Lucinda was verging on being a dangerous being. Thank goodness she had killed herself and not someone else.

Esther had her large notebook ready to record the more important decisions. Hector Evans would jot down the minutes of the meeting. Soames, as a businessman, was treasurer and would take hall bookings. It would be handy for people to make them in the Stores. Esther always arrived early for meetings so she could get her thoughts together. On this afternoon's agenda were the decisions about what the nearly completed hall should be called, when the official opening day should be held and who should do the honours of opening it, and what sort of occasion it should be.

She was surprised when the first committee member came in. 'Good heavens! Honoria, this is a first for you. You're twenty minutes early and you usually arrive when a meeting is nearly over. Is there a problem?'

'Not in the least, I just happened to have got on early today. Thought I'd pop along early for a tête-à-tête. When I know when the hall is to be opened I shall plan to spend the winter in sunnier climes, my first time away since the war broke out. Not much choice really, with so many countries still suffering the ravages. I'm thinking of the Caribbean, somewhere not too native.'

Honoria sat down on the right of her sister at a separate table.

She snapped open her beige handbag and slid out her cigarettes. A minute later she and Esther were smoking, sharing a cheap tin ashtray, having to stretch out their arms to reach it. 'The thing is, will you be all right when I'm out of the country? It will be a few months. If you'd rather I didn't go then I won't. Of course, I can cut my stay short; you'd only have to make a call. Such a pity you can't come with me. Why not let me get you a passport? The contacts I used to sort out those beastly blackmailers could easily get you a passport that even the most diligent customs officer would think was real. They got you the necessary papers and ration cards. You can trust them, darling.'

Esther shook her head emphatically. 'I'm too afraid to take the risk. Their man wasn't careful enough and was quite easily caught. He might have spilled the beans. He might not have known who asked his bosses to put up the hit but it might have led to you and then to me. I'd kill myself rather than face a day's questioning. The truth would be discovered and I couldn't bear that. You know what they'd do to me, the scandal would be unprecedented and all I have is my name, my good name. I'd love to go abroad like we did in the old days but I'm quite happy in my home. I never thought I'd have such a big home where I can be the lady of all I survey. I'm quite content to put my life and energy into Nanviscoe, to be thought of as a do-gooder battleaxe. You go away, Honny, and enjoy yourself. I'll be fine.'

'But if something should happen, if you took ill for instance and your servants called in the local doctor instead of our chap. He'd see . . .'

'Don't worry, I'll leave strict instructions that only Levinson must be called in. Anyway, I'm as fit as a fiddle. I always pay others to do anything remotely risky, like the Templeton boy to clear out the cellars. I don't drive or ride so I'm not likely to have an accident. There's years yet before we need to worry, but thank you, Honny dear. I appreciate your concern, your ongoing love. Now let's change the subject; someone else will turn up any minute.'

They kept a solemn thoughtful silence, finishing their cigarettes and pressing out the lipstick-stained stubs.

'Are you still seeing Soames Newton? I don't know how you could.' Esther spoke with distaste.

'Well, the history between Soames and me goes way back; he was once a presentable young man. He knows how to please, has been happy like me to make it an on-and-off arrangement. It's off right now, maybe for good you'll be pleased to hear. Soames couldn't be more delighted that Delia suddenly met a well-deserved grisly end. He's looking for a new wife, an agreeable companion.'

'Mmm, good luck to him.' Esther lost interest in gossipy news and turned to her notebook. 'I've got suggestions for the items on today's agenda. It's good knowing I'll have your support in all cases.'

Twenty-Six

'It's all decided, dear Dor, the termagant has had her way,' Greg said with theatrical flourish, throwing his panama expertly to land on the arm of his sitting-room armchair. He flopped down comfortably beside his hat.

'Make sure you put it on the hat stand when you get up, don't leave it to me,' Dorrie said, not glancing up from the child's seaside poem she was going over word by word. She was always aware of Greg's actions even if in another room. 'What's decided?'

'The hall details, not that one expected any different, but I like the name Mrs Mitchelmore put forward and I voted for it. The Peace Hall, to honour all those who fought and worked so hard to win peace for our nation. Opening is to be November twenty-fifth, a month before Christmas Day, enough time to plan a seasonal bazaar to raise funds for ongoing costs. Must get some sort of heating put in. Guess who's going to open it?' Dramatic pause.

Dorrie looked up and considered. 'Mrs Sanders, she produced a great deal of money to start the building off.'

'No.'

'Mrs Mitchelmore, she was part of the driving force behind it.'

'No.'

'Your good self; ditto.'

'No.'

By Greg's handsome grinning face Dorrie knew it was someone totally unexpected. She had another stab nonetheless. 'Mr Walters, the headmaster.'

'No, you're getting close though.' Greg steepled his long fingers and put them in under his chin.

'Very well then, I give up,' Dorrie declared in the weary, getting-bored way she had done as a girl with her brother. 'Who is to open the new hall?'

'The children,' Greg hooted in a triumphant manner. 'I think it's the best idea Petherton's old dear has ever had.'

'You mean the village children?' Dorrie asked, her delight matching his.

'Indeed I do, all of them, rich and poor, big and small. Mrs Mitchelmore had already approached Walters and he was enthusiastic about the idea. The motion was carried unanimously, and the children are going to sing a medley of popular tunes, and dance for us. The headmaster will call in Belle to teach them a new dance to victory music. I can't think of anything more appropriate.' Greg rubbed his hands together with relish. 'The people of Nanviscoe built the hall. We don't need some outside dignitary to open it. The war was fought to keep the following generations free and it's the right thing to do for the young ones to open the hall. The hall will always mean something to them.'

'You've had a very successful afternoon then. I'm so glad.' Dorrie laid her writing book and pencil down. 'This calls for a drop of rhubarb wine.'

'Don't be shy. A large drop,' Greg stretched out his hands in cheer. 'I can't believe the hall has come from an idea to near completion in so short a time. See what happens when people pull together.'

Sister and brother drank to the success of the hall. They had no doubt it would be put to good and regular use.

'Was Charlie there?' Dorrie asked.

'Yes.'

'How did he seem?'

'The same as usual. We did the right thing, Dor. You telling me what Verity had realized and me having a word with Finn. His stomach upset was good timing, although Fiona confided to us both it was due to too much drink and not an allergic reaction. He's set only on illustrating your poems and getting back to work at Petherton. We prevented a very sticky situation.'

'We did indeed. We never know,' Dorrie ruminated, 'of the passions that run beneath the surface of others.'

'A good thing too in most cases. Life is pretty settled now Verity is happy working for Jack, she's a different girl than the one who came to us miserable with all her confidence crushed. Let's hope nothing comes along to stir up a cold wind.' A bit later Greg went upstairs to change for gardening and went outside with an eager Corky snaffling puppy-like about his legs.

Dorrie carried on refining her work. Rather than publish a book herself at first, Dorrie, with Finn in agreement, was following a suggestion from Verity. She and Finn were to produce ten illustrated children's poems and send them off to a literary agency in London, people Verity knew and had got in touch with on their behalf. Verity had advised: 'They'll know the best publishers to approach, ones who will trust their opinion. Will save you a lot of time in the end, Aunt Dor.' Finn was also going to send in some of his old pictures and do some new work to send to the same agency, illustrations aimed at other categories, fantasy and supernatural, non-fiction such as nature, aircraft and real-life historical characters, and maps and charts. He had a gripping talent for any medium. Dorrie and Greg believed in his skill even if no one was interested in her poems.

The telephone trilled. Dorrie went to the hall. She was startled when she was connected to the caller, not so much because it was her brother Perkin but because of the pain and humility in his tone.

'Hello, Dorrie, it's good to hear your voice,' he spoke breathily into her ear.

'I don't think it will be for long, Perkin,' she scolded into the mouthpiece hoping her ire with him blasted all the way into his superior brain. 'But first tell me if there is something wrong. I didn't expect to hear from you again really. You were beastly to me the last time we spoke when I rang you over my worries about poor Verity. I don't suppose this concerns your only daughter? If you want to speak to her I'm afraid she's out. She has a very good job which she enjoys.'

'It does concern Verity, actually.'

Dorrie got the impression he was near to weeping, almost unheard of for the immovable Perkin, so sure of himself, uninterested in others' opinions unless they were male and of equal standing. Her sister-in-law Camilla was fully behind him, one of those wives who believed the man was the hunter and provider and his wife was gratefully to bear his children, keep his house and totally support him in all things. Dorrie's ginger eyebrows rose quizzically and she sat down on the telephone seat. This was going to last more than a minute or two. 'Well?'

'Oh, Dorrie,' he breathed, a watery catch in his voice. 'Please don't be abrupt with me. I feel sick to the core and I need you to be Dorrie the caring, good listener, your good self. Can you do that for me, please?'

Perkin was pleading with her. She was worried and felt the cold trickles of fear, while her heart warmed up for her brother, six years her elder. 'Don't be afraid, Perkin. I'm sitting down. Go ahead.'

'I'm sitting in my chambers, Dorrie, still wearing my wig and gown.' Again came that watery catch in his throat. 'I've just sentenced a man to hang, always a terrible thing to have to do, for me anyway, please believe me, but if the law allowed me to send this man to prison for life I would have done it, willingly. He'd murdered two men. When I'd heard his full case I wished he had pleaded insanity but he did not. He boldly stated that what he had done he did calmly and calculatingly and did not regret a single instance of it. He was a war hero, had been a POW escaped from Colditz, recaptured and tortured. He caught dysentery so severely he nearly died. When he finally was brought home he needed months of nursing care. I'm sure you would have read of this poor chap's trial in the newspapers and listened to it on the wireless. Can't mention names and places, of course.

'The saddest of things is after discovering he had lost his parents and sister to the air raids, he tried hard to make something of a future for himself. Got a position in a veteran friend's factory office. Met a girl, a typist, and fell in love. They got engaged. After enjoying dinner and a show one night he saw her home to her flat, left her to happily set off the next day to stay with her people until the wedding, a week away.' Perkin's voice was raw and agonized. 'But the young lady never reached her parents' home. On the way to the train station she was kidnapped and violated by a pair of drunken thugs. What they did to her was unspeakable – I'll say no more about that. The defendant was forced to wait for five anguished months until her body was found in a blitzed building, about to be bulldozed down. Every day and night, barely eating or sleeping, he had gone out searching for her.

'It soon circulated who the main suspects were. They had even been heard bragging about certain details of their vile crime around the time they had committed it. The defendant quickly tracked them down to their local pub, walked calmly in with a handgun in his pocket, approached the two men and just as calmly shot them between the eyes. He put the gun back into his pocket and asked the landlord to phone the police. He's had a lot of sympathy and calls for clemency, but he stated in court that he now had nothing else to live for, wanted to die and be with his beloved and asked people not to campaign on his behalf.

'Dorrie, it's the most moving and tragic thing I've heard in ages. It's really got to me. My heart is breaking for that poor chap.' A dull thud informed Dorrie he had thumped his chest. 'After all he'd done for his country and all he'd been through, that two rotten evil swine could do that to the woman he loved . . . No wonder he couldn't bear it and killed them, no wonder he wants to hang rather than go on living. From the start I kept thinking about Verity, my own daughter, what it would have been like if something so dreadful had happened to her on the way home to me and Camilla. Yet all the while we slated her simply for not loving the man we thought was the most suitable for her – and well, for us, Camilla and me, as a son-in-law. Verity begged us to believe Urquart couldn't be trusted. She was right. He spent a few weeks sowing wild oats then pounced on a gawky American heiress to announce his engagement to, someone who'll be compliant with all his wishes. He didn't care the slightest for Verity. He didn't have a single trace of love or respect for her, and to my eternal shame, nor did Camilla and I. We didn't care about her feelings. She would have had a dreadful life with Urquart, yet we punished her for realizing it and having the sense to break off with him. Thank God she did. To think it took something like someone else's misery to see I'd been so unloving and horrid to my own daughter.'

Perkin was now sobbing his heart out. 'I'm s–so sorry, Dorrie . . . t–tell her for me . . . p–please . . . do you think she'll forgive us?'

'Of course I will tell her, Perkin dear, and Verity will be very pleased to hear it. I'm pleased too and I'm sure she'll forgive you and want to put the past behind her. Verity doesn't bear grudges.' Dorrie had great sympathy for her brother; it took a good man to admit his faults, and she would not rub salt into his wounds by telling him how wretched Verity had been left by the extent of Urquart's malicious behaviour.

'As soon as I get home I'll talk to Camilla. I'm sure she'll see things my way; she's beginning to say she misses Verity. Then we'll both write to her separately and say how sorry we are. What time does Verity arrive home? I say "home" because Verity wrote that she considers her home is with you and Greg now. I'll ring her and explain and apologize to her. I don't suppose she'll want to come up here to see Camilla and me again but I'll stress we'll be very happy to see her and have her stay at any time. We'll be proud to take her out to dine at the Ritz and show her off to everyone. My duties end at the courts next month, Dorrie. I'm going to retire. Dare I ask if we can come down and stay with you for a few days to spend time with Verity? Would you smooth things over with Greg for us – well, try to, for Verity's sake?'

'Yes to both,' Dorrie replied cheerily to soothe Perkin, although she wasn't sure how far she would get with Greg. He and Perkin had been at war throughout all their childhood, playing tit for tat to a fine degree and few kind words had passed between them since.

'He doesn't know how blessed he is to have such a lovely, intelligent, vibrant daughter.' Greg had raged after Verity's arrival. 'We lost our only children. He's still got two.'

After Perkin's heartfelt goodbye, Dorrie returned to her chair and considered all he had said. She rehearsed what she would say to Greg, how she would implore him to allow bygones to stay in the past. She knew the story of the condemned man Perkin had spoken about; Dorrie had read all about it in *The Times*. Poor man. It was easy to understand how he had been driven to murder, even to applaud the fact he had removed two sadistic evil beings from the world. That had not been the case of the paid killer who had shot Mary Rawling and Neville Stevens. One thing Dorrie was still chillingly worried about was that the person or persons who ordered the executions must be local, probably harbouring a secret they would go to the last and final wicked length to keep under wraps. Could it have been something to do with the war? She thought not. Mary Rawling had worked on Meadows Farm throughout the war and had not ventured beyond the village boundaries. There was no possibility she could have discovered anything in the way of national espionage. Neville Stevens had been a motor mechanic at Wadebridge, and had been denied enlistment into the Forces because of his colour blindness, but he had joined the Home Guard. He was most unlikely to have discovered something Top Secret. Their murders were done over plain and simple, deadly blackmail.

Dorrie admonished herself. *Why still be bothered about it?* Everyday concerns were enough to keep in mind. Making Greg see that Perkin really was sorry for shunning Verity and planned to make amends was enough for now.

Twenty-Seven

A bonfire was about to start at Meadows House. With Verity at his side, Jack had lit a brazier in a secluded spot far from the back of the house, near a marshy pond. Down at their feet were three boxes of the dolls and other things Lucinda had disturbingly destroyed. The large vaguely circular pond was fed by the stream, currently wending its way over the stony bed, its surface sun dappled with darts of bright light that kept it from falling into stagnation and decay. Dragonflies hovered and danced about the reeds and bulrushes, but the couple did not notice the quiet simple way of nature.

'When it's all reduced to ash I'll throw the ash into the pond as a sort of atonement for Lucinda's slip from mindfulness,' Jack said, his voice registering low and decisive belying his lack of comprehension.

Verity saw the late child-woman's destruction as committed out of perilous lunacy but she never offered her thoughts to Jack. She said soothing remarks like, 'Poor Lucinda, she could not have known what she was doing.' And, 'I do feel for you, Jack.' Or, 'Life wasn't fair to your dear Lucinda, but take comfort that she's at peace now.' Verity couldn't help thinking it was a good thing Lucinda had taken her own life. Someone in the state of mania who could rip apart dolls, her much loved and constant companions, and paint them red to signify a lust for blood, would most likely have been horridly capable of butchering her husband or his servants in their beds. Red paint might not have sufficed Lucinda's mad condition for much longer.

It was a blessing, she thought, that Jack did not see things her way, and that his poignant memories of his tragic wife would always stay untainted by the deepest terrible truth. Verity had gleaned from the occasional remark by Cathy or the Kellands that they shared her view but were stringent to keep up a sorrowful pretence for their master's sake. When Jack had announced the child-woman's room was to be stripped bare, that all her dolls (the complete and undefiled ones) and all her things were to be given to an orphanage, Cathy had said under her breath, 'Now we can get back to *normal*.' Kelland had said, 'No need to lock a certain door ever again.'

Verity wondered if the house steward had slyly locked his mistress in her room last thing at night and unlocked it before Jack had risen. Verity had hoped Jack would have wanted to burn all Lucinda's strange stuff, for they gave Verity the jitters; at times she had even felt some of the dolls had stared at her with Lucinda's gorgeous eyes, hate-filled and maniacal against her for loathing her dolls. But, of course, Jack only saw his late wife as a wronged innocent.

'We can't just get rid of her dolls and things. I don't want to sell them off and make profit by them. Have you any suggestions, Verity?'

'Well, I suppose you could give them to a charity,' she had offered, hating to even discuss the wretched caboodle.

'To sell, you mean? No, not that, they would only end up languishing in a variety of rich girls' nurseries. They should be played with, dressed and redressed. I'll get on to the Salvation Army and they can hand them out to an orphanage and other worthy poor children.'

Verity had secretly shuddered, praying that none of the dolls and things would pass on any sort of curse to their new owners.

'Stand safely back, Verity,' Jack said kindly, taking charge of the burning. 'I'm just glad of your support. I'll feed the fire.'

Hugging her cardigan round herself, Verity watched in a sort of awful mesmerized trance as Jack tossed the wax, bisque and cloth limbs, heads, torsos and wads of torn-off hair, to sizzle, stutter and hiss diabolically in the flames. The stink of the glue was acrid and Verity stepped further and further back to prevent her nose and lungs being fouled. *Let this be a complete cleansing and let Jack then leave that poor wretched creature forever in the past.*

At the end as the last obscene doll part was burning out of existence and the flames were beginning to die down, Verity felt dirty all over her skin and hair and her lungs soiled and choked.

Jack saw. 'Oh no, I'm sorry you've got so grimy, Verity. I shouldn't have wanted you to stay so long. Please do go inside and ask Cathy to run you a bath, while you have plenty to drink.

Mrs Kelland can make you something hot and soothing with honey in it. I'm sure Cathy will be glad to lend you something to wear. Please don't go home yet. I've asked Mrs Kelland to make us a light cooked tea. You will stay?'

His plea was hopeful and needy, but also persuasive. Verity was happy to stay, she was hoping to. She liked everyone attached to this property, and now the ghost of poor Lucinda had been purged there was nothing left to pass a gloom over it, a gloom of bad regretful memories for Jack.

Cathy's clothes were not going to fit Verity's taller, curvier form so she sat down to the meal clad in Mrs Kelland's best dress, its generous width pulled in with a tie belt. Her legs would have been too much on display and so the cook-housekeeper had also loaned her a skirt to wear under the dress, pleated over and held fast by a couple of safety pins. The result should have made Verity look like a bag stuffed with potatoes but she actually appeared rather fetching, although old-fashioned. She smelled of coal tar soap and dabs of Mrs Kelland's violet scent that the woman had insisted she put on her wrists. Her wet hair was pinned up in a high bun giving her an exotic Latin look. 'I've helped dress ladies before when the occasion has called for it but I've never turned one out looking like you, though you still come across just as lovely, Miss Verity,' Mrs Kelland had declared, amused, as Verity was, by the end result.

'I'll return your clothes tomorrow and thank you, Mrs Kelland.' On the cusp of the moment she had given the woman a hug. 'You all make me feel so at home here.'

'Well, you said it, miss.' Mrs Kelland went off to her kitchen chuckling a certain chuckle.

The implied meaning was not lost on Verity. *At home here.* That was a not unwelcome notion.

'You look charming, Verity,' Jack said gallantly, at the foot of the stairs. Verity had taken so long relaxing in the deep Victorian bath and getting ready that Jack had beaten her in cleaning up for the meal.

'I think I rather do,' she smiled, accepting his waiting hand. As for him, he was enticing and virile in a white open-neck shirt and cravat, his potent muscles bursting against the fine linen of his shirt.

'Are you hungry?'

'Ravenous.'

He eyed her for many long seconds. 'Let's eat.' He escorted her into the dining room as if they were about to dine at a regal banquet, but once at the table – a long shining beauty set with a simple silver vase of roses – he brought the mood back to natural friendliness and engaged her in light-hearted banter.

In utter contentment they munched their way through breaded ham, and egg and parsley flan, boiled potatoes and salad leaves. Dessert was a delicious strawberry mousse. 'Just about all from my own produce,' Jack said proudly. 'And thanks to the best company I've had in absolute ages the food has never tasted so good.' Until now he had only gone through the motions of living, regularly getting drunk and bedding the temptress kind of women to seek refuge from the numb coldness in his mind.

Verity accepted the compliment with a salute of her wine glass. 'Jack, when do you next want me to do some work for you at the farm office?'

'I don't; there's nothing there for you to do,' he replied frankly, although he lifted his wine glass to his cheek and was smiling round it at her.

'Oh, does that mean you don't require my services any longer?' Verity asked the question in a serious tone edged with disappointment, yet her heart gave a series of tingly leaps. Jack's winning smile gave away his intention to keep her in some way in his life. Verity wanted nothing more than to stay in it in some capacity.

'We can say that officially you're my personal assistant, if you like. One thing pressing on my mind is to find out what happened to my sister Stella, and my brother Tobias. I only have my father's word that Tobias is dead. It's true Randall cut off Stella without a penny. She wrote to me a few times, just sketchy notes, saying she was working in medicine and was about to go overseas, there was nothing more after that. But what I really want from you, Verity, is to be my companion.' He put his glass down and reached for her hand. 'Would you like that?'

She placed both her hands round his. 'More than anything, Jack.'

'In this house?'

'Yes.'

'Together with me forever – you know what I'm asking you?' He lifted her hands to his lips and kissed them gently.

'I do.' She pulled the huddle of their hands and kissed them as he had done.

'It was not exactly a romantic and conventional proposal but we're two people who've been through enough of life's experience and don't need that. We're on the exact same wavelength; we've helped each other move on from the past. Agreed, Verity?'

'Agreed, Jack. Totally.'

He released her hands and drew her up from her chair and fully into his arms, gazing smilingly and tenderly into her eyes. 'You won't have to worry about me going astray. That's all out of my system and it was an empty way of running away from my woes anyway, to forget them for a while. I'm in love with you, Verity, darling. I fell for you hard and fast when I pulled up beside you in the car that day. I hope one day you'll fall in love with me too.'

Wrapping her arms snugly and now possessively round his neck and stretching up on tiptoes to kiss his sensuous mouth, she whispered huskily, 'You don't have to wait for that to happen, Jack. I've been in love with you for a long while.'

Twenty-Eight

Finn had been back at Petherton for two weeks. He had burnt up all the rubbish from the first cellar, tending it gravely, using a rake to ensure nothing fell out of the towering blaze and escaped to create danger or mayhem elsewhere. Each time he threw on another old box of odds and ends or piece of unwanted furniture he did so with incensed relish. The day after his agonizing hangover he had shredded every picture of Belle Lawry and thrown them into the stream, also destroying the ethereal image he had forged in his mind about her.

'I'm no longer a fool over you, woman,' he bellowed inside his head, his face burning in the heat, his eyes full of smoke. 'I'm no longer under your spell. I'm not a slave to your enchantment. Hate me, would you, for admiring you, for thinking I'd loved you. Offended you, did I? Not – as – much – as – you – have – offended – me.'

He had hurled a broken standard lampshade into the crackling, roaring conflagration and snarled aloud. 'What kind of woman are you? You only had to warn me off, put me in my place. I was never any danger to you. If you love your bloody Charlie so much how could you see I was possibly a rival to him? If you're that jealous and protective of your marriage then God help any woman who takes a fancy to him.'

Much later, when raking the embers and ash together to form a neat circle he quietly asked the world at large: 'Is anyone really what they seem? My father certainly wasn't. Julius Urquart wasn't. And the woman I thought was a pleasant housewife and mother turned out to be oversensitive and two-faced, not really a friend to me and Mum at all. Anyone else would have laughed and shrugged off my infatuation. I wasn't about to jump on her and rape her, for goodness sake!'

He grinned smugly. He had done much to put the prickly Lawrys right. During the time he had spent entirely at home illustrating Mrs R's poems, Belle Lawry had called at Merrivale once, bringing a little basket of fruit and expressing the neighbourly sentiment of hoping Finn had recovered from the dyspepsia. Finn sketched and painted in the guest bedroom where the light was best, where no tall trees cast any shadows. Often he had Eloise in with him lying on a thick blanket chuckling and kicking her chubby legs and shaking and chewing on her toys. He heard Belle's voice gaily calling hello and he felt sick deep in his core. His passion for the woman had turned into loathing and disgust; he did not recognize that he was deeply hurt and felt betrayed. To his bewilderment and shame he felt too embarrassed to face her yet. He didn't want to set his eyes on the woman for a very long time, until he could meet her eye to eye and behave as if she was no more than a friend's mother. He was glad to stay mates with Sam. He didn't see much of him because it was the busy fruit-picking season, but Sam had popped in with Jenna, bringing Tilly with them, and Finn had fussed round Tilly as if she was the only girl ever worth knowing. Sam would no doubt tell his parents that Finn was 'sweet on' Tilly – a snub to the Lawrys. Tilly's dainty oval face, with its long curling lashes and cute bow lips, was perfect for Finn to ask her to sit for him, and portray her likeness as one of Mrs R's fairy princesses. This meant they spent time alone on Tilly's day off. Finn always walked her back to Petherton on his arm and kissed her goodbye on the cheek.

Fiona had come upstairs to him. 'Did you hear who has arrived, darling?'

'Uh-uh,' he replied, a paintbrush between his teeth but expressing an uninterested sigh.

'Why not take a break and join us for coffee?'

'Ask her to accept my apologies, Mum,' he had said grimly, getting on with the woodland glade scene. 'I can't leave this right now.'

'Of course, darling.' Fiona had ruffled his hair and given him a quick hug to show she was proud of him. Finn loved this, his mother doling out affection. 'Eloise has drifted off. I'll pop her into her cot.'

While Belle Lawry was there, instead of transferring a sketch of Tilly the fairy princess to the glade and painting it, Finn darkened the scene and added another character from the theme – the Warty Witch.

After the bonfire, he had been given the job of whitewashing the cellar, making it lighter and not so intimidating, and then neatly to fit in the items Mrs Mitchelmore had decided to keep, and finally to pen a list of the spoils and hand it to Mrs Mitchelmore.

Now he was striding down the servants' passage with Mrs Mitchelmore to start on the second cellar.

'You won't find the stuff down there is as old, Finn,' she said, jangling a big bunch of keys. 'A good part is what I'd had put in after I married my husband. It's quite tidy I think. Put aside anything you think might be rubbish and I'll come and take a dekko. What I really want you to dig out is the trunks of dressing-up clothes and lug them up to the morning room. You know which room that is, don't you?'

'Yes, ma'am,' Finn said. He had the whole layout of Petherton in his mind after discovering an old map and taking a close study of it. He reckoned there was plenty of scope for hidden passages and rooms in the old place. He teased Tilly about being careful when she dusted or she might find herself suddenly swung into a creepy unlit smugglers' lair infested with gigantic cobwebs or stumble over the skeleton of some heinously murdered wretch.

'Don't be daft,' she had giggled but then glanced all around fearfully. They were outside in the yard where Finn was taking a smoke and Tilly had sneaked a free minute to join him. 'You don't really think so, do you?'

'Oh, you're priceless, Miss Dimples,' he had roared with laughter. 'Don't worry, if you disappear I'll come and rescue you.'

Tilly had smiled down at her hands shyly, displaying her delight that he had a particular name for her. It meant she was special to him. Mrs Teague, the plain cook and laundry woman, stressed to Tilly she was a lucky maid indeed to have such a personable, clever young man courting her, 'but don't forget to keep your hand on your ha'penny and keep your ankles crossed. Don't go the way of the sinful. Besides the mistress'd skin you alive for letting her down.'

'I wouldn't dream of doing what you're meaning and I don't need telling how lucky I am to have Finn,' Tilly had replied cheerfully, thinking in her head of floral headdresses and bridal veils.

'Now we have a proper village hall with its own little stage and curtains, I'll produce dramas and pantomimes, concerts and the like. Costumes will be called for and I can get that off to a flying start, my sister and I dressed up, child and woman for fancy-dress parties. Let me know as soon as you've put something in the morning room. Oh, and you, Finn, I will call on to play the role of the handsome hero, ah, ah no arguments.'

'If I must act I'd rather play the villain,' he said firmly. Mrs Mitchelmore, he had found, liked a bit of dispute even if she did not countenance being beaten.

'I dare say you will at some point; people go for handsome villains. To change the subject, how are you getting on with your project? I must say I do like your artwork. You portrayed to a T the essence of Petherton, all shabby gentility with a hint of the mysterious, now up in the hall. I understand Tilly features in fairy princess form in this effort by you and Dorrie Resterick. I heartily wish you well in following your chosen artistic career, Finn. It would be a crime if you couldn't make a good deal out of such a God-given talent. You may draw Tilly here in the grounds, if you'd like. Just ask me about when and I'll tell you where. Actually, something might be discovered in the dressing-up clothes for her to look the part.'

'Really?' Finn replied, delighted at the honour she had bestowed on him. Although she would have the Summer Fair nowhere else but in her grounds she extended no other invitations to Petherton. The more time Finn spent here the more he liked her. She was the stuff of the British Raj. If she had been captured in enemy occupied territory in the war she would have given the Germans or Japanese a hell of a time. Finn could picture her rallying the women and children in an interment camp, proud of her sweaty rags and greasy tats of hair and her malnourished, sore-ridden body – and torture scars for speaking out in defiance. 'That's very kind of you. I like coming here.'

'Thought you did,' Esther said stoutly. 'Consider yourself my odd-job man when I need a spot of painting done or similar.' She unlocked the cellar door further down the passage, nearer to the kitchen, and Finn propped it open. 'Same rules apply; there is a window down there but it's not to be opened for security's sake, probably wouldn't budge anyway, so do come up regularly for air and water. There was enough whitewash left, wasn't there? Good, there's no rush. I'll leave you to it.'

Finn had already shifted the bench alongside the wall and lined up the lanterns on it. His bicycle flashlight was in his crib bag. Leaving his bag on the bench and taking the flashlight and lanterns to light once down inside the cellar, he descended the solid wooden stairs with the exhilarating expectation and hope of an explorer of Africa.

He got off to a bad start. On the third step down his head smacked into a low beam with a loud thwack that rocked him and brought him down hard on his backside and sliding down hitting his back on the next four steps, stopping with his elbows on the step above. He had managed to hold on to his flashlight but lost grip of the lanterns that plunged down into darkness in a nerve shattering clattering and smashing of glass. 'Damnation!' he yelled, and much worse. Mrs Mitchelmore had obviously not been down here. She was a stickler for detail and wouldn't have forgotten that treacherous beam.

'Finn, are you all right!' Tilly called down to him.

'I think so.' He sat forward. 'Owahh!' Sharp hot needles of pain shot through his head, backside and back.

'I'm fetching Mrs Mitchelmore,' Tilly cried.

Finn was too muzzy in the head to make out what she had said. Stabbing bright stars of light flashed under his closed eyelids. 'Bugger, hell and . . . and . . . I've made a hash of things in the first minute.'

'Stay where you are, Finn.' He heard Esther's loud order. 'Matilda and I will soon have you up and out.'

Finn didn't know if he had languished on the stairs for minutes or hours but it passed through his foggy brain that his employer and Tilly carried him up to the daylight, quickly and easily. He felt the flashlight pulled from his grasp. Then Mrs Mitchelmore said, 'Ah, I see the problem, a hefty great low beam. This cellar was badly planned. That must be painted white. I'm so sorry, Finn. I had no idea. We'll get you into the servants' parlour, it's closest and you can lie down on the settle. I'm sure you'd prefer Matilda to clean the nasty bump on your head; the skin has been broken and needs to be bathed in antiseptic. Have a mug of hot sweet tea, that will do the trick, haven't got any sugar at the moment but there's some honey. If you see double or can't keep your balance I'll run you over to the doctor in the old jalopy.'

'Are you seeing double?' Tilly asked while she dabbed at his bulging bruised and bloodied bump an inch above his headline.

'Don't know, got my eyes closed, that's stinging like anything.' He liked Tilly being up close to him, slender and gentle and moving softly. She smelled as fresh as spring.

'Nearly finished. Mrs Teague will have your mug of sweet tea ready. We'll join you and take our morning break. There's some scones left over from yesterday's teatime, we'll be having those. That will make you feel better,' Tilly said chirpily.

'You make me feel better.'

'Do I?' she whispered. If he had been looking at her he would have seen her sweet face light up with joy and hope.

Finn didn't answer but wrapped his arms round her trim waist and leaned against her chest. He could hear her heart fluttering and feel one small breast under his cheek.

'Eh, saucy,' she pushed him away smoothly, giggling in embarrassment. 'What would Mrs Teague say? And the mistress if she saw?'

'That's what I like about you, Tilly; you know how to behave properly.' Finn grabbed her hands and squeezed them lightly, affectionately.

There was a rattle and quick steps. 'I did hear,' Mrs Teague said, 'and she's very glad you acknowledge a decent girl when you see one, young man.' The cook had bustled in with a loaded tray. 'Make sure you keep it that way. Tilly's a good chapel girl. She goes every Sunday to the little chapel along By The Way lane. I'll be keeping an eye on you, but you'd do well anyway to treat her with the utmost respect or you'll have Denny Vercoe with his hands at your throat. He's her guardian, don't you forget it. Well, sit him down at the table, Tilly. The sooner he drinks this special brew the better for him.'

Short, stringy, apple-cheeked and sharp-eyed, Mrs Teague, her greying hair in a hairnet under her cap, took her seat at the head of the table. 'We're too early for Ellery but he likes his tea stewed anyway. Butter his scones, Tilly, and put them in his place. Scones for you, Finn?'

'I don't feel like eating right now, thank you, Mrs Teague,' he said politely, parking next to Tilly at the table. 'And you need not worry about Tilly. She deserves to be treated right and properly and that's what she'll get from me.'

'So it's official that you're walking out together then?' Mrs Teague persisted, her eyes boring into Finn.

Tilly halted in spreading butter on the scones and stopped breathing, as red in the face as the dish of raspberry jam on the tray. Hanging on to the breath, every scrap of her crying out in the hope she was part of a romance, she glanced at Finn.

'If Tilly agrees,' he replied, smiling at her. 'If she'll have me. Will you?'

'O–of course, I'd love to, and Mrs Mitchelmore doesn't seem to mind. She's always been good to us, hasn't she, Mrs Teague?'

'She has indeed, and don't you forget it. No taken advantage or you'll have me to answer to, maid. I came here in service as a twelve-year-old in Mr Sedgewick's day. I started as scullery maid and worked up to parlour maid, was nearly a full complement of servants in those days with a battleaxe housekeeper. I left when I married, sadly had no children, but when my man died Mrs Mitchelmore took me back. There was just her here by then. Yes, she's a good mistress. We're a nice little group here, almost like a family, Finn Templeton, so don't you dare spoil it.' She smiled at last. 'Otherwise, you're very welcome as Tilly's young man.'

'I'm relieved to hear that,' Finn said, sipping his tea, a welcome whet to his dry mouth. He grinned. 'You were scaring me, Mrs Teague.'

He leaned sideways and kissed Tilly's cheek. Then disquiet came. *What was he doing?* He had more or less pledged himself to Tilly with an engagement of marriage in the not too distant future. *You fool!* He couldn't just let her down, she was too good and sweet and lovely to do that to. But he did like her, very much, and he enjoyed her company. He would just have to go along with it. Let the future sort itself out.

'How did you and Mrs Mitchelmore get me up so easily from the cellar?'

Mrs Teague cut in – Finn was to learn that she did most of the talking at the servants' table. 'It was the mistress, she more or less carried you on her own. I was watching. Tilly only had to hold your head. The mistress is a strong woman. She was a good nurse for old Mr Sedgewick – God rest him – lugged him in and out of bed and into his wheelchair like a good'un, she did. She's made of good stout British stuff, isn't afraid to put her hand to a few repairs about the place. If she'd married Mr Sedgewick when he was a young man there might have been children; an heir. Wish there was, with her sister Mrs Sanders also not having children, only God knows what'll happen to Petherton in the future. Never heard the sisters mention they got cousins or any relatives. All I know about them is they said they've moved around a lot and come from a military background. Still, Mrs Mitchelmore is a lot younger than me so I'll either be dead or nicely retired when she passes on – she's given me to understand she's set aside something for me in my old age. And you needn't worry, maid.' She eyed Tilly and jerked her head at Finn. 'You'll long be married with a family by then.'

Tilly gazed at Finn all aglow. His stomach sunk to his working boots. What had he got himself into? How could he have been so stupid and careless? He was in too deep to simply cut himself off from Tilly. He would just have to let things run, for now.

Tilly smiled at him and he found himself smiling back. Things could be worse, he supposed. Tilly was Tilly, after all, lovely, open and genuine.

Twenty-Nine

Summer had given way to autumn, and on a typical blustery day of grey skies and yellowing leaves fluttering down from the trees, Dorrie and Finn were in the library of Sunny Corner going over the final scripts, typed by Verity, and the accompanying artwork. They agreed the rhyming stories, one incorporating a woodland fairy princess who had lost her wings, and an elf, a pixie, a bunny, a squirrel, an ancient talking oak tree and a wise young owl who help her to find them, were ready to be packaged and posted to the literary agency in London, suggested by Verity. Dorrie would make the trip to the post office.

'I don't know anyone there personally,' Verity had said. 'I rang around and they're recommended by Angela Blakely-Smythe. You remember her, Aunt Dor? The chubby, spotty school friend you kindly allowed to join us one summer hols while her parents swanned off to Monte for several weeks. Angela was always giggling and playing pranks. She's turned out to be a curvy glamour puss, by the way. She knows all sorts of people. Angela says it's your best bet really, but she's given me a few more names and addresses you might like to try. I suppose things are still a bit tricky after the war. You've had an interested response to your initial letter, and Jack and I are keeping everything crossed for you.'

'Satisfied, Finn?' Dorrie asked, referring to her rhyming.

'More than satisfied, Mrs R. Let's go for lift-off. I'm not expecting great results for my contribution, it's likely to be seen as a bit raw, publishers probably like to keep to their own illustrators, but that doesn't matter as long as they want your stories. They might be able to do something with the other stuff I'm enclosing for war or ghost books. Not unexpectedly Guy has offered to pay to have loads of books published. He's such an expert at emotional blackmail of the good intentioned kind, says it would be nice for Eloise. We can always think about that if we're rejected.'

'Well, I don't care about myself,' Dorrie said, stroking Corky's smooth head just plonked on her knee. 'I'm quite happy to keep my writing private. You're the one who has to have a future, Finn.'

'I've a better opportunity all round now that Guy is sponsoring my fees at the private art academy at Wadebridge, after Christmas. Living in, I'm going to miss Eloise like mad but it's for the best. Mum can cope now and I've got the long-term future in mind. Now I've made enough for Denny to fix me up with an old Norton motorbike it won't take me too long to slip home at the weekends and holidays. Guy is driving Mum and me to meet the principal, Dame Rosalind Keats. I'm looking forward to seeing her, she sounds quite a character.'

'And will you miss Tilly also?' Dorrie tilted her head at him.

'Little Miss Dimples? Every time I see my drawings for our joint effort I'll see Tilly, the fairy princess. Of course I'll miss her, she's my sweetheart.' He smiled then reddened. 'Never thought I'd be saying something like that.'

'She's a lovely girl,' Dorrie said, glancing away to avoid embarrassing him. She was pleased he had moved his affections on from Belle Lawry but she was concerned at the thinly veiled animosity he bore against Belle and Charlie. Dorrie was convinced she and Verity had not been wrong about Finn having an unhealthy infatuation with Belle, or that Charlie had noticed it. On the one occasion Dorrie had been in Finn and the Lawrys' joint presence she had noticed Charlie casting Finn dark searching looks and Belle had practically ignored Finn after a desultory hello. At least Sam seemed not to have noticed anything amiss. 'Another drink, Finn? Hot chocolate? Jack got hold of some from somewhere and gave it to Verity.'

'Yes please, and is there any more of Mr Greg's fruit loaf?'

'There is indeed. Come along to the kitchen, it's cosier in there.'

Once in the kitchen, his long legs spread out from one of the three easy chairs set in a snug corner, Finn asked, 'Where is Mr Greg?'

'At the hall with Hector Evans, Denny, Soames Newton, Johnny Westlake and of course Mrs Mitchelmore planning its grand opening. They're also finishing off the electrical wiring. Mrs

Mitchelmore has suggested choosing the eldest and the youngest child at the school to cut a ribbon together, and then we shall all sing Trelawny and the national anthem and get on with the festivities. I like that idea.'

Dorrie brought the tray of hot chocolate and cake and sat down beside him. Corky stationed himself for effortless cake begging at her feet. From here they had a direct view into the range's roaring fire behind its grid. With the wall clock ticking lazily the woman and boy settled down to chat companionably.

'I shall also miss you when I'm away, Mrs R. I'll be sure to pop down here every weekend. You're one of my favourite people.' Finn touched Dorrie's freckled hand and gave her a winning smile.

'Oh, Finn.' Dorrie felt her eyes fill up. 'You'll have me in tears; that's one of the nicest things anyone has said to me. I'm very fond of you too.'

Finn gobbled down a chunk of cake. 'You've got your brother the judge and his wife coming down soon, Miss Verity's parents, for the engagement do. It is going to be here?'

'Retired judge,' Dorrie corrected him. 'No, it's to be at Meadows House, just a small dinner and not a do at all. It's what Verity and Jack want, everything including the wedding next year to be low key. They want to enjoy their engagement and make changes to the house. There might be a bit of an atmosphere while Perkin's here. Greg still hasn't forgiven him for disowning Verity for breaking off her last engagement. I think Greg was hoping that he would be walking Verity down the aisle one day, but now that Perkin and Verity have reconciled over the phone, of course Perkin will resume that honour. Camilla is a terrible snob. I'll be glad when they've returned home, to tell you the truth.'

'Must be hard work acting as peacemaker but you're made for it; you've certainly brought peace to our home.'

'That's nice, the way you said home and not house. What have you got there?'

Finn was turning a small square dog-eared sepia photograph over in his fingers. 'This fell out of the box of a pair of binoculars Mrs Mitchelmore kindly gave me from the stuff I hauled out of her second cellar. I didn't open the box until I got home. I was going to take it back to her but something made me think better of it and to show it to you.'

'Oh?' Dorrie put on her half-spectacles and took the photograph from him. It was a fairly good image of a young officer, probably serving in the Great War, and a young woman in a large garden. It could have been taken anywhere but even the slightest glance revealed the woman was Honoria Sanders, perhaps with a friend or old flame.

'Read the writing on the back. It's what got me puzzled.'

Turning the photo over Dorrie read aloud, 'To Honny, darling. A snap of you and Chester. With love, Mother x.'

'Mmm, I didn't know about a Chester; there has never been a single mention of him.' Dorrie studied the couple portrayed again.

'That's why I've held on to it until now. I've been in Mrs Mitchelmore's drawing room and there are many photos of the sisters but none of this Chester chap. Makes you think that he must be a dark family secret. He could have run away in battle. Seems he must have done something pretty shameful, don't you think? I came across nothing else connected to him.'

'Yes, I think you could be right, Finn,' Dorrie said quietly, but deeper thoughts she would keep to herself turned her insides to ice. '*know about Ch . . . bring money to Merryvale . . .*' The ripped part of the note Corky had rooted out sprang up as if literally before her eyes. Could this Chester be the Ch in the blackmail note? Chester who? Honoria Sanders had many ex-husbands and even the most determined gossips had not divined how her former surnames had run. Twelve years ago Sedgewick Mitchelmore had gone to Harley Street to consult a top heart specialist and returned with Esther as his bride. She had been a powerful figure from the outset and taken over the village's dealings so rapidly and efficiently she had met little opposition, rather mainly with relief and a hint of subservience. She wasn't the sort one felt easy to question and her stock remark had always been, 'Never mind about me. I do what I can for Nanviscoe for my husband's sake because he cared so much about it.' Divorced Honoria had turned up soon after and bought Sawle House and the sisters had become a prominent feature as if they had lived in the village almost from its origins.

'Mrs R? You've been quiet for ages.'

'Oh, have I? I'm sorry, dear.' She saw Finn had demolished his cake and quaffed his hot chocolate. 'I'm sure you did the right thing about not giving this photo to Mrs Mitchelmore. If she wanted this Chester's existence acknowledged she would have talked about him before.'

'You think he was a bad'un?' Finn asked as he got up to leave.

'It's likely he was, but he is really none of our business. If he does or did have great meaning to Mrs Mitchelmore I'm sure she's keeping private snaps of him. It might be best if the photo was burnt and we agree to never mention it again.'

'I'll go along with that. I have a lot of respect for Mrs Mitchelmore and I'd hate to be the cause of her being cut up about something. Can I leave you to destroy it? Thanks.'

Finn kissed Dorrie on the cheek as he always did now when saying goodbye and then he was gone.

Dorrie rose and went to the range. Before picking up the iron tool to lift the top plate to drop the old photo into the amber-pink flames, she again studied the writing on the back. It set her into troubled thinking.

Thirty

Tilly and Jenna were sitting cross-legged on the creaky double bed Jenna shared with her sister Maia, the younger by four years. The girls were binding up their neck-length hair in strips of rag to make it wavy the following morning. Tonight, as Mrs Mitchelmore was spending a rare weekend with Mrs Sanders, Tilly was going to squeeze into the bed with Jenna and Maia. The three girls loved these occasions and would giggle long into the night, sneaking downstairs at some point and bringing back cocoa and biscuits.

The little room, in which was squeezed a nightstand, had a curtain across an alcove where the sisters hung their clothes on a rod. Thanks to Jenna and Jean's seamstress skills the whole family had more clothes than most, mainly made up from bundles of clothing that Denny had procured. The bed was spread with a pretty multicoloured quilt of Jenna's own making. The walls were donned with a long mirror Denny had removed from an old wardrobe and a variety of gaily painted shelves he had put up for the girls' belongings.

'How's your new quilt coming along?' Tilly asked, her voice muffled from the next rag she had between her teeth.

Jenna was busy stitching another quilt for her 'bottom drawer'.

'About halfway done. I want to crochet some cushion covers. Dad's got hold of some good used woollens – you'd be surprised what well-off people sell him for next to nothing. They usually plump for him doing them odd jobs or some gardening owing to what their kind call 'the servant problem'. Mum and I are going through it all tomorrow and set the girls to unpicking and winding up balls. If there's any left over after enough has been set aside for Dad, Adrian and the little ones to have a new jumper or cardie, she's going to let me have some for the cushion covers.'

'You'll have a lovely room when you and Sam get married. You'll be living at The Orchards, so you won't have to worry about getting a whole houseful of stuff together.'

'I hope so,' Jenna replied, tying her last rag then looking down glumly.

'Something wrong? You and Sam aren't having problems, are you?' Tilly wriggled closer to her cousin.

'Sort of . . .'

'What do you mean, sort of?'

'I'm not sure but sometimes I get the feeling Sam is losing interest in me.' Jenna shrugged.

'But he always seems so keen on you,' Tilly protested. 'Has he said something then?'

'He moans that he gets fed up always having Dad breathing down our necks,' Jenna said, aiming a vexed look at the floor-boards. From below, Denny could be heard roaring with laughter.

'But Sam should understand Uncle Denny is only being protec-tive of you. You're not quite sixteen yet and Sam won't be seventeen until next January. What does he expect? Here, he's not pestering you to do anything . . . naughty . . . is he? Uncle Denny would have his guts for garters.'

Jenna glanced at the door, looked back then leaned towards Tilly's ear. 'He's always putting his hands on my bosom when we are alone.'

'And you let him? Or do you push his hands off?' Tilly gasped.

'Does Finn try anything with you?'

'No, never, he only pecks me on the lips because he says he respects me. He says we'll take things slowly and do things properly.'

Tilly's tender face was aglow with smiles. Finn treated her as if she was a delicate petal. He held her hand and he hugged her gently. He left her at Petherton's back door with a kiss on either cheek then a warm touch on her lips. He always spoke kindly to her, he laughed with her and never at her, and asked often if she was all right. He had even brought her back a little gift when he returned from seeing his new academy principal. The two-inch glass angel with tall wings she would treasure forever. He had said, 'I'll be away all through the week but we'll see each other nearly as much as before.' Tilly couldn't be happier with her courtship.

Her sister Cathy at Meadows House envied her. 'I wish someone like your Finn would come to the House,' she'd lamented, 'or I'll end up as an old maid.'

'Your time will come,' Tilly had reassured her.

With sighs of woe, Jenna said, 'You're lucky.'

'You said that with heartfelt envy and . . .' Another description wouldn't come to Tilly, then she was worried. 'Heck, he hasn't tried anything else, has he?'

'No of course not – and he wouldn't get very far if he did.'

Jenna had lied on both counts. After going through the cocoa and biscuits routine, when Tilly was fast asleep and little Maia snuggled in between them and sucking her thumb, Jenna lay awake in the darkness on her side, weeping silent tears.

A few weeks ago Sam had surprised her by slipping into the house while her parents were out making their monthly visit to Jean's mother, who years ago had gone to live in nearby Helland. 'Thought I'd take the chance to see you all alone for once,' Sam had said cheekily.

'I can't stop for long,' she had said at the sewing machine, distinctly uncomfortable at his unexpected appearance and the sly twist in his eyes. 'I promised Mum I'd get all this done before she gets back.'

'I won't hold you up for long. I've got work to get back to too. I just want a proper cuddle, that's all.'

'What does that mean?' She'd stayed rigidly where she was but he was soon yanking her into his tight embrace. He didn't aim his lips at hers but nuzzled her neck and throat, forcing her head back uncomfortably. His breathing was heavy and snorting.

'Gently, Sam, I don't like this.' She struggled to get free.

He loosened his grip on her. 'Sorry, Jen, this better? It's just that I want to be with you so much. Let's nip into the front room and cuddle on the settee.'

'I'm not sure about that if you're going to maul me about. Swear there will be no wandering hands. Don't forget I'm under age, apart from Dad being out to get you, you could go to prison.'

'I'd never do anything to hurt you, Jen, you can trust me. I promise I won't be rough with you. You do want to cuddle up with me, don't you? We've been going steady for weeks. I love you. I just want to hold you. There's nothing wrong in that.' He ended by sounding aggrieved.

'Do you really love me, Sam?' Jenna searched his flickering eyes.

'I've loved you for ages. I told you how long it took me to draw up the courage to ask you to be my girl. We deserve a little time on our own without all your brothers and sisters in the way, following us around and cracking silly jokes. Please, Jen. Why do you think I'd want to hurt you?'

That swayed her. 'You're right, there's always someone about, and anyway Dad should trust us. I've never been flighty. I know what's wrong and what's right. I'd never do anything to let my parents down. Let's spend a while being close.'

The front room wasn't kept just for special occasions with so many people living here, and Denny and Jean did not believe in keeping the room cold and mainly unused. To them, life was for living not for acquiring fancy things to protect behind glass or in cupboards. The fire was kept in with logs and the wind-fallen sticks that were thirteen-year-old Adrian's job to forage. Standing in front of the second-hand upholstered long settee that was adorned with crochet throws and knitted cushions, Sam held and kissed Jenna more thoughtfully for a long time.

He eased Jenna down and sat with her encircled in his arms. He glanced about. 'I love this room, and it's lovely being here with you like this.' He kissed the top of her head.

Feeling safe, cherished and happy now he was being gentle with her, she wriggled in closer to him, tucking her legs up on the seat. 'Yes it is.'

'I asked my father about, um, the facts of courting. I can ask him anything, we don't get coy in our house.'

'With so many children there's not a lot of coyness here really,' Jenna joked. 'I'll let you in on something. Mum's expecting again.'

'Well, there's still plenty of room for another baby, even another set of twins.' Sam paused, then he spoke while reddening as if his face was nearly on top of the fire. 'Um, Dad said that if a couple want to do everything they can use a rubber thing so there's no risk of a pregnancy. He said he didn't know about it when he was young but he doesn't regret having me.'

'You're not hinting at anything, are you?' Jenna said crossly, pushing his arms away from her. He had ruined the wonderful rosy romantic atmosphere. 'If you don't respect me, Sam Lawry, then you had better leave this minute!'

'I was only saying, Jen.' There was hurt in his tone. 'For

goodness sake, I thought we were so close now we could discuss private matters. If you don't trust me perhaps I should go.'

'No, don't do that. I'm sorry, it's just that . . . forget I said anything.'

'It's all right, treasure, I understand you want to wait until we're older, when going the last mile will be special to us both. Sorry for being an inconsiderate sod. It's lovely just being here like this.'

He held her in light arms for some time and Jenna was pleased, but no matter how hard she tried she couldn't bring back the bliss of those first precious moments.

Using his thumb, Sam gently rubbed behind her ear. He had forgotten his father's advice at the outset to always start off tentatively with a girl and he had ravished poor Jenna like she was a piece of meat. Charlie had detailed the places he called the erogenous zones on a woman, the most intimate ones he had named had turned Sam's face and neck to flames. 'Don't go on until she's totally at ease and accepting what you're doing. Remember most of all, my son, have your fun and sew your oats for many years before you settle down. Whatever you do, don't get yourself tied down with that Vercoe girl, she's nice enough but you don't want to end up part of that ragbag family, breeding brats and ducking and diving for a living. Don't forget she's not out of the woods yet; her age. There's a big wide world out there. Your mother and I love having you home but we'd also like to see you break out and do something with yourself.'

It was time for another kiss. Carefully placing his hand on the side of Jenna's face he brought his mouth to hers and kissed her long and thoroughly.

Enjoying his kisses, Jenna responded and soon relaxed into them. Sam was caressing under her chin and she liked that. Every few seconds he stopped touching her with his moving fingertips as if signing that he was taking things at her pace and comfort. Sam put his palm lightly on her collarbone and slowly, slowly tip-fingered his hand down until it was on the swell of her breast. It gave Jenna a delicious tingly feeling and she didn't want it to stop. She allowed Sam to slip his hand in under the neckline of her dress and over her chemise to lie fully on her breast. That was going to be his limit, she decided, but the gentle tweaking with his thumb and forefinger and massaging was utterly exquisite and she was filled with desire between her thighs.

She had told Tilly the truth. Sam had not tried anything she didn't want him to do. When his hands had left her bodice and travelled down and inside her underclothes she had ached and panted for him to do more. She had shifted for him when he'd hoisted up her skirt, freed himself and then after some fumbling and desperation he drove home inside her. The pain was too much for her to bear but only for a moment, and then she had striven with him, feeling as if she was rising ever and ever towards some sort of heaven. The heaven came for her and Sam an instant after, and he'd lain on her out of breath but still making guttural noises of pleasure and she felt like a woman for having pleasured him.

Pulling apart from her while still keeping them lying down he'd pushed down her skirt, saw to himself, then held her in his arms. 'Oh my God, I never thought it would be as beautiful as that. You all right, Jen? Did I hurt you? You did like it? You seemed to.'

'It was wonderful, Sam, because it was with you.'

'I didn't think you'd want to but you did. It's natural, isn't it? No wonder people do it all the time.' He kissed her lips then lay down his head to settle his breathing.

After a few silent moments Jenna's mind tumbled over with other considerations. 'We'll have to get engaged now, on my sixteenth birthday on December first. You'll have to ask Dad, he's old-fashioned like that.'

Sam was silent. She shifted to see his face. The firelight was flickering across it and suddenly he didn't seem like the quiet Sam of old, who had taken ages to pluck up the nerve to ask her out.

'You do want to get engaged, Sam?' Worry and an edge of shame dug into her.

'There's plenty of time for that, Jen. Just because we've done it once don't mean we have to do it again,' he said. But she had not liked the way he was smiling.

'You did use one of those things you mentioned?' Her whole inner self was aflame with indignity. What did Sam really think of her now?

'No I don't have any yet; I need to go into town to a pharmacy. Didn't think we'd go so far today. We've got nothing to worry about, you can't get pregnant the first time.'

Jenna had heard that before and her mother had declared it was an old wives' tale. She felt sure Sam would soon get some of those 'rubber things'. He might ask his father more advice about them. Charlie Lawry would know what they'd done. Sam had taken it for granted, because of her eagerness to have sex with him, that they'd be doing it again. Jenna had felt sick.

She felt sick now, unable to get to sleep while Tilly and Maia slumbered peacefully in their innocence. She was due on tomorrow and was praying she actually would get away with her first, and all too willing, frisky encounter.

Thirty-One

'It's not the same as marrying a man who will inherit a title, but at least Jack's a well-off landowner.' Camilla Barnicoat gazed down over her aquiline nose at the surroundings of her future son-in-law's drawing room. 'He's a good catch for you, Verity – considering the circumstances. That cheap coffee is still bitter on my tongue. Could I have a sweet sherry?'

Please . . . Why do people like you, Mother, think it's fine not to use the manners you insist from everyone else? Verity rose in her long, sleeveless aquamarine evening dress and went to the drinks cabinet. Before lifting the sherry decanter, she made a cross face behind her mother's back. 'Sherry for you too, Aunt Dor? Randall Newton sent for this vintage from one of Spain's best vineyards so this, Mother, should be pleasing even to your palate. I'm glad you approve of Jack – well, more or less.'

While her father, who was very much like Greg in looks but shorter, minus a moustache and a pale complexion, had on arriving at Sunny Corner swept Verity off her feet, kissed her effusively and once again begged her to forgive him for cutting her off after she had ended her engagement, Camilla had air-kissed Verity and murmured, 'Nice to see you, dear, you do look well.'

Perkin had cleared his throat. 'You've got more to say to Verity than that, Camilla.'

'Yes, well,' Camilla bristled in the disapproving manner in which she had treated Verity for much of her childhood. 'I'm sure we're both very sorry we didn't realize the true nature of a certain man, but I do think you could have ended with him, Verity, in a way that would have humiliated him and not us. Well, can we go inside? I'm dusty and dishevelled and feeling not a little travel sick.'

'Sorry not to have taken account of *your* feelings, Mother,' Verity had said, stiff with resentment.

'Well, it's in the past now and best left there.'

Verity's joy at finding the true love of her life and the wonderful future she was sure she would have with Jack, and her father seeking such a heart-wrenching reconciliation, were enough for her to want to leave things as they were with her snobbish, uncaring mother, otherwise she would have told Camilla to push off straight back home.

'An excellent sherry,' Camilla twittered in surprise, taking another sip and washing it round inside her mouth.

'You haven't looked round the house yet, Mother. Would you like to?' Verity asked.

'Indeed not, I'd rather wait until you and Mr Newton have made all your changes. This house gives me the shivers. Don't you think it's morbid taking over from a disturbed woman who killed herself here? I'm sure I would insist on living somewhere else entirely.'

'You're not Verity,' Dorrie interjected. 'And she knows very well what she is doing. She and Jack will have a very successful life together.'

Camilla shrugged dismissively. 'That is all that matters, isn't it? Verity, with clothes still requiring ration coupons I've brought my wedding dress down with me, if you'd care to wear it, but don't feel obliged to. Feel free to have it altered in any way you choose. Or make your arrangements and send your father and me the bill.'

Verity's eyes grew wide in astonishment. 'That's very thoughtful of you, Mother.'

'Well.' Camilla waved her sherry glass about. 'I don't feel I have the right to interfere with your new plans. You're very close to Dorrie. As the wedding will be in the local church here, you have my blessing to arrange everything together. Just let me know your colour scheme so I don't wear something that clashes, and what I can do towards the catering.'

'Golly, Mother.' Verity's mouth sagged down. 'I never thought you'd say all that. I'd be delighted to wear your wedding dress, with the odd alteration. I've always loved it; so much pearl and crystal detail.'

'Oh, I'm not entirely a battleaxe, you know.' Camilla smiled humorously and looked a bit less like an overdressed matron. 'Hope you don't mind if your father and I shoot off the day after tomorrow. We're off to take the liner to New York for a month or two to stay with my cousin, Margery. It was our immediate plan once Perkin announced his retirement. He needs a holiday so.'

'Of course I don't mind, Mummy.' Verity slipped back into her more usual way of calling her mother.

'I'll tell Margery about your gorgeous diamond engagement ring.'

'Would you mind if I went off to spend time with Daddy? Jack's taken him and Uncle Greg to the billiards room but I don't think they'd mind if I joined them.'

'I'll have another sherry, dear, then you may go.'

When Verity had flitted from the room, Dorrie nodded at the sister-in-law with whom she had little in common. 'You've made her seem like a little girl again. I'm so glad you're on the best of terms once more.'

'It wasn't all mine and Perkin's fault, the estrangement,' Camilla said, sipping her drink as if she really needed it. 'She should have come to us and explained how Urquart had treated her. Instead she stormed in on us when we were entertaining old Lord and Lady Mycliffe and raged about how she had told Urquart he could go to hell and that she hoped he'd dropped dead in the street. She frightened poor Lady Mycliffe and she is easily confused these days. Naturally, Perkin and I were furious with her behaviour, and after the poor old couple asked for their car to be brought round, there was the most dreadful quarrel. Things were said . . . well, as I said it's all in the past now. Thanks for looking after her for us.'

'I thought there must be some things Verity hadn't told Greg and me. I overheard her on the telephone to Perkin saying how sorry she was too,' Dorrie said in a satisfied voice. 'Now we can all look forward to the future.'

'I didn't mention it before – well, it was hardly important . . .' Camilla dipped her head and Dorrie knew a gossipy titbit was forthcoming.

'Oh? Do go on.'

'That Sanders woman, the fast one who lives close by here, Sawle House, I'm talking about, we passed it on the way here. I came across her three or four years ago. We were at adjoining tables at the Dorchester, taking tea. She was with a major in the

Guards. Well, the friends I was with told me that she was very good about entertaining officers – the previous week she had been there with an admiral. She's much married, you know. How does she behave here? All fur coat and no knickers, I dare say. Has she given Greg the come on? Or Jack? He's a very attractive man.'

'Actually, she conducts herself in an exemplary manner,' Dorrie answered swiftly, hoping this conversation would soon end. Jack had been one of Honoria's casual lovers. Verity knew and understood that his philandering had been his way of easing his loneliness, but it would be horribly embarrassing if they came in now from the billiards room. 'She's been a brick to Nanviscoe. She put up the money to start the building of the new village hall.'

'How disappointing.' Camilla finished her sherry and went to the piano. She loved to play and sing the big band tunes. 'I was hoping to learn a tasty morsel to take back with me and pass on after New York. Oh well, I dare say I'll meet her properly at the wedding. It was a shock to learn a member of her family owns Petherton. Chester something, isn't it?'

Dorrie did not reply but piped up, 'Do play "In The Mood", Camilla. I so enjoy the swing music.'

Dorrie didn't listen to Camilla's accomplished playing. She was trying not to shiver with the shock at what seemed confirmation to her outrageous assumption after she had burnt the sepia photo Finn had showed her of Honoria and an officer called Chester. It hadn't taken much imagination to dismiss the C in Chester and rearrange the remaining letters into Esther. Could she possibly have been right? Surely it was preposterous, laughable. Was Esther Mitchelmore, for some reason, really a man, posing as Honoria's sister while she was in fact Honoria's brother Chester? There was no doubt she was a strong woman. She had nursed old Sedgewick with the strength of two nurses, and only recently she had carried Finn, a strapping youth, almost single-handedly up from the cellar. She did things in a planned regimental way, naturally dealing out orders. She was very quiet about her private life. Words of Honoria's came to Dorrie from a wartime WVS meeting: '*But be careful, Esther, dear.*' Everyone present there, including Dorrie, had taken the words to be sarcasm as the sisters bickered, but had it been an affectionate warning of some kind, perhaps not to give herself away? No, it was too ludicrous. The very thought that Esther Mitchelmore was actually a man called Chester was farcical . . . Or was it?

If it was true there could be deeper connotations. Mary Rawling's scrap of blackmail note had stated that Ch— was known about. Ch— must surely have been the Chester in the photo. A man living as a woman would want his secret kept at all costs. Dorrie could imagine Esther Mitchelmore being the sort of person unafraid to take a gun to a pair of cold-hearted blackmailers, but the killer had been a paid thug. That didn't seem Esther's way somehow. Could it be Honoria's? Seeing things as she now did, Dorrie saw that Honoria was staunchly protective of her sister. Honoria was known to have mixed in unsavoury circles. She could be a very dangerous woman.

If all these terrible conjectures were right then it would be a terrible thing to allow Camilla – always on the outlook for society tittle-tattle – to meet Esther Mitchelmore and Honoria Sanders.

Thirty-Two

Dorrie made her way to Sawle House, her tummy burning with sickly acid, keeping her ears as sharp as Corky's for danger, and her nerves stinging as if attacked by a swarm of wasps. She felt she was about to dangle herself on the edge of a precipice. She was en route to see Honoria Sanders and she must be vitally careful how she broached 'the matter' with her.

As fate would have it Honoria was walking away from her high wooden gates, striding out in slacks and brogues, silk headscarf, white-blonde curly fringe and pouting scarlet lips. She had a Morris Eight but loved to walk.

'Hello Dorrie,' she waved. 'Isn't it a lovely day? I love all these scrummy yellow and brown leaves blown about everywhere, don't you?'

Dorrie enjoyed crunching through dry late autumn leaves and hearing them crackling underfoot but today the sweeps of leaves alongside the bottom of the hedgerows were soggy from the recent downpour of rain and she was watching her step.

'Hello Honoria, I've set out to see you actually.' Dorrie forced her reply out cheerily – after all, she could be facing a murderess.

'How nice. Shall we walk together? Along here – I so love being in among the trees, especially those around Merrivale.'

'You do?' Dorrie knew stabs of alarm.

'Why, of course, and I know why you've come to see me.'

Honoria's usually warm eyes narrowed to slits sparking with malice.

Dorrie tried to turn and run but her feet felt iced to the ground. Her heartbeat thundered as if it would explode against her ribs.

From her coat pocket Honoria whipped out a handgun and shot Dorrie cleanly between the eyes.

Dorrie awoke with a loud cry, slapping her hand up to the chillingly real piercing pain in her forehead. Wiping the perspiration off her face and neck she reached, trembling, to sip from a glass of water. A previous nightmare had featured Esther shooting her dead in a busy Faith's Fare, after curling up her lip and screaming at her, 'Traitor! I thought you were my friend.'

'I am your friend, Esther,' Dorrie had whispered through the night, while gripped with the horror of her dreamt death. 'That's why I'm seriously considering getting a warning to you somehow. If the world, through Camilla, was to find out you are really a man, your life would become unbearable. You'd be hounded out of everywhere you go. You would probably go to prison for tricking Sedgewick Mitchelmore into a sham marriage and inheriting his estate.'

Now, having suffered a second nightmare, Dorrie knew she must steel herself and go ahead and try to save her friend from unimaginable torment – Esther could be thrown into a male prison.

Putting aside the possibility of endangering herself (her suspicions might be wrong after all – and she hoped they were) she was sure it would be best not to approach Esther but Honoria, in a roundabout way using natural chit-chat; Dorrie now saw Honoria as the driving force between the sisters. The following mid-morning she set off for Sawle House.

Honoria's long-serving maid-of-all-work showed her into the spacious, rather sumptuous and sensually endowed drawing room. 'I'll fetch Madam down from upstairs. We've been packing for her long winter trip.'

'Thank you, Letty. So you're wintering in sunnier climes? I know Mrs Sanders finds English winters wet and dismal.' There was always a sense of pleasure within Honoria's home and Dorrie felt soothed. Surely she had been letting her imagination run away; surely her presumptions about both sisters were absurd.

In a wrap of sultry perfume Honoria entered the drawing room. Every muscle in Dorrie's body tensed. Honoria was wearing the exact same clothes as in her nightmare. Dorrie slapped on her friendliest smile. 'I'm sorry to interrupt you, Honoria. You see, I'm feeling at a loose end . . .'

'Darling Dorrie, you could never be an interruption,' Honoria purred effusively, kissing Dorrie heartily on both cheeks then folding her in a warm hug. Dorrie felt crushed by her friend's heaving bosom. Bracelets jangled on both of Honoria's wrists.

Dorrie laughed as she always did at these times but the embrace today unnerved her. 'Letty can carry on without me. I only get in her way really and she's sweet enough to tolerate me. She's my absolute treasure.

'Let's have a large drop of rum to clear the tubes, just the ticket for these colder days. My second husband, or was it my third, was a great believer in it warding off the evils of colds and 'flu. So you're feeling a bit low, poor darling. Has it something to do with the recent stay of your sister-in-law? I've heard via the jungle drums that she's a bit of a nightmare.'

The last word, apt to the present situation, unsettled Dorrie but Honoria had offered the ideal opening. 'You're correct on both counts actually. I do find Camilla very trying.' While sipping the rum, the exotic smell and taste of the strong nectar giving welcome warmth to her shaky insides, Dorrie sat on the end of one sumptuously plump sofa next to the crackling grate. Honoria lounged like some smouldering screen siren, her feet in fluffy slippers, on the sofa opposite.

Dorrie gave an account of Camilla's views of Verity's future, Jack and the wedding. 'It was such a relief that she's leaving the arrangements to us, although I have the sneaking suspicion that when we get nearer the date Camilla will come down and interfere with everything. When I mentioned as much to Verity, she scoffed and said her mother had just better not dare do any such thing. I suppose I'm just being silly but I do want Verity to have the perfect day.'

'You're never silly, Dorrie. You're a brick and the most wonderful person. Thank God Verity had you and Greg to turn to when her parents threw her out. In my opinion parents should accept their children exactly as they are and support them through thick and thin.' Dorrie felt that last was said with feeling. 'Just make it clear to the old bat that every arrangement made is set in stone and non-negotiable.'

'Well, I could do but I'm not sure I have the right. Verity is not my daughter.'

'You've been her mother for the last few months and this Camilla has gladly left the wedding schedule to all of you here, so of course you've got the right.' Smoking from a jet cigarette holder, Honoria grinned catlike, with relish. 'Put the bitch thoroughly in her place. I would. You try to, Dorrie, go on, I dare you.'

Dorrie smiled at the other woman's mischievous expression. 'Verity will have the wedding she wants, I swear on that. You've encouraged me; I always get a lift from you, Honoria.'

'It's what friends and neighbours are for. Another tot of rum, darling?'

'Just a tot, please.' While Honoria was reaching for the rum decanter, Dorrie plunged in. 'Actually, Camilla said that during the war she was with friends in the Dorchester and one of them knew you, mentioned something about you and a relative – um, Chester, I think it was. I can't say I recall you or Esther mentioning a Chester. Camilla is a prying woman, if she were here she'd question you like a dog gnawing at a bone. I hope I'm not speaking out of turn – I thought perhaps you and Esther might have suffered a sad loss . . .'

Honoria passed over Dorrie's replenished glass, looking strangely solemn and very sad. She was silent for a while. Dorrie could see she was chewing over something in her mind. Honoria exhaled so deeply Dorrie grew anxious she would pass out, and on that melancholy sigh Dorrie knew she had nothing to fear from her friend.

Honoria shook her head resignedly. 'I knew this day would come, but at least I know I can trust you, Dorrie. I'm going to reveal something to you that I trust you to take to the grave. There was a Chester. He wasn't a blood relative. He was Esther's first husband, and quite frankly, he was an evil bastard. It's to my lasting sorrow that I introduced him into Esther's life; he was my lover and when things between us fizzled out he swept poor Esther, who had fallen for him, off her feet. Our parents adored him, he had such charm, and they called him the son they had always hoped for.

'I didn't know for years he was cruel and controlling to Esther, and that he was free with his fists. She put a brave face on things and he was very careful not to leave a visible mark on her. Poor Esther thought if she bore him a son he'd change and respect her but when she had finally conceived he beat her in one of his drunken rages. It brought on a late miscarriage. She was nearly seven months along, and not only did she lose the child she also lost her womb and nearly her life. It left her terribly physically and emotionally scarred. Now she can't stand the thought of anyone seeing her disfigured body.

'She came to her senses and came to live with me. It was a relief when Chester was killed in a motor accident some months later. It meant dear Esther didn't have to go through the trauma and indignity of a divorce. You can understand why he has never been mentioned. Esther had quite successfully shut that part of her past out of her mind. Then she met Sedgewick Mitchelmore and made a new life for herself. As you can imagine, Dorrie, I'd do anything – *anything* – to stop her being hurt in any way again.'

'Oh yes, absolutely, Honoria, because Greg and I feel the same away about our family members, and you have my word that this confidence will never pass from my lips. I've forgotten about it already.' Dorrie downed the last of her rum, angry with herself. How on earth could she have thought Esther was really a man? Dorrie might be the reliable, down-to-earth one in her family but she had also been more than a little shameful . . . But there was the matter of whether Honoria had paid a thug to kill the two young blackmailers for Esther's sake. She would think it all through on the walk home. 'Tell me, dear, where are you off to for the winter?'

Thirty-Three

Finn had a visitor. 'Your mum said it was all right to come up. See you're drawing again and got the baby with you.' Sam stood awkwardly in the doorway, gazing at Finn who was on his bed, back against the pillows and headboard, sketching Eloise who was perched against his drawn-up knees. Sam never knew how to take Finn nowadays. Finn had not been to The Orchards for ages and he no longer asked after his parents – well, his mother – as he used to. Sam felt he must have offended Finn but Sam didn't know what he had done.

'Looks like it, doesn't it? Sit down then, don't dawdle in the bloody doorway,' Finn grunted. As it happened he didn't have any issues with Sam but he preferred, when he had the time, to be with Eloise and to have her all to himself. It was going to be a horrible wrench leaving her throughout most of each week when he started at the art academy.

'I've managed to get hold of a couple bottles of Coca Cola,' Sam said, flopping down in the tub chair, which was liberally covered with Finn's cast-off clothes. 'It's handy out on the rounds, you can swap anything for some extra fruit or veg.'

'Great,' Finn said, reaching out a hand for the opened drink without tearing his eyes away from his sketch of Eloise shaking her rattle. She made a grab for the bottle. 'No, no, sweetheart, you can't have this. You finish off your own bottle.' Tucking Eloise into the crook of his arm he put her bottle of diluted rose-hip syrup to her eager lips. All three in the bedroom glugged down the drink in their own bottles.

'I got these as well.' Sam thrust back his shoulders in pride as he threw three little packets on the bed.

Finn picked them up. 'Rubber johnnies! What do you want those for?' He was suddenly contentious. 'You better not be hoping to get fresh with Jenna. She's a decent girl.'

'Course not!' Sam coloured in guilt but hoped Finn would think he was merely embarrassed. He gathered up his trophies.

Jenna was refusing a repeat of their love-making unless they got engaged, but Sam only wanted some fun and sex now, not his future mapped out for him. 'I'm thinking of looking around, and hopefully the johnnies will come in useful.'

'Things fizzling out between you and Jenna then?' Finn looked Sam steadily in the eyes. 'Tilly says Jenna's been quiet about you lately.'

'I like Jenna, but she's just my first girlfriend. I'm not ready to settle down yet,' Sam said, mildly desperate. 'You do understand, Finn? Can you say something, please? You look like a ruddy judge.'

'Have you told her?'

'I've been trying to but I don't want to hurt her. She's a lovely girl but not the girl for me.'

'She's going to be hurt, can't be no other way, but she'll be more hurt if you keep her wriggling on a line. You chased after her, not the other way round, and you owe it to her to tell her properly and clearly. You're doing nothing now, why not get over to By The Way and speak to her privately. Don't be a bastard and keep her hanging on. Girls hope for more than us.'

'But it's Saturday, all the kids will be home from school and Denny tends to be in the yard. Jean will invite me inside and I'll be surrounded by Vercoes.' Sam cursed himself for it gushed out of him as a pathetic wail.

'Are you a man or a mouse?' Finn growled, dumping his drink down with force. 'Or a chicken-hearted ninny or a nasty bastard?' *Like your shitty father.*

'All right, I'm going.' Sam sprang up and scooted for the door. 'See you.'

Sam wasn't sure if he would try to see Finn again. His parents had for some reason turned against Finn, murmuring that he wasn't what he seemed. Sam decided he had no clue as to what Finn was really like; he was not a good friend to him anyway, that was certain. Finn was surly and confrontational. It was time to break with him too.

As Sam clattered down the stairs, Finn cuddled Eloise, delighting in her making bubbles on her rosebud lips. 'Hopefully that's the last we'll see of that crummy idiot.'

* * *

'Come down here, old girl – you too, Verity!' Greg bawled excitedly up the stairs.

'We're busy, Greg,' Dorrie called down from the landing. 'Verity is about to try on the wedding dress. I take it your exuberance has something to do with the phone call just now?'

Greg pounded up the stairs like a man half his age. 'Certainly was. That was a reporter I was speaking to, not one from the local rags but a top national. They've got word of how quickly the community here rallied together and built the new hall. They want to cover it, come down with a photographer and make a big thing of it as an encouragement to the whole country. They want to interview the main organizers and speak to the children who will officially open the hall. Said if we want to rethink it they could organize a VIP to help open the hall. They suggested a member of the Guinea Pig Club, a badly burnt war hero, as we're not interested in dignitaries and film stars. Just think of that, what an honour! What's the betting the next phone call will be from the venerable Mistress of the Manor organizing an urgent committee meeting?'

Greg was right in a way. The telephone rang almost immediately from Petherton but it was from Honoria, not Esther. She asked to speak to Dorrie.

'Dorrie, I'm afraid I've got some bad news. Esther hasn't been well for the last few days. She's been having terrible stomach pains and I've been staying with her. She collapsed this morning. I'm so worried I'm driving her up to Harley Street without delay. Somebody or other rang a little while ago about the village hall but I fielded him over to Greg's capable hands. Sorry I can't stay and chat, have to get on. I'll ring you from London.'

Before Dorrie could say how sorry she was about the news, Honoria said goodbye and cut off the call.

'Problems?' Greg asked.

'What is it, Aunt Dor?' Verity said. 'You look upset.'

'I'm taken aback. That was Honoria. It seems Mrs Mitchelmore is seriously ill and Honoria is about to take her up to London to see a top specialist,' Dorrie explained. She wasn't really surprised. She was pretty certain this sudden onset of illness of Esther's, who hadn't been seen out and about for a while, was a cover story. Through Dorrie's disclosure to Honoria, she was being faced with the prospect of her first marriage becoming known. Esther would be invited to Verity and Jack's wedding, and if not before, she would be bound to meet Camilla who might spill the beans. But why be so worried about it? From a scrap of paper, two people had apparently somehow discovered 'the truth about Chester', had tried blackmail and had been put to death for it – the most extreme measures for Esther or Honoria or both of them to take (if they really had) over a case of domestic violence? Esther had been a widow when she married Sedgewick Mitchelmore, all decent and above board; no bigamy. It would be painful but not crushingly humiliating to become known as a battered wife. But Esther had suffered an even more painful event. One of the most excruciatingly painful things to happen to a woman, Dorrie knew, was to lose her child. Esther's husband had viciously beaten her child out of her body. She might have been able to live with her husband beating her but perhaps not with him being responsible for the death of her child. Could Esther have wanted revenge? It was understandable. Could she have killed Chester by design or perhaps unintentionally in heart-break or temper? Had Chester really died in a motorbike crash? Had the crash been faked? Dorrie would never know for certain; she had no intention of looking into the man's death. She might have been silly in believing Esther was really a man, but she felt it was not fanciful to wonder if the facts pointed to Neville Stevens, a sneak thief, discovering some sort of evidence that Esther had murdered Chester. That he had told his lover Mary Rawling, that together they had made a blackmail bid, all leading to Honoria, through her dubious connections, to hire a professional assassin. It seemed a likely explanation to Dorrie for the manner of the couple's deaths, rather than them falling foul of a black-market gang.

Now it seemed to Dorrie that the sisters had been concocting a story to enable them to slip away from the village, probably by Esther declaring she would spend a healing winter abroad with Honoria, and neither would come back. By the time Camilla came down for the wedding the lady of Petherton would not be important enough for Camilla to seek gossip about. The reporter for the national newspaper had shunted the sisters' plans urgently forward, in a different direction.

Dorrie expected she would hear from Honoria quite soon but she doubted (and hoped, of course, not wanting Esther to be really ill) that Esther would have gone anywhere near Harley Street.

Thirty-Four

Tilly ran into Dorrie's open arms and sobbed on her shoulder. 'Thank you so much for coming, Mrs Resterick. Finn and I are struggling to leave Petherton. We can't believe Mrs Mitchelmore's got cancer, that she's never coming back.'

'I know, dear, I find it hard to believe too.' Dorrie stroked Tilly's soft hair where it hung below her little felt hat. She smiled at Finn, standing on the gravelled path, holding Tilly's small brown suitcase and few bags of belongings, while clearing his throat and wiping a tear from his eye.

Taking a mighty swallow he came towards them. 'I was really fond of her. She was always very good to me. Mrs R, do you know how long she's got? I've heard Mrs Sanders is taking her to Switzerland. Do you think the doctors there will know some sort of advanced treatment that will give her more time?'

'We can hope and pray, Finn, but Mrs Sanders says Mrs Mitchelmore is being very brave and doesn't want anyone to worry about her. Whatever happens she will be well looked after. Verity will be along soon in Jack's five-seater to take you and me to Meadows House, Tilly. You'll have a good position there.'

'It will be lovely working with Cathy. Mrs Mitchelmore has generously paid me two months wages, and Mr Jack said I don't have to start work straightaway, but I'd rather get stuck in, don't like being idle and there's lots of work going on in the house. Mrs Mitchelmore is such a kind lady, she's given Mrs Teague and Ellery enough to retire on early and they're going to share a cottage.' Tilly moved a few steps away and stared at the shabby old house. 'I wonder what will happen to this place now.'

'I guess it will have a new owner eventually,' Finn sighed.

'But it won't be the same, and Nanviscoe won't be the same without Mrs Mitchelmore running the place so well.' Dorrie summed up the feelings of the three.

'Will you step up to the mark, Mrs R?' Finn asked.

'Oh, most definitely not, organizing and planning isn't for me. I'd rather be available for others, if you know what I mean.'

'Definitely do,' Finn told her affectionately. 'Hate to think how Mum and I and Eloise would have fared without you helping us from the start. Oh God though.' He threw out another sigh. 'It doesn't seem right that Mrs Mitchelmore won't be here for the opening of the village hall.'

'I'm sure she'll be thinking of us all on the day. Mrs Sanders says she's arranged for the newspaper article to be sent to Mrs Mitchelmore, and that also Mrs Mitchelmore has written a little speech for Greg to read out on the day.'

'So she'll be there in a way, bless her,' Tilly sniffed. 'Well, better go to the gates. It's very kind of Miss Verity to come and collect me. Finn is going on to the hall to help put up the opening bunting. Funny, you never know what's going to happen in the course of a year, do you? Never thought I'd be working at Miss Verity's bridal home and . . . and poor Mrs Mitchelmore . . .' She shook her head and sobbed again.

Finn put the baggage into one arm and wrapped the other arm round her shoulders. 'Don't cry, Tilly. You'll be closer to Merrivale from now on. Mum will be there when I'm away at the academy, and I'll never let you down, not ever.'

Dorrie allowed them to walk on ahead of her, smiling in sweet emotion. Finn and Tilly didn't know it yet but they would be linked together for always, soul mates. She could tell by the way they gazed deeply into each other's eyes. They walked in synchronization ensuring their bodies kept touching. They were in line in every way.

The little company reached the gates. Someone was running towards them pell-mell, her hair flowing out behind her in a stream of tangles. It was Jenna. She was weeping as if in utter despair. 'You've got to do something, Finn. Dad's going to kill him!'

Verity drove wildly along the lanes and brought the car to a screeching halt outside The Orchards, making the tyres smell of acrid burning rubber. Denny's mud-splattered van was parked skew-whiff across the lane, making it impossible for motorized traffic or horse and cart to pass, showing his anger and speed at getting here. Verity, Dorrie, Jenna, Finn and Tilly spilled out and hurried towards the cottage kitchen door. Shouting, shrieks and scuffles and thudding sounds took them running down through the back garden and into the leafy windfall-strewn apple orchard.

'Dad!' Jenna screamed hysterically at Denny, who was pounding Charlie Lawry's chest with his fists. Charlie was equal in the fight and butted Denny hard in the guts. The men had been at it long enough for both to have suffered cuts and bruises. Dorrie grabbed Tilly to stop her rushing at the men to try tearing them apart. 'Stop it! For heaven's sake, stop! I don't want this.'

On the other side of the battlers were Sam and Belle. 'It's too late for that, girl!' Belle yelled in fury. 'See what you've done? Get your beast of a father and yourself off our property.'

Hearing the aggressive interchange and needing to catch their breath, the two bloodied men staggered apart to the sides of their respective children.

On the way there Jenna had filled in the reason for Denny's furious venture to The Orchards. Finn now loathed the gypsy-like beauty who had once filled his dreams, and now presented her visage as a gorgeous revengeful witch – no one must challenge her precious family no matter what rotten deeds they had committed. He bawled at her. 'You can't blame Jenna alone for this. Your cowardly bastard of a son got Jenna pregnant. Nothing would have happened if he hadn't pressured her into it, that's for sure.'

'Oh, you know that, do you, criminal's son?' Belle hissed, advancing on Finn with her hands on her hips, while glancing antagonistically at all the Vercoes. Weeping and sobbing in anguished gulps, Jenna shook violently and Tilly joined Dorrie in holding her up.

Belle continued taking her venom out on Finn. 'Who are you to judge? Tell me that. Not so long ago you looked at me with eyes filled with lust. Dir-ty lit-tle swine. How dare you? As soon as I knew I cut myself off from you. That's the reason you don't come here any more, do your girlfriend and your mother know that? My son says that girl was just as willing as he was. The reason why his bullish father is here on the warpath is because Sam doesn't want to marry the girl. Sam told her he'd acknowledge the child and provide for it. He doesn't love Jenna. He doesn't want to settle down with her or anyone yet. He was honest with her. He knows he's done wrong and will have to bear the brunt, but he has the wisdom to know a forced marriage would only make them both miserable in the end.'

Suddenly Sam charged at Finn. 'You were trying to get at my mother? I'll kill you!' Before he could smash his fist across Finn's face Finn raised his arms in defence and took the blow.

'Please!' Dorrie managed to make her plea cut through all the anger and malice. 'This isn't helping anyone. Can't you see all this is just one of life's occurrences? Finn had an intense schoolboy infatuation on Belle. Sam and Jenna have done what young people have done and regretted through the ages. It's sad they won't be getting married, but there it is. What good is fighting and fury going to do anyone? The facts aren't going to change. There's a baby involved in this, a baby that deserves to come safely into the world and to receive only love and care from its parents and both sets of grandparents. The baby will be related to the Lawrys and Vercoes. I suggest those involved calm down and go into, or back to, their homes. If a go-between is needed you know where I am.'

No one moved or spoke, twitched a nerve or took a deep breath. Dorrie and Verity exchanged rueful looks. Then the soft snivels of Jenna were heard. Dorrie and Verity's hearts went out to the girl. She was the one who would have to face the public shame and bear the baby, a daunting prospect for a woman who was still really a girl.

Wiping blood and sweat off his hairy face, Denny blasted one last look of enmity at Sam and then Charlie. He went to Jenna. 'Come on, dry your eyes. I'm taking you home. Me and your mother will look after you. A new baby is welcome in our home even if it isn't elsewhere.'

Dorrie watched as the Lawrys formed into a protective huddle. Sam and Charlie stared down at the ground. 'Thanks for what you said, Dorrie,' Belle said, looking grave and critical. 'I'm sorry you and Verity got involved in this. It's not your family problem. We'll sort this out ourselves.'

Finn looked at Tilly, his expression worried. Dorrie was sure of his thoughts – what would Tilly think of him now?

Tilly simply put her hand in his. 'Let's go.'

Jack Newton's car was filled again and was off for its original destination. Finn got out at the crossroads to walk to the hall. He waved goodbye to Tilly, watching until the car disappeared.

'Poor Jenna, I can hardly believe she's got herself into trouble,' Tilly said in a small voice, from the back seat. 'I'm sorry about all this, Miss Verity. I promise I won't let family troubles affect my work or, um, let myself get into the same situation.'

'I trust you, Tilly, and I can see how much Finn cares for and respects you. As for Jenna, these things happen. During the war I typed up a lot of official papers for a charity that placed a lot of fatherless babies into adoption. It was very sad. At least Jenna has the support of her family, including you and Cathy. Cathy will be shocked to hear the news. You must spend the afternoon together to do as you please.'

'Yes, madam, thank you,'

'Miss Verity will do for now and next year Mrs Newton. Aunt Dorrie, are you all right? You're very quiet.'

'I'm fine. It's just all these sudden dramas and changes. As Tilly says, a lot can happen in a year –, well in just a few months really – but I must remember most have been for the good. Hopefully all will go smoothly at the hall opening.'

Thirty-Five

Up on the little stage of the smart Peace Hall, which smelled strongly of fresh paint and new timber, and buzzed with excited chatter and the clinking of teacups, Greg raised his arms and called for hush.

'Thank you, thank you, everyone,' he said in a loud happy voice as a shuffling quiet spread in an interested wave over the gathering. 'I have here a message from Mrs Mitchelmore and it was now, after the grand opening and the press had gone, that she specified she wanted it to be read out. Dorrie, are you sure you don't want to do this? It was you who Mrs Mitchelmore wrote to.'

'Not in the least,' Dorrie replied, sitting at a long line of trestle tables with Verity, Jack, the Templetons, Guy and the Vercoes. Jenna was there, chivvied along by her parents, sadly having spent every moment quiet and strained. The news of her 'little problem' had not yet become common knowledge, and the Vercoes and Lawrys were keeping a careful distance from each other.

'Get on with it, boyo,' called out Hector Evans, and everyone laughed.

'Right then, here goes, it's only fitting the dear lady has the last word. It's dated five days ago, from Geneva. "My dear friends and neighbours of Nanviscoe. I'm so sorry to have suddenly left your midst, but in my trials, I am fully confident that I have left you in the very capable hands of the Peace Hall committee. I am also deeply saddened, as is my sister, Mrs Sanders, that we could not be with you there today, but we will take pleasure in what will be, undoubtedly, your pleasure. I urge you all to enjoy your splendid new hall, built with the sweat of your brows, and allow no one to spoil the future occasions you have in it. May God bless you all. Yours, with my affectionate regards, Esther Mitchelmore."'

There was a thunderous round of clapping and whooping and a spontaneous outbreak of 'For she's a jolly good fellow.'

Thirty-Six

While the opening-day fun went on, Dorrie caught Finn's elbow and nodded to him to go outside with her. Fitting to the occasion the sky had been a peaceful pale blue with lazily drifting white clouds and the sun shining down warmly, and now the winter daylight was waning like a cover of protection.

'I wanted to speak to you alone, Finn. I've had another letter, from the agent. Read it, dear, and see what you think about it.'

Finn's eyes moved over the typed letter. 'So he likes your rhyming story but thinks my style of artwork isn't right for the current market. He wants to try to link you up with another illustrator.' Finn nodded. 'That's fair enough.'

'Are you very disappointed, Finn?' Dorrie was hopeful. His face had not dropped like a stone; he was taking the rejection well.

'Not really. I've thumbed through a few more kids' illustrated books and my artwork isn't as rounded and as cuddly as is theirs. I think that's what the agent means. I certainly don't want to change my style, but you go ahead, Mrs R, and see what happens.'

'It's not something I really want to do, Finn. I rang the agent and asked him to return everything in the postage-paid reply envelope. Fiona has mentioned that if things don't go ahead she'd like to turn the work into a decorated scrapbook for Eloise. There's always the option we can try again in the future with something else. Greg and I are planning to have some of my poems made up to sell with the proceeds going towards the upkeep of the hall. We're hoping you'll agree to add some of your illustrations.'

'It's a great idea, Mrs R.' Finn hugged Dorrie and planted a hearty kiss on her cheek. 'I want to concentrate on my studies for the next two years and I can do that without worry, knowing you'll be close by Mum, Eloise and Tilly too. Best thing that ever happened to us was meeting you.'

'Oh, Finn.' Dorrie shuffled her hand into her cardigan pocket for her hanky. 'You'll have me in tears.'

'Will Mrs Sanders let you know when . . . time's up for Mrs Mitchelmore?'

'I'm sure she will, Finn – and because when she last got in touch she said Mrs Mitchelmore was buoyant and bubbly, I hope it will be a very long while yet. Shall we go back in?'

Proudly, Finn took Dorrie back in on his arm.

Dorrie enjoyed the rest of the day. It was the best event ever held in the village. The first of many to be held in this hall, Dorrie thought contentedly, and all boosted forward by Honoria's generous monetary donation. If Honoria and her sister had conspired in two terrible (although in each case, she felt, rather understandable) crimes, then Dorrie was happy for them both to remain enigmas.